THE
LOCKED
WARD

ALSO BY SARAH PEKKANEN

House of Glass
Gone Tonight
The Ever After
The Perfect Neighbors
Things You Won't Say
Catching Air
The Best of Us
These Girls
Skipping a Beat
The Opposite of Me

WITH GREER HENDRICKS

The Golden Couple
You Are Not Alone
An Anonymous Girl
The Wife Between Us

THE
LOCKED
WARD

A NOVEL

SARAH PEKKANEN

ST. MARTIN'S
PRESS

NEW YORK

First published in the United States by St. Martin's Press, an imprint of St. Martin's Publishing Group

EU Representative: Macmillan Publishers Ireland Ltd, 1st Floor, The Liffey Trust Centre, 117–126 Sheriff Street Upper, Dublin 1, DO1 YC43

THE LOCKED WARD. Copyright © 2025 by Sarah Pekkanen. All rights reserved. Printed in the United States of America. For information, address St. Martin's Publishing Group, 120 Broadway, New York, NY 10271.

www.stmartins.com

Designed by Steven Seighman

Library of Congress Cataloging-in-Publication Data

Names: Pekkanen, Sarah, author.
Title: The locked ward : a novel / Sarah Pekkanen.
Description: First edition. | New York : St. Martin's Press, 2025.
Identifiers: LCCN 2025006976 | ISBN 9781250349514 (hardcover) | ISBN 9781250349521 (ebook)
Subjects: LCGFT: Psychological fiction. | Thrillers (Fiction). | Novels.
Classification: LCC PS3616.E358 L63 2025 | DDC 813/.6—dc23/eng/20250214
LC record available at https://lccn.loc.gov/2025006976

The publisher of this book does not authorize the use or reproduction of any part of this book in any manner for the purpose of training artificial intelligence technologies or systems. The publisher of this book expressly reserves this book from the Text and Data Mining exception in accordance with Article 4(3) of the European Union Digital Single Market Directive 2019/790.

Our books may be purchased in bulk for specialty retail/wholesale, literacy, corporate/premium, educational, and subscription box use. Please contact MacmillanSpecialMarkets@macmillan.com.

First Edition: 2025

10 9 8 7 6 5 4 3 2 1

For Amy Casey Smith and Chris Smith,
friends who turned into family

Deep vengeance is the daughter of deep silence.

—Vittorio Alfieri

THE
LOCKED
WARD

CHAPTER ONE

GEORGIA

You awaken slowly, struggling to surface, like you're swimming up through mud. Your arms and legs ache, and grit burns your eyes. A headache throbs rhythmically at the base of your skull.

Your mouth feels sticky, as if your lips have been sealed together.

Your eyes flutter open, and as they take focus, you see you're in a dimly lit room. It's tiny; the drab beige walls seem to press in on you. The drop ceiling is beige, too. There's nothing on the walls. Nothing to orient you. Nothing familiar at all.

The sharp, tangy aroma of bleach fills your nose, but it can't mask the odor beneath it. If despair had a smell, it would smell like this room.

You have a good nose, a sommelier told you only a few nights ago—back when your life was your own—after he decanted a hundred-dollar bottle of wine and you identified notes of leather and blackberry.

You feel too weak to stand up, but something deep within you is screaming at you to try. Then you realize your arms are cuffed to the sides of the bed. So are your legs. You're splayed out, completely helpless beneath bright green paper pajamas.

You strain as hard as you can, but the Velcro cuffs—red bands for your wrists and blue for your ankles—don't yield.

"Help," you croak in a voice that sounds nothing like your own. You try to swallow but your mouth is too dry.

Then you hear something that makes you wish you'd stayed silent. A man's voice: "You're awake."

Your heart shudders as you glimpse him seated on a plastic chair down by your feet. He wears burgundy scrubs and a somber expression.

When you see his face, it all comes rushing back to you, a tsunami of memories, sending terror spiking through your veins. You remember why you are here.

And you know no matter what you say or do, you will not be allowed to leave.

You are no longer Georgia Cartwright, a thirty-two-year-old woman with a job as a high-end wedding planner, a city apartment with a wall of windows, a weakness for ugly dogs, and a love of running.

From this day forward, you are the newest resident of the locked ward.

CHAPTER TWO

MANDY

It's the Crime of the Decade!

The early-morning headline explodes across my iPhone as I scan it through bleary eyes.

I read the first few paragraphs: A woman from a wealthy, socially prominent family is accused of bludgeoning her younger sister to death at the family estate in Charlotte, North Carolina—just ninety minutes away from my one-bedroom apartment, but essentially in another world. Pathological jealousy is the presumed motive.

Then I scroll through more updates involving war, famine, and the breakup of my favorite celebrity couple. I recently made a resolution to avoid checking social media first thing in the morning because it supposedly causes depression. I'm not sure the news is any better.

I stretch my arms above my head, then reluctantly pull myself out of bed. One of my employees took last night off, so work was especially hectic. At least I was filling in for my bartender Scott instead of the short-order cook. I'd rather pull beers and mix Jack and Cokes than stand over a deep fryer any day of the week.

I step into my bathroom and twist the knob for hot water in my shower, then hesitate. I thought I heard a faint noise in the distance just before it was muffled by the sound of rushing water.

I listen hard and hear it again: the bright music of my phone's ringtone.

Everyone in my life knows I work nights and not to call before 10 A.M.—which it isn't even close to now. It could be spam. But something is urging me to turn off the shower and walk back into my bedroom.

My phone is on my nightstand, flashing the words *Private Caller.*

Probably a salesperson, I tell myself. But some deep-seated instinct overrides my logical brain, pressing me to answer.

"Amanda Ravenel?" The man's voice is raspy and urgent.

"Who's asking?" I counter.

"My name is Milt Daniels. I'm the public defender representing Georgia Cartwright."

My mind reels. It's the case I just read about, the one with the insanely jealous sister.

"Ms. Ravenel?" the man repeats.

My throat is bone-dry. If it weren't for the hard, smooth feeling of my phone in my hand, I'd assume I was dreaming. "I'm still here."

"Would you be willing to come see my client?"

I sink onto the edge of my bed, a feeling of surreality flooding me. Nothing about this call makes sense. I'd never heard of Georgia Cartwright until a few minutes ago. Why does her lawyer want us to meet? And how in the world does he even know I exist?

"Why?" I ask.

When he speaks again, his voice is gentler: "This may come as a surprise. Or maybe you've known for a while. Georgia is your sister."

I bark out a laugh. His words are nonsensical; clearly he's been given wrong information. "I'm an only child," I correct him.

"And you're adopted," he replies.

I rear back, blood rushing between my ears. That's not something I hide, but neither is it something I advertise. It's simply part of who I am, like my gray eyes and dark brown hair.

"Let me call you back. What's your number?"

I scrabble for a pen and scrawl down his number, then hang up and enter his name into a search engine.

He appears to be exactly who he claims. I watch a snippet of an old video in which he answers a question from a reporter, and his voice matches the one that was just in my ear.

My mind swims as I consider the information I have: He's a lawyer, one who relies on facts and data. And he's clearly checked me out if he knows I'm adopted. He must have a good reason to think his client and I are sisters.

But there's something more tugging at me, something that goes deeper than logic and reasoning. A piece of me has always felt missing, like a phantom limb. I've carried around a hollow emptiness for as long as I can remember. I've never been able to figure out why; I had loving parents and a good childhood—happier than most—and I've never had my heart shattered by a man.

The lawyer could be wrong.

But what if he's found the missing piece in my life?

When I call him back, he answers on the first ring.

"Why do you need me there?" I ask.

"Georgia wants to see you. You're the only person she has asked for."

If I go, I'll have to lean on my staff to run my bar, Sweetbay's. But they're competent, and it shouldn't be a busy night.

"There's one other thing." I clear my throat. "The news reported that Georgia is thirty-two. So am I."

"That's correct," Milt tells me. "She's not only your sister. She's your twin."

CHAPTER THREE

GEORGIA

"Breakfast is at 7:30," the man in burgundy scrubs tells you as he removes your thick Velcro cuffs.

He provides other information as you slowly sit up, wincing as your back threatens to spasm: "Lunch is at noon, dinner at 5:30. You can eat in your room, but it would be better if you came out and joined the others. Group activity is from 10 to 11 A.M. Today it's gentle yoga. You have phone privileges, though those can be taken away at any time."

It doesn't matter. There isn't anyone you want to call.

Your bed is a thin mattress atop a one-piece, bright blue plastic base that's bolted to the floor. It's the only item in the room now that the man has removed his chair.

"Would you like to use the bathroom?" he asks.

You give a slight nod, then slide off the bed, your feet landing on the floor. Someone put socks on you last night, the nonslip kind with rubber dots on the soles.

The aide presses his back against a wall, staying a full arm's length away from you. His eyes never leave you. He gestures for you to walk through the open door first.

You hear the scream just as you cross the threshold: *"She stole my glasses!"*

A woman about your age, wearing a light purple sweatsuit, is standing in the hallway, pointing at you, her voice outraged but her face slack and devoid of emotion.

You shrink back.

"Give me my glasses!"

The woman shuffles a few feet down the hallway, looking back at you the whole time. You feel the skin-pricking sense of other eyes on you. Other watchers. A tall, heavyset man with rumpled dark hair, in a green paper top and pants that match yours, stands in a nearby doorway, gaping at you. Others appear, creeping forward in nonslip socks, appearing from doorways and around corners. Like museum-goers gathered around a new exhibit. Like predators encircling prey.

"They smell fresh blood," you overhear a nurse say, a chuckle in his voice.

You are no longer a woman who loves sushi and hates Zoom meetings, who carries a bag with a sewing kit, stain remover, mints, and spare gold bands to every wedding she oversees.

You are fresh blood.

The aide points to a door. "Bathroom's here."

You step in, and he closes the door, sealing you inside. You begin to tremble, as if your body is trying to shake loose the stares that still cling to you, the hungry gazes you feel through the door. You reach for the lock. There isn't one. There isn't even a handle on the inside.

The only items in the room are a low metal toilet with no lid, a quarter roll of toilet paper resting in an indentation curved into the wall, a small bolted-in soap dispenser, and a plastic sink with two buttons instead of taps.

Bile burns your throat, and you lean over and dry heave into the toilet.

"Everything okay?" the aide asks as he peers in the door. There are eyes and ears on you everywhere. Even when you're crouched over the toilet. Even when you're sleeping.

"You need something in your stomach," the aide tells you. "Come on."

You rise on trembling legs and step out of the bathroom.

There's a long, low-to-the-ground table in the center of an open room at the end of the hall with individual paper trays of toast, scrambled eggs, oranges, and little cartons of milk and juice. Every face at the table turns to you.

A man waves a piece of toast, calling "Well, hello there!" in a bright, overly solicitous tone, the kind salespeople use as they approach. His eyes are vacant even as they stare at you.

Others stop chewing as their gazes roam over your face, your body. Are you an exhibit or prey?

You know the schedule for today but not the rules. Is it more or less dangerous to reply?

The aide gives you a tray of food, which you clutch in both hands. "You can eat here," he says, pointing to a low plastic chair. You have an assigned seat, like in preschool.

You don't move. The seat is between the woman with partially grown-out pink hair that reveals the natural blond underneath and a man whose green pajama top is gaping open at his chest, exposing a thick mat of hair, a Roman numeral tattoo, and a keloid scar. You won't be able to breathe, sitting that close to them. Penned in on either side.

"Fine, you can eat in your room this morning," the aide sighs. "But you need to go to activity."

He follows you as you walk back to your room and sit on your bed, placing the tray next to you. You open the cardboard box of cranberry juice and drink it in one long, thirsty gulp. The tray holds a plastic spoon and fork, but no knife.

You look around your room again. You're used to sizing up spaces in a glance; it's a professional skill. The room is eight by ten feet. There's no closet. The floors are linoleum. There's a window that isn't really a window; it's covered with a glaze and a tightly woven metal screen that lets in only the faintest wisp of light.

There's one item in your room you didn't notice before: a small dome affixed to your ceiling. You've seen this item in hotels and shops. You know exactly what it is. The dome is made of plexiglass to keep the camera inside from being tampered with or broken.

Even though you're in an empty room with a watcher standing in the doorway, other eyes are still observing you.

You are no longer the daughter of one of the wealthiest families in North Carolina, accomplished equestrian, daily Wordle player, expert on dozens of types of flowers suitable for a statement wedding bouquet, and passionate fan of deep-tissue massages.

You are Case Number NC-0416729.

CHAPTER FOUR

MANDY

She's your twin.

The lawyer's words reverberate in my mind as I ring the doorbell of my old therapist's office. After my parents died, I went to see Dr. Lisa Galper to help me cope with my grief. She encouraged me when I told her I wanted to quit my boring marketing job and take over my parents' bar, Sweetbay's. She's a good sounding board, and I've learned to trust her judgment.

I haven't been here in more than a year, but Dr. Galper agreed to squeeze me in for an emergency session this morning.

She opens the door, the spring sunlight glinting off the top rim of her silver glasses.

"Mandy, it's good to see you again. Come on in."

I bypass the couch and take my usual chair next to the small gas fireplace. She settles in across from me, a fresh yellow notepad on her lap.

I don't waste time with preliminaries. I blurt out my story, my voice jagged with emotion. When I finish, Dr. Galper is silent for a long moment, her brow wrinkling. I know she's considering my jumbled narrative, untangling the knots and distilling it down to its emotional core.

"This must feel completely disorienting," she finally says.

"Yes! It's so bizarre—how could I have a twin and not know? My parents obviously didn't know, either. They would've told me."

"Do you want to see this woman who claims to be your sister?" she asks.

"I'm incredibly curious. But it's a little scary, too. She's accused of murder. What if we're not related and she's a psycho?"

"If she is, why did she pick you?"

Her calm is contagious. My mind becomes more centered as I formulate a plan.

"I could find her date of birth and see if it matches mine—it's probably public record somewhere," I say.

"That would be a good start."

"It's just . . ." My voice trails off.

Dr. Galper waits me out, letting me gather the courage to voice what I need to, her eyes steady on mine.

"I want to see her. I think she really is my sister. I can *feel* it."

She jots a note on her legal pad, the first she has taken. "It might be better to wait until you have more information. Why the rush?"

"Shouldn't I at least go and hear what she has to say?"

"Mandy, I would caution you against plunging into a relationship with this woman too quickly."

I can read between the lines. I know what Dr. Galper is getting at; we've discussed this particular element of my life before.

A lot of women I talk to—especially when they're downing margaritas at my bar—confess their struggles with men. They scrutinize two-word texts, wonder about guys' ulterior motives, and strategize how to make the men they're falling for want to be with them, too.

I'm the opposite. Men have always been easy for me; I enjoy their company, and when I feel chemistry, I sometimes act on it. It's female friendships that confound me. They're so nuanced and complex; it's like there's a rule book I can't decipher.

Maybe because I grew up without siblings or cousins around, I've never fit into a group with its unspoken hierarchies and social codes.

What worked for me was having one best friend, someone I did everything with. It's rare for me to find someone I truly click with, but when I do, we can become as close as sisters.

Twice in my life, though—once when I was fourteen and again in college—my best friends were abruptly taken away from me, tearing gaping holes in my life. The summer before ninth grade, my closest friend Melissa's family moved to California for her father's new job, and though we swore we'd write and call every day, we gradually lost touch. Then, in college, my roommate, Beth, transferred midway through our junior year after she was sexually assaulted by a guy she'd gone to a party with.

Dr. Galper thinks these losses are why I struggle with female friendships, jumping in too quickly when I find someone I click with and scaring some women off. *You're not the type of person who can have lunch with a friend every few months and catch up*, she told me. *You crave something much deeper. But that's not everyone's preference.*

Now I pull my laptop out of my tote bag. "I was wondering if we could look at pictures of Georgia together."

"You haven't already?" she asks.

I shake my head. "I'm nervous. What if we're identical?"

Something flickers in her eyes, but she nods. "Sure. Let's take a look."

The images spring onto my laptop screen. At first, I can barely glimpse them before yanking my eyes away. It's the visual equivalent of touching a hot stove. Seeing Georgia's face shocks me to my core.

I know her instantly, even though we've never met.

My hair is dark, while Georgia's is streaked in shades of red and gold. Her features are more delicate, and she is reportedly five foot seven to my five foot five. Those aren't the only differences between us, but the others are more subtle. In a photo taken at a charity event, she is captured in a dress of sapphire-blue silk, her hair an almost liquid cascade down her back, her wrist as graceful as a swan's neck as she holds a flute of champagne. She looks like someone born to money. Even if I put on the same dress and posed the exact same way, I could never look like that.

"What do you see?" Dr. Galper asks.

"We look kind of alike . . . She feels familiar somehow."

"You don't look all that much alike to me," she says gently. "I have to search to find a resemblance."

Her hand reaches out, as if to touch mine, but she pulls hers back before making contact. "You've had a lot of deep loss in your life. It's natural to yearn for a secret relative, but there are so many damaged people out there, and I don't want anyone preying on your vulnerability."

We talk a little more, but when our forty-five minutes is up and Dr. Galper suggests I schedule another session before agreeing to meet with Georgia, I tell her I'll get back to her.

I can feel her watching me as I go.

★   ★   ★

I head to Sweetbay's, knowing I won't be disturbed since we don't open until 4. I sit in the silence of a wooden booth, searching for every scrap of information I can find on Georgia Cartwright.

In pictures, Georgia presents as exactly who she is: a former debutante, a product of the finest girls' boarding school, a glittering fixture in the moneyed Southern social set. She exudes charisma; not only does it leap off the pictures, but I see it in the way people in the background are turning their faces to her, like she's the sun on a chilly day.

We may share DNA, but in many ways, we're opposites.

I look beyond the photos, absorbing the facts of the case. The victim's name was Annabelle Cartwright. It was her birthday, and a grand party was thrown at the family estate in her honor. Annabelle was found shortly after midnight on the floor of the dining room, her blood soaking into the heirloom rug. She'd been smashed in the temple with a heavy sterling-silver paperweight in the shape of the letter A. It was a birthday gift Georgia had just given her younger sister.

Georgia was discovered looming over her sister's body, blood on her hands and clothes, her expression vacant. The first police officer on the scene ordered a seventy-two-hour psychiatric hold for Georgia and summoned an ambulance to take her to the psych ward because she appeared to be in a dissociative state. Yet the press seems to have already convicted her.

Georgia looked like the girl who had everything, but there was something off about her even as a child, a neighbor confided anonymously to a tabloid.

One of Georgia's aunts was blunter in an interview with *The New York Times*: *Georgia wanted to be an only child. She was so jealous when her little sister came along. She never got over it.*

And the most searing quote of all, from Georgia's mother: *She is no longer my daughter.*

I grew up seventy miles away, yet worlds apart from Georgia. My dad was a bartender and my mom a waitress until they had saved enough money to buy Sweetbay's. I inherited their house and bar after they died, him of a heart attack and her of a stroke I'm convinced was caused by a broken heart. It wrenched me to sell the house with the family room addition my father had built with his own hands and my mother's garden with her prized espalier—an apple tree she trained to grow so its limbs spread flat against our wooden fence.

I couldn't bring myself to sell Sweetbay's, too. I guess when everything shatters, you try to hold on to whatever fragments remain.

Now I look up above the liquor bottles lining the bar shelves, staring at the picture of my parents I keep on the highest shelf. Next to it is a keepsake they gave me the day I was born: a small bronze St. Michael the Archangel figurine in a leather pouch embossed with the words *Protect Me Always*. Customers often come in with stories of things my parents gave them, too—a ride home after too many shots, a shoulder during a divorce, a few bucks to keep the lights on. Georgia might have grown up with all the advantages, but I suspect I was the lucky daughter.

My mom and dad said they had never met my birth mother, who requested the adoption records be kept sealed. I was told only that she was very young, refused to name the father, and wanted no future contact.

I do one final search as the skin on the back of my neck prickles.

Georgia and I share the same birthday, December 14. We both turned thirty-two a few months ago.

I close my laptop and tuck it into my shoulder bag, then check traffic. It should take me an hour and a half to get to the psych ward where Georgia is being held.

I call Scott, my bartender, and ask him to open Sweetbay's, saying I have an appointment and I'll be in later this evening. Then I phone Georgia's lawyer and tell him I'll be there at 2 P.M. I head into the parking lot and unlock my Honda, wondering what I'm about to walk into.

I'm the only person Georgia is willing to see. Why? And how long has she known about me? If she's telling the truth, we shared a womb and a blood supply, pressing up against each other for months. We were as close as it is possible for two people to be, suspended in our own private world. Then we were split apart.

I turn on the engine and head for the highway, struggling to keep from speeding.

My actions aren't driven by curiosity or yearning. I *need* to see Georgia. I'm terrified yet exhilarated, my emotions linked yet contrasting. Just like me and my sister.

Sister. How easily that word flows into my mind, like it has been tucked into a deep cranial fold all along, in a place that predates memory and knowledge, just waiting for the right moment to emerge.

CHAPTER FIVE

GEORGIA

Here are the things you cannot do on the locked ward: possess a pen, earrings, shoelace, drinking glass, or pair of fingernail clippers.

You can't wear your own clothes until you are no longer deemed a suicide risk. Fabric can be twisted and used as a noose; same with belts. You can't drink coffee that is hot enough to burn yourself or others. You can't choose your own mealtimes. You can't have trash bags because you can use them to suffocate yourself or others. You can't lock the door to your room because there is no lock.

Here are the things you can do: You can watch a skinny guy with pale, pitted skin raise a fist, yelling that he's going to kill the man next to him for hiccuping, and see four male aides swoop in and hustle him away. You can wear green pajamas that identify you as a patient of this floor in case you manage to escape.

During art, you can follow the therapist's suggestion and use stubby crayons to color a picture of something that makes you happy.

After lunch, you can step into the rooftop courtyard and look up at the lone, skinny tree growing in the center, straight as an arrow, as if it wants to get as far away from this place as fast as possible. The only other items in the courtyard are two plastic picnic tables with attached benches that are bolted to the ground. Their bright colors stand out against the dingy cement floor and towering, reinforced metal fences. You can't see any other buildings or people on the outside.

You're as isolated as a bird in a cage in the middle of a desert because this facility was built on top of a hill, originally designated to house tuberculosis patients in the early 1900s. You learned about tuberculosis in school: It was called the "white plague" and rendered victims listless and pale. The patients here could be their ghosts, drifting aimlessly through the halls a century later.

You can also lie in bed and count the number of dots in the ceiling tiles, losing your place over and over and going back to the beginning again.

You can feel yourself slipping away, your identity dissolving, as if acid is dripping over it. There's no shiny mirror in which to see yourself, only reflective metal. No journal to jot down your secrets. No smartphone that once held your busy calendar and an album of the cutest ugly dogs you've spotted.

You also have no visitors scheduled, even though they are allowed to come. Your parents wish you didn't exist; your mother spat those very words at you as you were taken away. You don't have a boyfriend or husband, and even if you did, you wouldn't want him to see you like this. The press would eat their own families for the chance to get in and shout questions and blind you with cameras flashing like fireworks, but they're not permitted.

Friends? Sure, you have them, but you can't endure seeing them. They'd be a reminder of everything you've lost, with their layered gold necklaces and jasmine-scented perfume and wide-open futures. If they hugged you, you would shatter. Then they would disappear through the series of locked doors that lead to the outside. And the staff would notice your emotion. You would be viewed with suspicion. The eyes on you would sharpen.

The only way to survive is to be like the others and fade into a ghost. To embrace the strange rhythms of this place. To completely lose track of time in the hopes that it will go faster until one day, you can convince the doctors and the judge that you're rehabilitated and no longer a danger to anyone.

Unless Mandy comes. Then everything will change.

But maybe she won't. You could spend years here without having a single visitor.

You have reached number 642 of the dots in the ceiling tile when a nurse enters your room.

"Mandy Ravenel is here to see you," he says.

CHAPTER SIX

MANDY

"You're going to want to take that off." A nurse named Becca points to my necklace as we step onto the elevator. "Earrings, too."

Before I can ask why, she says, "Last week a PhD student studying deviant behavior came in and wore a lanyard. A patient wrapped it around her neck and tried to strangle her. We got him off her in time, though."

Her tone is matter-of-fact. Like this sort of incident is as unremarkable as mentioning that we're taking the elevator to the top floor.

I slide my hoops out of my ears and tuck them into the pocket of my slacks, then unfasten the gold chain from around my neck and do the same with it.

I wonder which patient tried to kill the student. I spent a little time researching some of the people who live in this facility. They include a young man who stabbed his father more than a dozen times and buried his body behind the garage, a middle-aged woman who tried to burn down a shopping mall because she heard voices telling her to, and a vicious gang member presumed to be sane but canny enough to have worked the system. And those are just the ones I know about. Currently twenty-two patients reside on a single floor of this hospital, accessible only through a series of locked doors.

What is it like for her here, the ex-debutante who graduated from Vassar and planned six-figure weddings and loved to run half marathons? I've read so much about the case I feel as if I'm getting to know Georgia in a superficial way, like she's a character on a TV show. But I have no understanding of what makes her tick.

My heartbeat accelerates as the elevator climbs to the fifth floor. We step out. The first thing I notice is the hallway is completely empty. The second is the heavy silence. The only noise that reaches my ears is my own shallow breathing.

"You can store your purse here," Becca says, punching a code into a small locker. I comply and she secures the door.

Becca reaches for a phone on the wall and speaks into it: "I have Georgia Cartwright's visitor. We're about to come in."

She hangs up, then takes a few steps to a solid-looking brown wood door that's significantly shorter and narrower than a standard door. Above it is a sign: *No videotaping or photography permitted.*

My sister would have been escorted through it only two days ago. With every footstep of hers I trace, I'm drawing nearer to her.

My skin tingles as Becca fits her key into the door and opens it. I follow her into a claustrophobia-inducing space. The ceiling is low, and there are no windows. The air feels thick and stale.

Becca pulls the door shut behind us and I hear a loud click. We're sealed in this tiny area now.

"This is called a trap," she tells me. "You can't open one door unless the other one is locked."

Becca reaches for a key again—I can't tell if it's the same one—and fits it into the second small wooden door.

She looks back at me. "Stay behind me as we enter, please."

My mouth dries up. I nod, and she opens the door. I step into the locked ward.

The first person I see is a woman who has pink-mixed-with-blond hair. She's drifting through the hallway, her face slack. She catches sight of me and changes course, heading directly for me.

To my right is the nursing station, which resembles nursing

stations everywhere: There are desks and computers and charts and busy-looking employees.

There's one huge difference.

The entire station is surrounded by thick protective walls of plexiglass. And the only way in is through another locked door. One of the nurses on the inside opens it and quickly ushers us in.

We're in the station before the woman with pink hair reaches me. I wonder what she would have said or done if we'd come face-to-face.

"You're going to meet Georgia in a private room, but there will be a watcher in the doorway," Becca tells me. "If at any time you want to end the visit, signal to him. Excuse me a moment."

She turns to confer with a colleague while I take in my surroundings.

A disheveled-looking man with a scraggly beard is standing on the other side of the plexiglass, gaping at me. I meet his eyes, and he lifts his palm and bangs on the glass.

"Turn away from him," Becca instructs, not even raising her eyes from the chart.

I shift my body and take in the nurses and aides instead. Most of the employees on this floor look uncommonly fit and strong. And three-quarters are male. A nurse who has to be six foot four is slipping on latex gloves and filling a syringe with a gold-colored medicine. Another—with giant, tattooed biceps—is working next to a CB radio with a big sticker on it that says *Security—Press 11*.

There's a cupful of miniature pens, half the length of traditional ones. It takes me a moment to realize why: If an employee takes a pen out of the nursing station and leaves it near a patient, it can't be gripped and used as a weapon.

In the distance, I hear a woman arguing with someone, her voice shrill and jagged. I watch as a couple of burly nurses clear the hallway, leading patients around the corner and out of view.

They don't want anyone to see me leaving the protection of the nursing station, I realize.

"Ready?" Becca looks at me. I swallow hard and nod.

She unlocks the door, and a male nurse—the one with the tattooed biceps—comes with us, staying slightly behind me and to one side.

Becca ushers me a few feet down the hallway and into a room with two chairs. They're set far apart. "Take the one closest to the door," she tells me.

There's nothing else in the room. I try to shift the chair to the side and can't; it's as if it were made from concrete.

"Georgia will be here in a moment. Damien is going to stay during your visit." She gestures to the male nurse standing in the doorway.

Becca leaves and my stomach tightens.

This air in this place feels thick and strange, as if it has absorbed the trauma of its inhabitants.

Footsteps approach. I jerk my head toward the door. My body tightens.

A figure appears in the doorway. I look into Georgia's eyes for the first time.

CHAPTER SEVEN

GEORGIA

You can't take your eyes off her.

It isn't curiosity or desperation or envy. It's more primal than that. A powerful current is arcing between you. She feels it, too. You can tell by the way her body jerks slightly, like she received a mild physical shock.

Maybe you feel it because she is your only hope. Or maybe it's because she is part of you.

Mandy looks exactly like she did on the video you saw last month. The private investigator who found her for you sat at her bar and ordered a soda. A tiny camera on a button on his shirt filmed your sister filling the glass from the bar spigot, impaling a wedge of lemon on the rim, and sliding it forward, as if she were offering it to you.

You were mesmerized by her efficient manner and easy smile. You played that video again and again, greedily hoarding details about her: her neat, unpolished fingernails; her straight dark eyebrows over light gray eyes; the hollow between her collarbones.

And now she's here. You have to walk past her to claim the chair opposite hers.

The aide who brought you matches pace with you, staying between you and your sister. It doesn't matter. He can't break your magnetic link.

As you pass Mandy, you inhale her scent. She smells fresh and clean. You don't detect any perfume, but there's the faintest hint of something citrusy, probably from her shampoo or bodywash.

You sit down, automatically crossing your legs at the ankle and bending your knees to one side, as you were trained to do from a young age. You see her take in your paper top and pants and sticky-bottom socks before her eyes rise to your face again, drinking you in. She looks anxious, uneasy. No. It's more than that. She *feels* anxious and uneasy.

You know this because it's as if you have slipped into her skin, as if your physiologies have seamlessly fused back together after being apart for three decades.

The aide takes up his post in the doorway, tilting his body to keep you within his line of vision. It would take him only seconds to get to you if you tried to attack your sister. Which you never would. Not this sister, anyway.

Mandy clears her throat. "Why did you ask for me?"

She's direct, no-nonsense. She cut to the crux of the situation without any extraneous questions or attempt at small talk. Somehow you knew she would.

You need to play this moment carefully. Everything depends on it. You are supposedly in a dissociative state, which you learned about years ago because you wrote a twenty-page paper on it for a college psychology class.

The topic interested you, so you did your research and spent late nights crafting your paper. It turned out to be the most important thing you learned in college.

That paper may have saved your life.

You keep your facial muscles slack, your voice and body devoid of expression. You speak in a low monotone—too low for the watcher to hear. This message is for your twin alone. Everything depends on how she receives it.

"I didn't do it," you tell your sister. "And if you don't get me out of here, they're going to kill me."

CHAPTER EIGHT

MANDY

She's lying. I just saw proof.

A moment ago, Georgia shuffled into the room, her eyes dull and her movements sluggish. With her lank hair and shapeless paper scrubs, she bears little resemblance to the chic, graceful woman I saw in photographs and videos.

Then she whispered her desperate message to me, and as her eyes fixed on mine, I saw complete awareness in them. It was as if she raised the cover of a trapdoor an inch and allowed me to peer into a secret compartment in her brain.

Behind her vacant expression is a razor-sharp, supple mind that she wielded full control over as she told me I had to get her out or she'd be killed.

Is she lying about that, too?

"Who is going to kill you?" I whisper.

She doesn't reply. She's perfectly still now, her mouth slightly open, her eyes downcast. She has latched the trapdoor again.

I search her face for answers. Instead, I find traces of myself: We both have a faint constellation of freckles across our cheekbones. We both have attached earlobes, and I see the markings for double piercings on hers. I have the same markings. The list tallies as my breath quickens:

Her eyebrows are straight, like mine. She reaches to scratch her nose, and she does it with her left hand. When I have an itch, that's the hand I use to scratch, too, because it's my dominant one. Only 10 percent of people are left-handed. Georgia and I are among them.

Dizziness crashes over me. I can't look at her face any longer.

I drop my gaze lower. Her nails are painted the shade of a ballet slipper, but on her left hand, the nail of her index finger is broken to the quick.

A vision flits through my mind: Georgia lifting the heavy sterling-silver paperweight—it was reportedly four pounds—and smashing it into her younger sister's temple.

"I didn't do it," she repeats in a faint, breathy whisper, and I flinch. It's as if she can peer into my mind, as if she is watching the violent scene play out along with me.

"Who did it, then?" I ask.

"Find out," she whispers. "Help me."

Who are you? I want to ask. She's intensely familiar and a stranger, all at once. Something inside of me knows her, remembers her. Because as odd as it is to be in this alien, disturbing place, on some deep level, it also feels exactly right.

"How do I know you're really my sister?" I ask.

Instead of answering, she does something so eerie, I rear back against my chair, trying to get farther away from her.

She reaches up, her hand slow and deliberate, and curls a few strands of hair around her index finger. Her eyes lock on mine as she pulls down her hand, stretching the hairs tight. I feel pinned into place; she seems to be sending me a strange, silent message.

She pulls her hair even tighter. It has to be painful, but she doesn't flinch or react. The tip of her finger is turning white from the circulation being cut off.

I wait for the aide to stop her from hurting herself, but her movements are so small and slow he probably doesn't realize what she's doing.

Her wide, unblinking eyes stay trained on mine as she gives one final tug, yanking out her hairs by the roots.

Then she rubs her fingertips together, and I see the red–gold strands drift to the floor.

"Test them," she whispers.

Georgia slowly begins to rise, and in a flash, the muscular nurse darts into the room, inserting himself between us. But she merely turns and begins to make her slow, unsteady way back out. She disappears down the corridor.

I look down at the hairs glinting on the white linoleum floor. A DNA test would definitively prove Georgia's claim. That must be what she meant.

I lean forward and pick up the thin strands of hair, suppressing a shudder as they tickle my skin like the touch of a spider's legs.

"Miss?"

The muscular aide has returned and is standing by the door. His message is clear: My visit is over.

CHAPTER NINE

GEORGIA

An hour after your sister leaves, you see your first takedown.

The skinny guy who threatened to punch another man for hiccuping is agitated again. He walks the wide halls, exhaling hard through his nose, his hands clenching and re-clenching into fists. You hug the wall as he approaches, hoping he doesn't veer toward you. Nurses and aides and a security guard are nearby, but the ones you can see are distracted, doing paperwork or interacting with other patients.

Eyes vacant, you remind yourself. *Don't show fear.* You need to be an octopus blending into its background, taking on the hues and topography of the locked ward. *This is just another test*, you tell yourself.

The man passes and your body relaxes a fraction—until you realize he's now behind you. His socks are soundless against the floor. If he tries to attack you, you won't know until it's too late.

Fresh blood, your mind whispers.

Ahead of you is a blind corner. You don't know if anyone—patient or nursing staff—is around it.

It could be empty.

Your instincts are screaming. You slowly swivel your head, looking behind you. Your heart leaps into your throat. The pale man with pitted skin is there, muttering under his breath, his stare locked on you.

Your pulse explodes. The closest nurses are a dozen yards away, behind plexiglass. None of them are looking your way.

"Pretty baby," the man croons. "Babies cry. Do you like to cry?"

He is between you and the nurses' station. There's no help nearby.

Don't make eye contact, you warn yourself, but it's impossible to pull away your gaze. He's smiling at you, his lips peeling back over crooked, chipped yellow teeth. It's the most terrifying smile you've ever seen.

"What's your name?" he whispers. He's coming closer, so close you can smell his vinegary scent. "Huh? You got a name, dontcha?"

A thin silver scar runs down his left cheek like a tear. His eyes aren't in sync—one of them drifts upward while the other stays pinned on you.

Your chest is so tight it's hard to breathe.

"*I've been through the desert on a horse with no name*," he sings.

The quick footsteps behind you turn your legs to jelly. Is it another patient or someone coming to help you?

"Josh, keep walking and let her pass by."

It's the aide who watched you while you slept. Relief crashes through your body, even as you realize he won't be able to protect you all the time. He can't. There are too many patients on this floor, too many doorways and corners, too many other tasks to distract the nursing staff.

"Just taking a lil break. No law against that." Josh cracks his knuckles.

The aide moves slowly, keeping his hands in front of him, as he positions himself next to you. You take a step back, then another, until he's closer to Josh than you are.

"Where's your room?" Josh asks you.

Your mind shrieks, but you can't release a sound. If they Velcro you to the bed again and Josh finds you, you'll be at his mercy.

"You don't need to know that, Josh. Come on. Keep walking."

"Pretty baby," Josh croons. "That's your name."

"I'm not going to tell you again," the aide says. "Keep walking, Josh."

Josh doesn't even acknowledge the man. He's fixated on you.

What did he do to end up here? you wonder. But what you really want to know is, what is he capable of doing now?

You realize you already know the answer. You'd know it even if you didn't see him threaten another patient, even if you hadn't taken in the silvery scar running down his cheek. You know it the way an animal instinctively knows when sizing up another animal, calculating whether to flee or fight: He's capable of anything.

Then you see other nurses and aides coming your way. There's a security guard, too. Six in all. The biggest nurse holds three syringes in his gloved hand. There's also a dark-haired female nurse, maybe forty, leading them.

The men remain a few feet behind Josh, spreading out in a semicircle, but the dark-haired nurse strides up to him, though she remains an arm's length away. She's wearing a knitted vest that holds all the colors of the rainbow over her scrubs.

She looks like she could be a middle school teacher or a saleswoman at a crafts store. Right now, she's the one in charge.

"Josh, you need to go to your room," she tells him, her voice crisp and authoritative.

"Why? I can take a walk."

"Make the right choice, Josh. Walk to your room now."

He sneers and lifts his arm, like he's going to strike her, and the hallway explodes into action. The aide nearest me grabs me and yanks me away as the group of men pile onto Josh. It isn't a melee, though. It's as carefully orchestrated as a dance.

Josh is splayed face down, each of his limbs pinned by a different nurse or aide. But he's still cursing and struggling. Then the big nurse holding the syringes squats down and injects them one by one into Josh's shoulder.

Josh instantly goes completely limp, all the fight in him squashed like a bug.

"Come on, Georgia," your watcher says, leading you away from the scene of the struggle.

You comply instantly.

You've just seen what happens when you don't.

CHAPTER TEN

MANDY

Two days. That's how long it takes me to uncover the truth.

I couldn't believe how simple it was to test Georgia's claim. DNA kits are sold everywhere from drugstores to the internet, with some specifically designed for potential siblings. I ordered one that promised rigorous reviews of markers and fast results. All I had to do was swab my cheek and send in my sample along with Georgia's hairs, paying for expedited shipping.

Even though I suspected it, seeing the result almost knocks my legs out from under me. I stare at the email on my phone, rereading the information that just landed.

Georgia is my sister.

I ease onto the counter stool at my kitchen island, my coffee and eggs growing cold. More than anything, I wish my parents were here to talk through my next steps. We'd sit at their round kitchen table, like we always did for important conversations. My mother would bring out banana bread or cookies, because one of the ways she showed love was by feeding us. My dad would write up a list of pros and cons, like he did whenever I had to make a big decision. I still have one of his old lists from when I was weighing whether to get a gecko for my tenth birthday: CON—*you have to clean the cage. PRO—geckos are awesome!* My mom, the quieter and more anxious of the two, would chime in with a smart question like: *What if Georgia is a murderer and she's released and begins to fixate on you?*

But in the end, they'd support whatever decision I made, even if they didn't agree with it. The greatest gift my parents gave me was steady, uncomplicated love. After they died, it was like an invisible safety net beneath me disintegrated, one I didn't notice I possessed until it was gone.

It's safer to keep my distance from Georgia. My parents would secretly hope I'd do that.

But Georgia is the only family I have left.

★ ★ ★

The grand stone Myers Park church is already filled with mourners fifteen minutes before the funeral begins. Hundreds of white flowers decorate the room. A harpist's fingers glide across the strings of her instrument, filling the hallowed space with an ethereal melody.

An usher hands me a program. I look down at the name written in embossed gold on the front: *Annabelle Cartwright.*

I couldn't stay away from her funeral, not after what Georgia told me. Over the last two nights while I tilted beer glasses under taps and cleared plates off tables, and as I lay sleepless in bed with the moonlight painting stripes across me through the slats in my blinds, I thought about what she'd said.

I didn't do it. And: *They're going to kill me.*

But she's in a high-security psych ward. Don't they all say that?

Now I look down at the program in my hand. In her photograph, Annabelle has wavy blond hair and a smile so big I can see her gums. She looks wholesome. Genuine. Beneath her photograph are the years of her birth and death.

She was only four months younger than Georgia. In a way, they were almost twins, too.

I'm just about to take a seat in the last pew when an anguished wail erupts from the front of the church. I'm still standing, so I have a clear vantage point down the aisle. A woman in the front row wearing a black veil is collapsing—but slowly, so it appears as if she's melting into the ground. For a moment, I fear she's going to crack her head against the unforgiving floor, but at the last second a tall, distinguished-looking man with a red tie catches her.

The music halts. Murmurs spread through the crowd like ripples across a lake: "Did she faint?" "That's Annabelle's mother." "Should we call an ambulance?"

Then I see the woman in the veil being helped to the front pew. Someone rushes over with a bottle of water, but she waves it away.

I recognize her from the news articles I've been devouring: It's Honey Cartwright, the woman who raised Georgia. The woman who told a reporter she'd lost two daughters on the same day.

"Can you imagine?" the woman next to me murmurs to her companion. "All she's been through. What a nightmare." Their deep drawls are much more pronounced than my light Southern accent. They look to be about Honey's age; they must be neighbors or friends.

If they know the family, they must also know Georgia.

I shift closer to them.

"I keep thinking of that Christmas pageant," the other woman replies. "Probably because it happened right here in this church. Do you remember?"

"I wasn't there, but I sure heard about it."

"I knew something was wrong with Georgia even way back then. That look on her face—it was like she was proud of what she did to little Annabelle. Like she enjoyed hurting her in front of everyone."

"And remember what Georgia did when Annabelle was in a stroller near a busy street? She could've killed her—" The woman cuts herself off as a hush falls through the crowd. The priest is approaching the pulpit.

I tune out during his opening prayer, and a reading of Annabelle's favorite poem by Mary Oliver, and the soloist's performance of "Amazing Grace." I refocus during the eulogy, but there's scant information in it. Georgia's name is never mentioned; instead, the priest focuses on Annabelle's volunteer work with the younger children in the parish, her hope of traveling the world one day, and her energetic, buoyant character.

I scan the crowd. The younger women—those around Annabelle's age—have sleek blowouts and are disproportionately blond. The older women wear glittering jewelry, and the men are dressed in dark suits.

Their faces are alternately stoic or tear-streaked or downcast. I wonder what lies behind their socially appropriate expressions. Memories must be roiling through their minds—not just of Annabelle, but also of my twin.

The people in this room have the key to the thing I desperately want: to understand my sister.

"God rest her soul," the priest concludes his eulogy.

"Amen," reply the hundreds of mourners as one.

What did Georgia do to Annabelle at the Christmas pageant? I wonder. And what else did she do to her younger sister?

There's a private reception for family and friends at the Cartwright estate following the service. The same place where Georgia allegedly killed Annabelle.

I need to find a way in.

CHAPTER ELEVEN

GEORGIA

The gray-haired man sits across from you in the same room where you met Mandy.

"I thought you'd be comfortable here, Georgia," he says. "But we can talk in the common area. It's your choice."

You don't reply or make eye contact.

You've been in danger ever since you were brought here, but this encounter is your riskiest yet. The man sitting before you is beginning an assessment so he can issue a recommendation of whether you're mentally fit to stand trial for murder.

North Carolina has the death penalty. But you won't last that long if you go to jail. You'll be dead within a week.

Does Mandy believe you are innocent?

You thought the bait you'd dangled would entice her to become involved. But maybe you miscalculated.

It wouldn't be the first time you'd misjudged a sister. You thought you knew Annabelle—everyone did, because she appeared so guileless and sweet—but she was full of surprises. Perfect Annabelle, who got straight As and called adults "ma'am" and "sir" and loved babies. No one would believe what she'd done if you'd told people about her scandalous secret. Or they'd find a way to blame you. Your mother always did, and your father was too cowed by her to challenge her.

Your parents never wanted to leave you alone with Annabelle. There were always eyes on you, just as there are here. From a very young age, no one trusted you around your little sister.

The man is staring at you. What does he see?

Your hands are icy and beginning to tremble. You slowly slide them beneath your thighs and rock back and forth slightly.

"My name is Dave Winters and I'm a psychiatrist," he tells you.

He doesn't look like a shrink. With his beefy shoulders, beer belly, and lumpy nose, he looks more like an avid Panthers fan. You can almost see him in the stadium, face painted blue, as he screams the crowd-favorite chant, *Keep pounding!*

But something tells you the mind behind that ordinary face is uncommonly sharp. That he deliberately crafts his low-key appearance—down to his ratty sneakers, plain khakis, and cheap watch—to his advantage.

"Do you know why you're here?"

You keep your gaze focused just to the right of his face, looking at his temple and deliberately softening the muscles around your eyes. You wish you could adjust your hearing, too, because his questions feel like nails driving into your brain.

"Do you understand the charges against you?" he asks.

You tell yourself to let his words bounce off you, like raindrops clinking onto a roof. They can't be allowed to reach you.

A person in a dissociative state is mentally disconnected from their thoughts and feelings—and even, in more severe cases, their memories and sense of identity.

You wrote that line in your college paper, the one that earned you an A.

A more severe condition is a dissociative identity disorder, once known as multiple personality disorder, in which an individual can have two or more "identities."

There's no way you would have been able to get away with faking the second, more severe condition. But so far, you've been able to pull off the first one.

"Georgia, do you know what day it is?"

It's the day of the Sullivan wedding. A church service with silk bows adorning the end of every pew and a curly-haired flower girl toddling down the aisle, holding the hand of the little ring bearer, to delighted murmurs. Eight bridesmaids in teal linen, the fabric identical but each design distinct. Lush cascades of blush-colored roses perfuming the air. An open bar with a signature drink, a Bali Breeze, in a nod to the honeymoon destination. A stunning six-tier seafood pyramid. Four dozen bottles of Veuve Clicquot popping open for the toasts.

You've got a binder full of details, but you don't need them to refresh your memory. That's your signature, like the Bali cocktail. You don't leave anything to chance. You don't make mistakes.

Until the night of Annabelle's party. You never saw the events of that night coming.

The first police officer on the scene, the one who walked into the dining room and discovered you standing over your sister's body while Honey wept and raged at you, was a family friend—the son of the chief of police, invited for Annabelle's birthday party. You briefly dated him when you were nineteen. He's been half in love with you ever since.

That must be why he pulled Honey off you and ordered the seventy-two-hour psychiatric hold rather than arresting you. One last gesture from his heart.

"Do you know why you're here?" the psychiatrist asks again. His voice is mild. His palms are flat against his knees. He exudes calm and patience.

He terrifies you.

Annabelle died moments before her birthday ended. She'll be forever frozen at the age of thirty-two.

So will you, in a way. It's as if a giant cleaver came down at the stroke of midnight, a reverse Cinderella effect, separating you into the woman of before and the patient of now. The life of Georgia Cartwright is so far removed from yours that it appears to belong to a different person.

"I'm going to order a fourteen-day stay," the psychiatrist says. "You'll be entitled to a court hearing, which will be held in this facility via Telehealth. You will be appointed a mental health representative should you choose not to attend. Do you understand, Georgia?"

You don't move. You don't even blink or breathe. You feel his eyes drilling into you. Then he stands up and gathers his things.

"I'll see you soon, Georgia."

Maybe you've passed his first test. Or maybe he sees right through you.

CHAPTER TWELVE

MANDY

I've never been to a house like this before. I doubt I've ever crossed paths with the people who live in it, either. It's a safe bet the Cartwrights don't shop at chain supermarkets or scour discount stores for designer knockoffs. They don't schedule flu shots at CVS or fly coach.

They exist in an alternate universe, one in which every path is gilded and every preference fulfilled.

At the base of the long magnolia tree–lined private drive leading to the Cartwright estate, several men in dark suits briefly stop each car that passes, peering inside. It takes me a moment to figure out why. Then I realize they're probably checking for paparazzi, given the intense media interest surrounding Annabelle's murder.

Being thirty-two and having girl-next-door looks gives me a perfect disguise. I could be one of Georgia's childhood friends, college classmates, or work colleagues. I sweep through the security checkpoint easily.

Uniformed parking attendants use hand signals to direct me to a back field, where I park my Honda in between a Cadillac and a Mercedes.

I wait in my car, pretending to check my makeup in my rearview mirror, until a powder blue Bronco pulls up and four women around my age step out. I trail them toward the house, drawing close enough that I appear to be part of their group.

Two unsmiling men with military-short haircuts stand at the front door, their eyes cutting through everyone who walks by. One of the women taps on her phone, revealing what looks like an invitation. The guard gestures for us to enter. I smile at him as I pass by.

I step across the threshold, then suck in a breath as I take in the scene: The marble-floored receiving hall is easily as big as the entire house where I grew up, and the enormous chandelier two stories up looks like it would crush someone to death if it broke free and landed on them. A massive impressionistic painting hangs on one wall, surrounded by pale yellow, textured wallpaper.

A server in black slacks and a crisp white shirt approaches, offering white wine or sparkling water from the tray balanced on his palm. I accept a glass of water and thank him.

Dozens of people are congregating in the entrance hall, while others are flowing into the adjoining room, which holds several groupings of cream-colored couches and chairs.

"Never buy a light couch or carpet," my mother told me once as we shopped at a Macy's sale for a new sofa. "The stains show much faster."

Apparently that's not a concern of the Cartwrights. The grand room is done in shades of cream and white, with occasional splashes of pastels. Flowers are everywhere—white calla lilies, roses, and tulips—filling the air with a cloyingly sweet smell.

And in the middle of the cream-and-white room is Honey Cartwright in her black dress, like a splotch of spilled ink on a sheet of paper. She's surrounded by a group of women, and another server stands at attention a few feet behind her. Mrs. Cartwright looks like a queen holding court with her handmaidens.

Even though her face is tear-streaked and her eyes are swollen, it's easy to see why she was won the title of Miss North Carolina when she was twenty-two.

This is where my sister once lived—at least when she wasn't at boarding school. Did she tiptoe in through the front door as a teenager when she was late for curfew? Did she have a crush on the Jonas Brothers and sneak Marlboro Lights out her bedroom window like I did?

"It was a beautiful service," someone murmurs next to me.

I turn and see a slender, balding man with bland features and owlish, watchful eyes.

"It really was," I agree.

"How do you know the Cartwrights?" he asks.

"I was friends with Annabelle in college." I give a sad half smile, then cast my eyes down, hoping he takes my brevity for grief.

"I'm Reece DuPont. And you are . . . ?"

Before I can reply, a ripple runs through the room. Heads swivel toward the front door. The energy in the room surges.

I see its source: the silver-haired man who caught Honey Cartwright when she collapsed at the funeral.

He stands in the open doorway, backlit by the sun. I can't see his face clearly at first. Then he steps into the room. He's handsome for an older guy—tall and fit, with perfect teeth and a few lines on his lightly tanned skin. But that isn't why I find myself staring.

I've read interviews with celebrities who exude a special kind of wattage, and more than one has spoken about their ability to turn it off and on. I'm guessing this man has that same ability, and he's running it full throttle now.

"Senator!" A man steps forward and extends his hand, pushing through others to get to the new arrival.

I've seen him before, in political ads and on the front page of the newspaper my parents used to get. He's Michael Dawson, the senior US senator from North Carolina, who is widely rumored to be a front-runner in the next presidential election.

The crowd parts for him as he makes his way to Mrs. Cartwright. One of her handmaidens vacates a chair so he can sit by the grieving mother. He murmurs something to her I can't hear, and they talk for another few moments before he takes her hand and briefly presses it before standing up again.

Where is Mr. Cartwright? I wonder. I've researched what he looks like, but I haven't seen him today.

No sooner has that question flitted through my mind than the senator turns and walks directly toward me.

My mouth dries up. Everyone is watching the senator's movements, so it feels as if everyone is staring at me.

Do they know I don't belong?

At the last second the senator veers to my left, approaching a man I hadn't noticed before who is standing only a few feet from me. That ginger-mixed-with-gray hair, the heavy eyebrows and ruddy, round-ish face—it can only be Georgia's father, Stephen Cartwright. The senator reaches out and hugs Mr. Cartwright.

This time, I'm close enough to listen.

"My deepest condolences," the senator begins. Even his voice seems presidential—deep and confident. "Your family is always in my prayers."

"Thank you, Michael," Mr. Cartwright says.

Mr. Cartwright doesn't use the elected title like everyone else. It's a clue that these men are not only close, but see themselves as equals.

"Words don't help much at a time like this," the senator continues. "That's why I'm giving you a promise instead."

If I'd been farther away, I would have missed it.

But for just a second, I see emotion twist Senator Dawson's face, breaking apart his polished veneer. It looks like genuine pain.

There's a person behind the facade—a man who cared deeply about Annabelle, I realize.

The senator's voice rises slightly, steel running through his words. "Justice *will* prevail. And Annabelle's memory will live on in all of us."

CHAPTER THIRTEEN

GEORGIA

You wake up screaming in the darkness.

You dreamt about Annabelle. You were yelling at her, telling her you hated her, raising your hand to strike her while she cowered. Then she was on the floor, all the life gone from her eyes, blood leaking from her skull.

"Georgia!" A nurse hurries through the doorway. "What's going on?"

You gasp for breath as you remember where you are. You've slipped out of one nightmare into another.

Your chest tightens as pressure builds behind your eyes. You're seized with the desperate urge to run, to hurl your body into the locked doors.

You try the tricks you've established to keep yourself from spiraling. You breathe deeply from your stomach, not your chest. You remind yourself of the things you can do here: You can draw and color. You can feel sun on your face in the courtyard on nice afternoons, even though the giant metal fence means you can't look at anything other than the sky. You can watch TV, though the screen is behind a layer of plexiglass that makes the images look cloudy. You can eat fresh fruit every day.

It could be so much worse, you tell yourself.

"Take this. It'll help you sleep." The nurse tries to hand you a small round pill and a paper cup of water. But you keep your arms at your side and your expression blank. Your college paper taught you that you can't be forced to take medication until you are ruled mentally incompetent, which you haven't been yet.

Your mind is fully intact. You need to keep it that way.

You've been terrified of going to jail because you know what will happen there. You've lost the power and money that provide a protective cushion around anyone with the Cartwright name, even the black sheep of the family. You'd end up in a maximum-security prison. A woman like you—privileged, soft, pretty—would be marked by a bull's-eye target. And not just by people on the inside.

You are desperate to avoid that fate.

A sharp noise comes from just outside your room. The nurse? Or is someone else approaching? Maybe it's Josh, the man with pitted skin.

You want to get up and look, but you can't. Not because your limbs are tied down—you no longer have a watcher or Velcro straps, now that you don't appear to be a suicide risk—but because your body is weak with fear. Your brain feels fuzzy; thoughts slip through it and disappear like minnows darting through a cloudy stream.

You listen as hard as you can, but there's no echo of the noise. Maybe your brain conjured it up. Perhaps your mind is beginning to turn on you.

Silent tears leak out of the sides of your eyes. You don't have the energy to wipe them away.

What will a month here do to you? A year? A decade?

You lie atop your plain, hard bed and look around at the nothingness of your room. Once, you went into a sensory-deprivation tank. You were weightless in the salt water, and when the lid of the tank was closed, you couldn't feel your body.

This feels like that.

For the first time, you think maybe jail would have been the easier way.

There is more than one type of death.

It just happens more slowly in this place.

CHAPTER FOURTEEN

MANDY

If you don't get me out of here, they're going to kill me.

Georgia's words are urging me to take a risk, driving me toward the room where Honey Cartwright is gathered with her friends.

I set my glass down on a table and edge across the threshold into the main receiving room. This may be the only chance I'll have. Everyone is focused on the celebrity in their midst; they all want to establish a connection with the senator who could soon be living in the White House. Maybe they'll get an invitation to sleep in the Lincoln Bedroom if they get in good with him now.

My target is elsewhere. It's the guest book splayed open on a stand just inside the white-on-cream room. Even from this distance, I can see the pages are filled with names of the people who know the Cartwrights best. Maybe through them, I can begin to unravel the mystery of my twin.

My fingers close around my phone. All I need is a few seconds to take a picture of the names written in the book.

I take a few more steps forward, then casually look around. A man seems to be scanning the crowd. A security guard? Then I see him lift a glass of wine and take a deep drink.

Security wouldn't touch alcohol on the job. He's not a threat to me.

I edge closer to the book, mentally rehearsing my movements. My phone is in my right hand, the camera already on. I reach for the pen that's next to the guest book with my left and scrawl an illegible signature. Then I tilt my body to the side and pretend to check my phone, frowning at an imaginary message while I click a photo.

I step away, still frowning at my phone.

"Was she your sister?"

The blood in my veins turns to ice. The man with watchful eyes—Reece DuPont—has materialized beside me. He's waiting for my answer.

How does he know who I am? My throat is too dry for me to speak. I can't read the man's expression. Maybe he's one of Georgia's allies. Or maybe he's about to call the cops on me.

"Tri Delt, right? Wasn't that Annabelle's sorority?"

Relief crashes through me. I nod and smile.

"What did you say your name was again?" His question is casual. His expression is anything but.

"Amanda," I say. Some internal warning keeps me from giving my last name.

He opens his mouth to speak, then whips around at the sound of a tremendous crash behind us.

I spin around, too, and see a waiter has spilled a tray full of drinks. Wine oozes across the floor, carrying shards of glass in its stream. Within seconds, a half dozen other waiters come rushing over to clear away the mess.

I use the distraction to step away before the blond man can ask me any more questions. I weave through the crowd until I reach the front door. I keep my head low and hurry to my Honda.

Even though it's a sunny afternoon and I'm in a place with high security, a shiver runs down my spine as I climb inside. I instinctively reach out and hit the button to lock my doors.

Only then do I look at the image on my phone. It's crystal clear.

I've now got the names of dozens of people who know the Cart-wrights.

But I don't think any of them know who I am.

Which means I can slip into their lives like a ghost, collecting stories and details about Georgia. I can begin to piece together who she really is.

CHAPTER FIFTEEN

GEORGIA

Mandy hasn't come back.

Your encounter must have jarred her to her core. She could be regrouping, trying to figure out her next steps. Or maybe your twin is carrying on with her life, chatting with her customers in the easy way you saw on the video. She could already have written you off.

But the research you did on her showed she's tough. A real fighter: She once leapt over her bar and dug her fingers into the eyes of a man who was punching a woman in the face. The guy, who'd been previously arrested for domestic battery, lost vision in one eye and sued. The judge ruled in Mandy's favor after viewing a video of the incident, and Mandy handed out black eye patches to customers that night for a celebratory party.

She's intensely loyal to family; instead of selling her parents' bar and using the money to travel or buy a Porsche, she quit her marketing job and took it over.

You're all the family she has left now. That has to mean something to her.

You've got one final card to play. Your gut tells you it's time to use it.

Your lawyer calls or visits every day, but during those encounters, you typically stay silent. The only time you've spoken directly to him is when you told him, in a low, halting voice, that you had a twin named Amanda Ravenel and you wanted to see her.

You shuffle to the plexiglass wall of the nurses' station closest to the patient phone and stand there until an aide on the other side asks if you'd like to make a call. You nod slowly, concentrating on keeping your eyes dull and unfocused.

"To your lawyer?" he guesses.

By way of answer, you reach out your hand for the phone. He tells you to hang on a second while he looks up the number and dials it; then he speaks into the receiver: "Georgia Cartwright wants to speak to Mr. Daniels . . . Sure, we can hold."

He stretches the receiver through a small opening, like a fast-food worker delivering a meal via a drive-through window. The phone receiver is the only potentially dangerous thing you've been allowed to hold. It's solid and fits easily into your hand. But the reinforced stretchy cord extends only a few inches beyond the opening, rendering the phone useless for anything other than its intended purpose. You lift the receiver to your ear and curl your body around it, so no one can hear you or try to read your lips.

When Milt Daniels comes on the line, you whisper another instruction to him. He repeats it, a question in his voice, but you hand back the phone to the aide without saying anything else.

There's something you need the lawyer to offer to Mandy. She won't be able to resist taking it. And once she does, she'll learn so much more about you.

The more she feels like she knows you, the harder it'll be for her to walk away.

The public defender's job is to save you, but he's young and overworked, and there's a good chance your parents and Senator Dawson will get to him or the judge. You have no faith in him.

You've put it all in Mandy.

But that faith begins to wane as the day ambles by, broken up by its usual segments of meals, art, group activity—today it's stretching—and outdoor time.

You grow worried. Maybe your lawyer decided to ignore your instruction. If he did, you are done for.

Just as you are beginning to despair, a nurse approaches you in the common room. Your breathing grows shallow. It's a struggle to keep your expression neutral.

"Georgia, your lawyer just told me someone is coming to pick up your things."

You don't have many things for Mandy to collect. You were brought in the back of your old lover's police car wearing your silver dress and shoes and jewelry and carrying a small clutch purse. You were told that your belongings were locked in a safe.

You close your eyes, imagining Mandy opening your purse and looking inside.

Your purse contains five items, the essentials most women carry with them when they go out for an evening.

The police almost certainly took one of them, your cell phone, as potential evidence in the case against you.

But the other four items should still be in place.

One of them will tempt Mandy.

CHAPTER SIXTEEN

MANDY

Happy hour at Sweetbay's is always a crowded time, especially since I started offering a five-dollar build-your-own-nachos bar, although my bartender Scott is probably responsible for some of our success, too. Women love him—and the way his muscles flex when he holds up a shaker to mix their drinks.

I'm carrying a case of Heineken out from the walk-in fridge in the back of my bar when I catch a glimpse of a man's reflection in the mirrored wall by the front door. My shoe skids on something slick and I nearly drop the beer.

It looks like Reece DuPont, the man who questioned me at Annabelle's funeral.

He's in a group with a few other guys, his back to me, in an Eagles cap and a T-shirt and jeans. He's wearing glasses today, which he wasn't at the funeral.

But I'm pretty sure it was his profile I caught sight of in the mirror.

"Excuse me!" I yell. I set the heavy box of beer on the end of the bar and make my way through the crowd, trying to get to the man.

Someone wraps an arm around my shoulders, their boozy breath warm against my cheek, and I instinctively elbow them hard in the gut, then spin around, my foot lifted to stomp on their instep.

"Whoa, Mand, what's up girl?" It's Ruben, one of my favorite regulars.

"Sorry." I lower my foot. My heart is pounding, and I realize my hands have come up to defend myself.

He rubs the side of his stomach. "Good thing I've got a lot of padding."

I look in the direction of the man again, but I can't see him anymore. It's like he evaporated.

I take a deep breath and order myself to get it together. "I haven't seen you in a while," I tell Ruben. "Are you cheating on me with another bar?"

He grins, showing an appealing gap between his front teeth.

"I got a job in Norfolk. I'm moving next week."

"Hey, congrats!" This time I don't have to force my enthusiasm. Ruben's been through a tough stretch lately, with his girlfriend breaking up with him and his being between jobs.

"Do a shot with us." He leans over the bar and orders six Fireball shots, passing a few to his buddies. It isn't unusual for me to have a beer while I work, but I steer away from shots. Not tonight, though. I'm so on edge I need one.

I clink my glass against Ruben's, then swallow the syrupy red liquid, feeling the burn down my chest. I lick the spicy cinnamon from my lips, then chat with Ruben for another few minutes. Before I move on, I lean over and discreetly tell Scott to comp his bill.

All the while, I keep scanning the crowd at the bar. Maybe it wasn't Reece I spotted, I finally acknowledge. I only caught that split-second glimpse in the mirror, and half the guys who come into my bar wear caps and T-shirts. And I've been preoccupied ever since I learned about Georgia. Today I took a wrong turn on the way to work today, a route I've driven countless times.

My mind could have been playing tricks on me.

Besides, how would he have found me? I didn't give him my last name, and no one at the service knew who I was.

Then my heart plummets as I remember the checkpoints. Maybe

there was invisible security, too. Like cameras to record every license plate that passed through. If mine was captured, it would be easy for someone with the kind of power the Cartwright family has to link it to my name and get the address of my bar.

I walk to the end of the bar and flip open the hinged counter. I'm being paranoid, I tell myself.

It hits me a split second later: That's exactly what I thought about Georgia when she claimed she'd be killed if I didn't get her out of the psych ward.

My eyes seek out the photograph of my parents on the high bar shelf. If they were here, we'd be in this together. I can feel my throat thicken, so I look at the St. Michael the Archangel statue they gave me, displayed next to their picture. The powerful message on its pouch—*Protect Me Always*—centers me.

I try to lose myself in the busyness of my bar, dealing with a credit card machine that's acting up, restocking the napkin holders, and collecting empties from the booths and high-top tables. I don't stop moving until the happy hour crowd has died down.

Once everything is under control, I grab a glass of ice water and head to my little office in the back, where I plan to get a start on payroll.

I unlock the door and see my cell phone, which I've left charging on my desk, has a new message. I pick it up and see the now familiar words in the call log: *Private Caller.*

The message is from Milt Daniels, the public defender. He wants me to come and pick up my sister's belongings.

CHAPTER SEVENTEEN

GEORGIA

You are no longer the newest member of this strange place that feels like it's floating through the ether, immune to the laws of the fourth dimension of time.

Another woman just arrived.

"She's a late breaker," you overhear a nurse say.

The staff speaks in a shorthand code you've begun to decipher. A 10–13 is a takedown. Some patients are frequent fliers. There are also first breakers like you—people who have never been admitted to a psych facility before. The woman coming today is a late breaker, so she must be middle-aged or elderly.

You're seated on the couch in the common area, in full view of the nurses behind the wall of plexiglass. You stay here whenever possible in case Josh comes around again. So you're among the first to see when the new arrival is brought in by the tallest male aide.

Your eyes flit toward her; then you drag them away.

You are always being watched. Cameras are everywhere in this place. Any sign of interest, any change in your affect, could be noted by the nurses and used in the case prosecutors are building against you.

Patients begin to gather, drawn toward this new source of energy, but she doesn't react to them.

"Hello, darling!" cries the woman who accused you of taking her glasses. "How are you today?"

You slowly move your head so you can study the new patient out of the corner of your eye.

She could be anywhere from forty-five to sixty. Her hair is a mix of brown and gray and cut short, she's full-figured, and her features are unremarkable, other than her mouth, which is pulled down, giving her a sorrowful expression.

Then you spot the thick white bandages on both of her wrists.

Most people are in here because they're a danger to others. The bandages tell you this woman likely falls into a smaller group of the patients, those who are a danger to themselves.

Plus, she's being escorted by one aide, not the four who brought you in. And he's not taking any special precautions, like wearing a spit guard or staying an arm's length away from her.

It seems horrible that someone who attempted suicide would be brought to this dark place. But you've learned it's the only part of the hospital designed to protect her from herself. And to protect the hospital against lawsuits, should she attempt suicide on the premises.

She shuffles down the hallway as several patients trail in her wake.

When she's out of your view, you slowly move your head to face the television. It's tuned to a children's movie about a dog who can talk, with the volume so low it's difficult to hear.

You can't see any clocks, but you're learning to gauge the time by the daily schedule. It's probably around 11 A.M.

Then the strangest thing happens. You feel a physical *click* inside of you, like an electric charge has triggered a deeply buried reflex, setting all your synapses firing.

And you know, beyond the shadow of a doubt, it's because Mandy is on her way to you.

You've read about twins who are so inexorably linked that when one of them is injured, the other feels pain. When you were in college, you experienced the phenomenon of getting your period at the same time as all three of your roommates, your physiological cycles effortlessly syncing. And you've heard about long-married couples who die within hours of each other, as if they've somehow willed themselves to stay joined in this world and the next. People connect in all kinds of mysterious ways.

Now it's happening to you.

You can *feel* Mandy's presence drawing closer. It's a tangible thing, as real as the fabric of the cheap sofa beneath your legs and the syrupy odor of the breakfast pancakes lingering in the air.

Maybe you're able to tune in to Mandy so deeply because in this place, your link to her isn't diffused by the noises and distractions of everyday life.

The sensation grows stronger with each passing minute and mile.

You close your eyes, imagining her hands on the wheel, those wide gray eyes fixed on the road ahead. And you know another thing for sure, deep in your gut.

Your sister is thinking about you right now, too.

CHAPTER EIGHTEEN

MANDY

I arrive at the hospital a little after 11 A.M.

I've visited patients before, but gaining entrance to the locked ward is an entirely different procedure.

I follow the same steps I went through when I first came to meet Georgia. The guard at the main front desk is the first gatekeeper. I give him my name and show my driver's license. Then I'm handed a stick-on visitor's pass and instructed to step to the side and wait. Everyone who comes to the main desk after me is told the room number of the patient they're visiting and given directions to it. But I need a special escort. After a few minutes, a young guy in burgundy scrubs comes down to retrieve me.

"I'm Tim," he tells me as he leads me down a wide corridor. We're still in the main part of the hospital, so medical staff and visitors are milling around. We pass a smiling man pushing a wheelchair that holds a tired-looking woman with a newborn cradled in her arms. A middle-aged couple comes out of the gift shop holding a helium balloon with the words *Get Well Soon* printed on it. A doctor in a white coat hurries past, sipping coffee from a paper cup, the rich smell of roasted beans wafting behind her like a cloud.

Are any of the patients and visitors aware of the alien world that exists just a few floors above?

Tim pauses at an elevator bank and pushes a separate button for the elevator at the very end.

"How's traffic out there?" he asks. "I do overnight shifts, but I'm heading home soon."

"Not too bad," I reply.

The elevator doors open and we step inside. Tim takes out his keys and touches a small circular fob to the control panel, then presses the button for floor five.

The doors close and we jerk up.

"Do you know how many things I'm picking up?" I ask. I've got a few reusable shopping bags tucked under my arm.

"No, but those bags should do it," he tells me. "It's whatever Georgia had on her when she was brought in that the cops didn't take. By the way, she's off her one-to-one, so you're welcome to bring back some clothes for her. Just no belts or scarves or shoelaces. Sweatpants without a drawstring, T-shirts, and sweatshirts are fine. No bright colors or offensive words on the clothes, though."

"'One-to-one'?" I echo.

"Sorry, that was when she had a watcher at all times. She hasn't shown any signs of wanting to injure herself, so she isn't considered an imminent suicide risk."

I have plenty of sweats and T-shirts. It wouldn't be a big deal to bring a few for Georgia. I'm sure the fabrics aren't as luxurious as the ones she's used to wearing, but she'd probably be more comfortable in them versus the paper pajamas she wore the last time I saw her.

Sisters share clothes, after all.

I try to picture Georgia slipping her head through the slightly frayed neck of my favorite dusky blue sweatshirt and pulling on the matching sweatpants. They'd be a little short on her, but they'd fit well enough. It would feel so strange to see her in them, knowing her microscopic skin cells were shedding and mingling with mine as our scents blended together.

The elevator opens to the silent hallway. Our shoes slap against the linoleum and echo as we approach the small wooden door. I wait for Tim to unlock it, but instead, he moves to the row of metal lockers built into the adjacent wall.

He finds one in the center of the row and checks something on his phone, then spins the dial and unlocks it using a combination I can't see.

"All yours." Tim steps back.

The only object is a small clutch purse, shining like a star in the dark hole of the locker.

"Where are her clothes?" I know Georgia was wearing a backless silver dress the night of the party; I saw it in a photograph published in *People.*

"Probably taken as evidence," Tim says matter-of-factly. "Guess you didn't need those shopping bags after all."

I reach for the purse, my fingers beginning to tremble. It feels unexpectedly heavy, and its clasp is intricate and elegant. I'm desperate to peer inside, but I don't want to do it with Tim watching.

"All set?" he asks.

I feel a stab of disappointment. I was steeling myself to go back into the psych unit. My sister is only yards away. If I could look through walls, I could see her.

"Can I see Georgia before I go?" I ask. "Just for a minute?"

"Hang on a sec." He picks up the phone and speaks into it. I wait, my fingers touching the sleek silver fabric of her purse. There's no blood on it, which must be why the police didn't take it. The purse feels strangely warm in my hands, as if it's a physical entity.

Tim hangs up the phone. "You can visit her briefly. Don't bring that in, though."

I give him back the purse, and he locks it up again.

Then he leads me through the two doors into the high-security unit.

I spot Georgia immediately. She's sitting on a couch in the common area, staring blankly at a television. I walk over to her with Tim matching my steps. Two other male nurses come out from the secure station and form a perimeter around me.

"I'm getting your things," I say.

Georgia doesn't acknowledge me. Maybe that's because she doesn't want anyone to overhear. But I can see a pulse beating at the base of her neck, like a bird's wings frantically fluttering.

"I'll be back soon," I tell Georgia.

A strange sensation floods my body. It feels like deep relief, as if someone has stretched out a hand and caught me as I've been sliding off a precipice.

I'm not in any danger, though. An eerie thought strikes me: Could I be tuning in to Georgia's emotions?

"We need to leave since this isn't a scheduled visit," Tim tells me.

I look up and see a man with pitted skin heading toward us. If he ran, he could be upon me in seconds. But his movements are slow and languid, like he's trying to walk underwater. He must be heavily medicated. Still, he's staring at me and I can tell he's trying to get to me.

I'm not the only one who notices. Another big male nurse quickly exits the walled-off station and blocks the man's path.

"Follow me," Tim instructs.

We're out the door before the man reaches us.

Tim whistles a tune I don't recognize as we walk back down the hallway. My stomach is still clenched, but this is everyday for him.

Tim retrieves the silver bag from the locker, then touches his fob to call for the elevator.

"I can take it from here," I tell him.

He shakes his head. "No visitors can be unattended until they're off this floor."

We ride down in silence. I'm acutely aware of the bag in my hands. I think of Georgia standing in her closet—it would be a walk-in and beautifully organized—and considering the evenings bags displayed on a shelf before selecting it.

Did Georgia tell her lawyer she wanted me to pick up her things because there's no one else in her life that would do it? Or did she have another motive?

Tim walks me back to the guard's desk and tells me to have a nice day. I wish him the same, then step on the mat that triggers the big, oversized doors and walk out into the warm sunlight.

I practically run to my car and jump into the driver's seat. I can't wait another second. I open the purse.

It holds four items: A Chanel lip gloss. A slim silver card holder with Georgia's platinum Amex and driver's license tucked inside. A travel perfume atomizer. And a set of keys.

I already know where Georgia lives; the tabloids showed images of her posh building named The Vue.

Now I know how to get inside.

CHAPTER NINETEEN

GEORGIA

"Would anyone like to talk about ways they make themselves feel better when they're upset?" the therapist begins.

He isn't the guy who looks like a Panthers fan. This man wears horn-rimmed glasses and looks like he's barely thirty. Even though his voice is casual, he keeps lightly tapping his foot against the floor.

He's nervous. You don't blame him. He's in a small room with six patients, including the giant man with the keloid scar. You spend most of your time sitting just outside the nurses' station, which means you overhear a lot of things. Yesterday a patient asked a nurse if it was true that man had stabbed his father and buried him behind the garage, a question the nurse brushed off.

Maybe it's a lie. Maybe the truth is even worse.

There are two young, strong aides sitting in chairs a bit apart from the group, but still, the therapist must know he's outnumbered. He can leave at any time, though, disappearing through the thick wooden doors that are a portal to the real world.

"Can anyone share ways they make themselves feel calmer and happier?" the therapist asks.

A tired-looking woman raises her hand. "I have one," she begins.

She twists around, looking behind her. "Aw, get off me," she says, her tone part affection and part exasperation.

There's nothing on her.

"What's your strategy?" the therapist asks.

"What I do is count to ten," she says. She looks back at the empty space again. "Knock it off, c'mon."

The therapist asks, "Who's behind you, Devina?"

A guy in pajama pants and a navy T-shirt speaks up. "She thinks it's a brown dog. He's always jumping on her."

The therapist frowns. "Um, is there a way you cope with the dog, Devina?"

You decide to escape in the only way left to you. You transport yourself into a different time and place: the day of your favorite wedding.

You thought you had the bride sized up when you met her. Rich and privileged tends to equal high-maintenance clients. But you were wrong. There was more kindness and love at this wedding than any you'd ever experienced. The bride and groom wanted to focus on their guests' comfort, so kids of all ages were welcome. A few baby-sitters were hired, and a private room with movies playing on a big screen and a table full of craft projects was set up adjacent to the ballroom. The bride wore her mother's dress, even though she could have found one that was more flattering, and the groom left an empty space at the front pew for his father, who'd died the previous year, with a boutonniere on it. The newlyweds surprised the bride's grandparents by asking them to come onto the floor for their first dance. Grandma spun around in her wheelchair while Grandpa did a few surprisingly fluid jitterbug moves; then he bent down to smooch his wife as the crowd cheered.

The day was pure love. You were there in the wings, watching it all, feeling a warm glow in your chest.

Then you're jerked back into the present as you feel something behind you. Something is brushing against the back of your neck, gentle as a whisper.

Goose bumps rise on your skin. You can hear his quick breaths and smell his vinegary odor. It's Josh.

He has crept up behind you and is running a fingertip along the back of your neck. You suppress a shudder and quash the instinct to jerk forward.

"Josh, won't you sit down?" the therapist says.

"Just gonna stand here for a bit," Josh replies. "Got a little cramp in my calf."

The therapist is too green to take control. From his frown, it's clear he wants Josh to sit down, but doesn't know how to make him. And the therapist can't see what Josh is doing; you're blocking his view.

"It doesn't work if you count quickly," Devina continues. "So what I do is, I take a deep breath between each number."

"Pretty baby," Josh croons, his voice so low only you can hear.

A scream swells in your throat, but you can't release it.

The therapist is oblivious to what's happening. But one of the aides must sense something is wrong. He stands up and takes a step toward you, and just like that, Josh walks to his seat and eases down, his legs splayed out.

Your body is rigid, fight-or-flight adrenaline coursing through it. Tears spring to your eyes, but you bite the inside of your lip, hard, and the shock of pain manages to staunch them.

Josh is even more dangerous than you thought.

He was smart enough to come up with a plausible excuse for lingering by your chair. And aware enough to bide his time.

This unit isn't very big. You can avoid dead-end hallways and stay in view of the nurses as much as possible. But it won't matter.

Josh will find you again.

There's no way out.

CHAPTER TWENTY

MANDY

Clouds of pink and purple blooms adorn the graceful crepe myrtle trees lining Georgia's street. I stand outside her building, looking up at the glass-and-steel structure silhouetted against the clear blue sky.

Her block is filled with high-end boutiques, a French bistro, and a gourmet coffee shop. It's easy to visualize Georgia moving through her neighborhood, popping into the corner shop for a morning latte or unwinding after a long day with a glass of wine at the bistro's bar.

I reach for her building's door and pull, putting some muscle into it because the thick glass is heavy. I step inside and see there's a concierge in a dark suit behind a desk. Another gatekeeper.

The reception area is gorgeous, with a soaring ceiling and arrangements of birds-of-paradise scattered throughout and furniture that encourages lounging. Classical music plays softly over speakers. It looks more like a high-end hotel than an apartment building. Maybe I should've worn something nicer than the jeans and Florence and the Machine T-shirt I changed into after I left the hospital.

"How can I help you?" the concierge asks as I approach.

Now that I'm close enough to see over the edge of his desk, I notice he has a row of monitors in front of him, allowing him to view all the public areas of the building.

I've thought about different options for what I could say, and nothing seems as simple and powerful as the truth.

I give my best winning smile. "Georgia Cartwright asked her lawyer to give me her keys. I'm going to collect some clothes from her apartment for her."

I hold up the keys on the Gucci chain.

The concierge's expression gives nothing away, but this has to be titillating for him. A possible murderess lived in his building. Even with all the camera monitors and other layers of security, danger lived and breathed here. Is it a story he relishes telling when he kicks back with the guys for a beer after work? Does he search his memory, finding details about Georgia that didn't seem significant at first—a dispute with a neighbor over noise, a certain hard glitter in her eyes when she was inconvenienced—and fitting them into the new picture he holds of my sister?

"Can you give me a moment?" the concierge asks.

I don't have much of a choice, so I nod. He gestures toward the seating area.

"Make yourself comfortable. There's a Keurig machine in the far corner if you'd like coffee."

The last thing I need is caffeine; I'm jittery enough. I take the first seat I see and swivel my body so I can look at the concierge.

He's on the phone. I can't hear what he's saying, but I see him holding the receiver. He looks at me, then yanks his eyes away when he notices I'm watching.

After a moment, he hangs up and stands, gesturing for me to come over.

"Since Georgia has authorized you to access her apartment, I can let you up. I'll just need to see some ID first."

A tinge of unease runs down my spine. I'd rather him not know my true name. But I can't see any way around it. I'm more eager to see Georgia's place than I am to preserve my anonymity. I hand over my driver's license, and the concierge takes down my name and address.

"There's one other thing." He looks up at me, still holding on to my license. "We've been getting messages for Georgia. One of her clients keeps calling. She and her mother even came by here the other day, but we couldn't let them into the apartment without authorization. They say Georgia has something that belongs to them."

I have no idea how to respond.

He continues, "Since you're one of her legal representatives, I guess I should give the messages to you. Hold on a moment."

I don't correct him. I don't want to say anything that would lose me access to her apartment.

The concierge clicks on his computer, and a moment later, a printer spits out a piece of paper.

He hands it to me along with my license. "Have a good day."

I thank him and tuck my license into my wallet, then fold the sheet of paper and put it in my purse as I walk to the elevator bank and press the call button. The doors to the middle elevator glide open. I step in and press *PH* for penthouse. Nothing happens. I press the button again, frowning.

Then I look down at the keys in my hand and realize there's a circular fob on the chain, just like the nurses from the locked ward use to access the fifth floor. It's another layer of security. I touch it to the sensor in the elevator, then press *PH* again. This time, the button lights up and the door close.

The elevator soars up. Through its glass walls, I watch the lobby retreat, growing smaller with each passing second. The concierge is staring at me, his face upturned.

I exit when the doors yawn open, stepping out onto a thick gray patterned carpet. Wall sconces provide soft lighting for my path, and the air smells lemony fresh. I walk down the hall to Georgia's home.

It takes me two tries to fit her key into the lock because my hands feel shaky and uncoordinated. Finally, the door yields. I step inside and shut it behind me, holding my breath in the silence.

Georgia's apartment is shockingly messy. It takes me a beat to realize why: The police must have searched it. Her sofa cushions are strewn on the floor, and all her kitchen cabinets are open, with the contents tossed on the counters. Dirt is scattered around the floor by a lush green plant, like someone dug through it.

Despite the mess, every detail of this apartment is stunning, from the panoramic view of the city to the walls of windows to the elegant pieces of furniture—the sectional sofa with a faux fur blanket tossed over an arm and a round industrial-style dining table made of metal and stone.

As my eyes sweep across the room, a sense of déjà vu grips me so strongly that the floor seems to lurch beneath my feet.

This place feels like home.

It takes me a beat to figure out why. Then my eyes widen as I look around again, taking in everything anew.

Though the styles and price points are different—and my living area is half the size—I also have a sectional couch and a round dining table. Mine seats four, and Georgia's seats eight. My sister and I both chose soft patterned rugs for our floors. The patterns aren't identical, but the colors are: We went for shades of gray and rose.

My heartbeat quickens as I hurry to her refrigerator. On the side, held in place by colored glass magnets, are several invitations—to a baby shower, a charity fundraiser, a save-the-date for a wedding. I open the refrigerator. Tidy rows of glass bottles of Perrier, a half-full bottle of chenin blanc wine, almond milk creamer for coffee, two Honeycrisp apples—my favorite—in the fruit drawer, ten brown eggs in a clear segmented container, and a bottle of capers, the same brand I buy to sprinkle atop my scrambled eggs.

My adrenaline is pumping, filling me with a giddy unease. Everything here feels new and sparkling, yet utterly familiar. Stepping into my sister's place gives me the sensation I've heard people describe as occurring when you meet your soul mate.

I spin around again, heady yet acutely focused, trying to take it all in. The pristine white orchid on the dining room table. The retro record player in the corner with albums pulled out of their holders and scattered on the floor. The Nest reed diffuser that perfumes the air with the scents of eucalyptus and mint. These are all features my apartment lacks. But when I glance at Georgia's music, in between Luke Bryan and Taylor Swift I spot a Florence and the Machine album.

Two rooms lead off the hallway. I peer in the doorways and identify them as her office and her bedroom. I walk into her bedroom first, gliding my fingertips lightly down the wall.

Entering this room feels like stepping into a cloud.

It doesn't look like my bedroom. But it looks exactly like the bedroom I'd create if I had unlimited money.

Despite the mess left by the police—an overturned mattress and covers on the floor—it's soothing and spare, with a soaring arched ceiling and walls painted the lightest of greens. The wide-planked wooden floors gleam, and a huge window frames the ever-changing cityscape. The closet door is slightly open, allowing me a tantalizing glimpse of the cashmeres and silks taken off their hangers and piled on the floor.

I sit down on the edge of her bed frame, and that's when I see it.

There's a paperback on Georgia's nightstand with a bookmark in the middle. A chill runs through me when I read the title: *The Age of Innocence*, by Edith Wharton.

I have the same novel on my coffee table at home; I bought it just last month.

A roaring noise fills my ears as I stare at the familiar cover. How is it possible my sister and I are both reading it now?

It can't be a coincidence; there are too many books in the world.

I feel like I can't breathe. I drop my head between my knees until my dizziness passes.

Then I force myself to focus. I need to consider other scenarios.

Maybe the DNA my twin and I share has dictated our choices, creating these uncanny overlaps—and potentially more that I have yet to discover. We wouldn't be the first twins to experience this; I read about two identical twin brothers, both named Jim by their adoptive parents, who were separated at birth and went on to lead eerily similar lives, down to driving Chevrolets, vacationing at the same Florida resort, and marrying women named Linda—before both Jims got divorced and remarried women named Betty.

But there's another possibility.

Georgia is a professional planner; she stages scenes for maximum impact.

Could she have staged these links between us before luring me here?

CHAPTER TWENTY-ONE

GEORGIA

The most dangerous animal on earth isn't the great white shark or a hungry crocodile or a mama bear. It's the human being.

You learned that somewhere—in a classroom, or maybe from an Instagram post. It wasn't terribly relevant to your life at the time. You took precautions, after all. You didn't walk alone late at night, and you always met men in public places for your first dates. Once, you even stepped out of an elevator in your doctor's building after a guy got on and stared at you instead of pressing the button for his floor.

Now you're constantly reminded of the unique capability of the human mind to plan ways to inflict harm.

The evidence is walking and breathing all around you.

You've eaten breakfast, and you're on the couch by the nurses' station, watching television. The channels here are restricted, which means nothing with even a hint of violence or nudity can be shown, but today you discovered HGTV is permitted.

It's as if you've been handed a glass of water as you're dying of thirst. The simple distraction, this segment of normalcy from your old life, allows your battered psyche to rest. You could sit here all day. You plan to, in fact.

On the screen, a peppy husband-and-wife team is helping a pregnant couple find their first home. She wants a sunny nursery. He wants a garage. She wants a cook's kitchen. He wants a yard.

As a wedding planner, you had a knack for guessing which couples would make it and which would be filing for divorce. It boiled down to how they handled the inevitable stresses that underlie every big life event. The groom who kept texting with someone during his wedding rehearsal—nope. The bride who blasted the groom's obnoxious mother for inviting eight extra guests to the seated dinner reception without telling anyone—yes; good for her for drawing boundaries. The couple who argued about everything, but argued fairly—another yes.

The pregnant couple seems like they'll be okay. He concedes a sunny nursery is more important than a garage. He mainly wanted one as a workspace. His wife looks at him lovingly as he talks about his plan to build the baby's crib.

The TV hosts, though—the supposedly happy couple? She bristles whenever he speaks. It's a safe bet they're sleeping in separate bedrooms.

Honey and Stephen—you no longer think of them as your parents—did too. Stephen often traveled for work, but when he was home, Honey complained about his snoring and banished him to the guest room. He never pushed back. For a man who was so successful and respected in the business world, Stephen was out of his league at home—reduced to a bit player in Honey's orbit. Once, back when you were in elementary school and Honey forced you to go to school despite your high fever and cough—"Nothing a lil medicine can't take care of," she'd said—Stephen tried to intervene: "Georgia really doesn't look well. Shouldn't she rest?" Honey whirled on him faster than a rattlesnake. "Do you want to quit your job and take care of the girls and run this household if you think you can do it better than me?" she screeched, launching into a tirade that had Stephen gulping the rest of his coffee and escaping to the office. Honey was still ranting while the maid cleaned up the breakfast dishes and the nanny drove you to school. As for Stephen, he got the message loud and clear: If he wanted peace—and he was a man who absolutely did—then he'd keep his mouth shut.

"We've found the house you want, but the kitchen needs to be renov—" the male TV host begins.

"*Fully* renovated," the female host cuts her husband off. He smiles without showing any teeth.

You see a slow, approaching movement out of the corner of your eye.

You release your breath when you realize it isn't Josh.

It's the new woman with bandages on her wrists. Her watcher accompanies her. She's also being followed by two other patients. She drifts into the room and stands near your couch.

The other patients—a woman with dark skin and deep hollows under her eyes and a short, heavyset man—do the same.

"I want to watch *The Price Is Right*," the dark-skinned woman declares.

"*Price Is Right*," the heavyset man echoes.

The watcher looks at you. "Georgia, the rule here is we need a consensus on what to watch. If one can't be reached, whichever show gets the most votes wins. Do you want to watch *The Price Is Right*?"

You shake your head slowly, just once.

"I'm sorry, but we have to change the channel. It's two votes to one."

Tears spring to your eyes. It's such a stupid thing, given everything that's happening, but this is the only escape available to you. Your throat begins to thicken. You're so tired and scared. And now the only tiny reprieve you've been granted from the black hole of your life is about to be yanked away.

Then the new patient speaks up in a voice so soft it's almost a whisper.

"I vote for HGTV."

The watcher turns to look at her. A smile breaks across his face. "Patty, I'm so glad you're expressing your opinion."

"So we're not watching my show?" the other woman huffs.

"If it's a tie, whatever was already on wins," the watcher says.

"I hate you!" The woman storms off, stomping her feet. Which must hurt since she's wearing socks. The heavyset man looks after her, then decides to stay. He lowers himself into a chair and begins pulling at his chin whiskers.

"Patty, would you like to sit down and make yourself comfortable?" the watcher asks.

She nods and walks over to the couch. She slowly eases down next to you. She looks so gentle and soft. You wonder what life did to her, to bring her here.

And then you realize something else.

You're in view of the nurses. And with Patty next to you, her watcher will remain close by. Josh won't be able to touch you now.

Patty was brought here to be saved.

But right now, she is saving you.

CHAPTER TWENTY-TWO

MANDY

I don't know how long I sit on the edge of Georgia's bed frame, trying to make sense of the overlaps in our lives. It's like we've traveled down separate, parallel tracks that repeatedly twisted back together, mirroring the double helix strands of the DNA we share.

It strains credulity that Georgia set all this up. She couldn't have known what kind of T-shirt I'd wear today or what book I just finished reading.

Still, the rich and powerful have ways of finding things out.

Georgia found out about me, after all. But she didn't contact me until she was accused of murdering her other sister. Why?

My cell phone buzzes, yanking me out of my thoughts and into the present. It's a text from my domestic beer distributor, letting me know his usual delivery will be delayed by a day. I reply that it isn't a problem, then pull myself to my feet.

I'm here to get some clothes for Georgia, items that can't be fashioned into weapons, I remind myself. Then I can keep digging into learning who my twin is and what she might be capable of.

I step into Georgia's closet and flick on the light. It's like walking into an exclusive boutique, one filled with a curated mix of classic pieces and sexy, edgier items. But her clothes have been pulled off hangers and left puddled on the floor, and her shoes are overturned and scattered around. The built-in drawers are open, with lacy bras and thongs spilling out, and her purses are a tangled mess on the floor.

I get to work setting things to rights, glad to have a concrete task to occupy my mind. It's a bigger job than I can finish today, but I pick up about half her clothes, smoothing out a black pantsuit with a deep V-neck and straightening a violet silk halter top, trying to figure out where each item goes before hanging it up. It's impossible not to covet her things as my fingers touch sweaters and coats, designer jeans, and gorgeous dresses in every shade of the rainbow. Georgia's shoes and purses are scattered on the closet floor, and I notice her feet are just a half size bigger than mine. Her Chanel combat boots are so exquisite it's hard to take my hands off them.

As strange and voyeuristic as this feels, it's also tantalizing.

What would it be like to live like this? If Georgia and I had been given to each other's families, this could have been my closet, my apartment, *my* life.

I choose some things that will work for Georgia, laying the items on her bed. Sweaty Betty sweatpants, a half dozen T-shirts, and a couple of sweatshirts. I start to put a bra onto the pile, then realize the straps could be used as a strangulation device. I add a pair of slippers instead.

I find an overnight bag in her closet and fold the clothes neatly inside.

I've finished what I came here to do.

It's a ninety-minute drive home. I could swing by the hospital and drop off her things, then go home and get some sleep.

But there's another option.

It's Monday, the one night of the week my bar is closed. Lately I've used the time to catch up on sleep or go on a Tinder date, since I'm not seeing anyone special right now.

I could spend the night in Georgia's apartment instead and drop off her clothes at the hospital tomorrow.

Surrounded by her things, I could begin to search for answers tonight.

CHAPTER TWENTY-THREE

GEORGIA

You awaken abruptly to find someone shining a sharp beam of light under your chin.

You blink, disoriented. You're suspended in the hazy transition between sleep and wakefulness. Then the knowledge of where you are comes smashing into you.

You can't believe how badly you've messed up. You've fallen asleep. You've let yourself become vulnerable.

This time you're lucky. The shadowy figure in the doorway is a nurse's aide conducting a C15. Every fifteen minutes, staff does rounds to make sure patients are in their beds. A light is shone on your chest to check for the rhythmic motion that indicates breathing.

You know the checks are performed every fifteen minutes because you've counted the seconds between them.

It's reassuring to know about the C15s. It's also terrifying.

All the cameras and eyes on this floor should be enough to ensure the safety of patients. But clearly patients have been able to circumvent these security measures. They've been able to slip out of their rooms undetected and harm themselves. Or others.

The medical staff no longer believes you are an imminent suicide risk. You've been moved to a new room, one without an overhead camera, and you're left alone at night now.

When you first came here, you thought things couldn't get worse. You were wrong.

Nine hundred seconds. That's how many ticks of the clock compose fifteen minutes.

There are so many ways a person can be hurt or killed in nine hundred seconds. A hard blow to the head could erase you instantly, like it did to Annabelle. Suffocation takes only a few hundred seconds, which means Josh could seal his hands over your nose and mouth and be back in his room, feigning sleep, by the time an aide shone a flashlight on his chest. Josh could do plenty of other things to you first.

You've tried to think of ways to protect yourself. The measures you'd take at home if you felt threatened—a deadbolt on your door, a can of Mace and cell phone on your nightstand—aren't options here. Anything that could be turned into a weapon has been removed from the patient areas. No sharp objects. No glass. No furniture you can lift. No phone to summon help.

The only line of defense you have is to lie awake at night and catch catnaps during the day on the couch in view of the nurses' station.

But you've failed at that, too.

You have no idea what time it is. It could be 10 P.M. or 5 A.M. You never realized what a privilege it was to have your phone charging on your nightstand while you slept, always ready to tell you the time, giving you a tangible way to orient yourself in the darkness.

You miss your soft bed and fluffy comforter. You miss the cold glass of Sancerre you enjoyed at the French bistro across from your apartment after a long day of work. You miss your neighbor's bulldog with the underbite, the one who joyfully snorted while you scratched his head.

You miss your *life*. You didn't appreciate it while you had it. You were too busy, too stressed, too distracted.

What you would give to have just one hour back of your old life.

You're spiraling, your chest growing tight, which is a luxury you can't afford. Panic is your constant companion, hovering behind a gauzy screen, always threatening to break through and consume you.

You conjure up a talisman to ward it off. You envision Mandy.

She came to pick up your keys today and told you she'd be back soon, which sent relief flooding through your body. She must have gone to your apartment, which means she is getting to know you. Did her gray eyes roam across the books on your shelves? That was always your favorite trick for getting a shorthand glimpse into someone's mind, by discovering what they read. Did Mandy look into the drawers of your bathroom vanity, smoothing on a bit of your face cream and sniffing your perfumes in their delicate glass bottles? Did she imagine what it would be like to be you?

And the most important question: Will Mandy help you?

All the evidence you've gathered indicates she will. Unless she believes you are guilty.

In that case, you may need to do something else to draw her in.

You stare into the dusky nothingness and will your mind to empty so you can try to tap into the link between you and your twin.

But before you can conjure the connection, an aide appears in your doorway again. The circular beam of light shines on your chest, like a target. A bull's-eye.

Don't fall asleep, you instruct yourself.

And then you send up two prayers, the most heartfelt ones you've ever willed. Each prayer is directed to a different sister.

Save me, Mandy.

And then: *Forgive me, Annabelle.*

CHAPTER TWENTY-FOUR

MANDY

Before I begin my search, I head down to the lobby and tell the concierge that I've been instructed to gather some paperwork and other items from Georgia's apartment.

"I may be here quite a while over the next few days," I say, trying to convey a touch of exasperation.

"No problem," he tells me. His face is pleasantly blank, but I'm sure he's bursting with questions. I decide to give him one tiny detail, a way of incurring a favor in case I need something from him later.

"The police tore apart her place, so it's taking longer than it should."

He leans forward. "I was the one who let them in when they showed me the warrant," he says importantly.

I nod. "I've also got to gather some clothes to bring to Georgia, since she's off suicide watch."

His eyes widen. He's clearly delighted I've given him a tidbit he can share.

I take note of the name on his plate affixed to his chest pocket: "Thanks for everything, Gavin."

Then I go back upstairs, and as I enter Georgia's apartment, I turn on a few more lights, since it's dark out now. I decide to start my search in Georgia's office. I figure I'll have my best shot at finding tangible information there.

Her workspace is done in shades of black onyx and cream, with four bouclé swivel chairs surrounding a round table. An arrangement of crimson-tipped roses that are beginning to weep petals is overturned on the table, with water puddled around it. There's a small desk off to one side with a computer mouse resting atop it, but no computer. The police must have taken it during their search.

On Georgia's walls are framed cinema posters of classic love stories—Rhett and Scarlett from *Gone with the Wind*, Ilsa and Rick from *Casablanca*, and Cary Grant and Deborah Kerr from *An Affair to Remember*.

There's a bookshelf in the corner, but instead of books, it's clearly intended for dozens of white fabric-covered binders. All of them have been pulled out and are scattered on the floor. It makes me wonder if police searches are deliberately messy.

I clean up the flowers, then pick up one of the binders. The name of a couple—*Anna and Matthew*—is embossed in gold on the cover. I flip through each page. Then I pick up another binder and look through it, then another.

Each contains a love story; it traces the path a couple took from engagement to ceremony. There are invitations to engagement parties and sample menus. Brochures for all sorts of wedding venues, from historical homes to luxury modern hotels. Images and sketches of gowns and veils. Scraps of fabrics and copies of handwritten vows.

Surely Georgia must have had all of this documented on her computer. This system of filing is as antiquated as the classic movie images on her walls.

Perhaps the folders were a backup for her electronic files, a tangible and lovely record of the special days she created.

Could the binder be what the bride-to-be and her mother are so desperately seeking? It makes sense, if Georgia and her computer disappeared and they need critical information about the upcoming wedding.

I reach into my purse and pull out the sheet of paper the concierge handed to me.

Caroline Evers has called, emailed, and come to the building in person seven times in the past few days.

She's desperate to get back something from this apartment. And I'm desperate to learn more about Georgia. So we each have something the other one wants.

I reach into my bag for my cell phone and dial her number.

She picks up on the second ring, sounding rushed: "Hello?"

"Hi, Caroline, this is Amanda. I'm returning the messages you left for Georgia Cartwright. I'd love to help you if I can."

"Oh, thank God! Do you have the Bible?"

"Sorry?" I ask.

"My great-grandparents' Bible. Georgia had it—she was going to get the cover repaired so we could use it for a reading."

"Okay, I'll look for it and—"

She cuts me off. "Wait, are you in Georgia's apartment now? Because I can be there in twenty minutes." She doesn't let me reply before continuing, "That Bible has been in my family for more than a hundred years. Every birth, death, wedding—it's all written down on the first few pages. I cannot lose it."

"I understand," I say. I want to meet Caroline, but not until I've had more time alone in Georgia's place. "I can meet you at Georgia's apartment tomorrow morning. Say 10 A.M.? We'll find the Bible."

"Yes." She exhales. "I'll be there."

I'm about to hang up when she lets out a half laugh. "I mean, who would've thought my wedding planner would be accused of murder two weeks before my wedding? It's insane!"

"It is," I agree.

"Maybe not my best choice of words . . . I mean, you must know Georgia pretty well, right?"

In some ways, better than you can imagine, I think. But all I say is, "Not that well. I never saw this coming."

"Right? She's this stunning, perfect woman. How does someone like that snap?"

"I don't know," I say. "Maybe everyone has a breaking point."

"How do you know her?" Caroline asks.

I make a split-second decision. I deviate from my planned cover to imply I'm working with Georgia's lawyer. If Caroline thinks I'm here in some official capacity, she might be less forthright.

"We're friends," I say. "I'm a neighbor. It's why she gave me an extra set of her keys, in case she ever got locked out."

"Oh, wow. Well, I have to say I'm happy she did. Have you heard whether they're going to try her for murder? Someone was saying on a talk show she may end up in a mental institution for life."

"I don't know," I reply.

"I— Oh, shoot, that's my fiancé calling. I've got to run. But I'll see you at 10 tomorrow."

"See you then." I hang up and get back to work.

I spend the next couple of hours looking through every binder in Georgia's office, lining them up on the bookshelf as I finish. I'm stunned—and a little disgusted—by the money some people lay out for a few hours of celebration. The bar bills alone are more than what Sweetbay's brings in during a month. There are calligraphed invitations hand-delivered in white satin boxes, Russian caviar stations, floral canopies made of orchids and wisteria over custom-built dance floors, and five-figure gowns. One bride-to-be flew her bridesmaids to Canyon Ranch Spa for a few days of pampering the week before the wedding. Another sent each of her four hundred guests home with favor bags containing a bottle of Veuve and a sterling-silver Tiffany photo frame.

I find the binder labeled *Caroline and Hayden* toward the bottom of the pile. I open it and see a receipt tucked into the front pocket from Stanley Bookbinding.

I use my phone to google the address. It isn't far away. And though it closed a few hours ago, it opens again at 9 A.M. Which means I can get the Bible before Caroline shows up tomorrow. If I do, she'll be relieved and will no longer have a reason to rush out. Perhaps she'll be in a chatty mood again.

My stomach rumbles, and I realize I've missed lunch and dinner. It's past 10 P.M. now.

I could order DoorDash. Instead, I find myself drawn into Georgia's kitchen. I take the eggs out of her refrigerator; according to the expiration date stamped on the cardboard container, they're still fresh. I open a lower cabinet and see the frying pan I need. I easily locate her olive oil, spatula, and a small bowl and whisk. It's almost like I already know my way around my sister's kitchen.

I uncork the bottle of wine and sniff. It hasn't turned. I pour a glass and sip it while my scrambled eggs cook. I don't have a nose for wine, but I'm confident of this: It tastes like money.

When my eggs are done, I sprinkle some capers over them and dig in. As I take the last bite, a deep wave of fatigue hits me. I haven't been sleeping well since I learned about my sister, and my emotions have been ricocheting all over the place.

I take my dishes to the sink and rinse them before putting them in the dishwasher; then, almost as if in a trance, I walk into Georgia's bedroom.

In the built-in drawers in her closet I find several nightgowns. I choose one made of pale blue silk.

I was going to lend Georgia my clothes. Now I'm borrowing hers. As sisters do.

I take off my jeans and T-shirt and bra, folding them and putting them on a closet shelf. Then I slip on the delicate nightgown, the silk whispering as it slides down my skin.

I wrestle the mattress onto the bed frame before finding fresh sheets in the linen closet and making her bed. Then I step into the gorgeous ensuite bathroom that boasts a soaking tub, an oversized shower, and a marble-topped vanity. Georgia's first drawer is for her cosmetics—for a naturally gorgeous woman, she sure has a lot—and the next one is filled with lotions, cleansers, and scrubs. I use my index finger to scrub my teeth with minty toothpaste, then turn off the light.

I slip beneath her fluffy, pristine white comforter. I barely have the energy to turn off the little lamp on the nightstand before I plunge into a sleep so deep and instant it's as if I've been drugged.

CHAPTER TWENTY-FIVE

GEORGIA

You lie awake in the endless night. Every moment that passes is excruciating. You have only your thoughts to occupy you, and they take you to a very dark place.

You've hit Annabelle before, feeling the satisfying crack of your palm against her cheek. You've wanted to hurt her so many other times—to rake your nails down her face, yank at her hair, knock her to the ground.

You've wished her dead more than once. Sweet Annabelle, who everyone adored. Who your parents always loved far more than they did you.

She was born four months after you were adopted. A miracle baby.

It happens that way sometimes, people said joyously. As if Annabelle were the prize and you merely the placeholder—a superfluous one now.

You stare into nothingness, hoping daylight will break before you do.

Then you remember the therapist's words from group today: *Think about something to distract you when your feelings seem overpowering.*

You call up a memory of the life you used to lead, tentatively bringing up the first image, like a tongue testing an aching tooth. It isn't too painful. So you let the memory bloom.

Your job was to guide brides, to smooth out any wrinkles in their paths, to make them feel special. You excelled at this. Whatever curveballs life has in store for your brides, and no matter how their marriage is challenged—because it will be one way or another—at least they'll always have the gilded memory you designed, directed, and delivered. What you created, in essence, was one perfect day.

You never promised to give them a happy union or change their lives. That was beyond your powers.

But a strange flip occurred recently. Your client Caroline Evers changed *your* life—permanently.

It started with a discussion about seating arrangements, one of the many land mines of wedding planning.

Caroline came to meet you alone, without her mother or groom. You were seated at a prime table of a restaurant renowned for its high tea service. The table was big enough for six, which you'd requested so you could spread out the various seating charts you'd created. Fresh scones with lemon curd and clotted cream, cucumber finger sandwiches, flutes of champagne and steaming pots of sweetly fragrant herbal tea, classical music playing—every detail was designed to cultivate a relaxed, elegant mood.

"I have no idea where to sit my birth mother," Caroline confessed moments after she sat down. Caroline is a gabber. In the months you've been working with her, you've learned about her sister's eating disorder, her colleague's torrid affair, and her recurring nightmare that she'll trip while walking down the aisle.

"My mom—who adopted me when I was a baby—will be at the head table, of course. But I don't want my birth mother and my half-siblings sitting in Siberia, you know?"

"How did you connect with your birth mother?" you asked, your skin prickling.

You always gave your clients your sole focus. Caroline's simple words ruptured your rule. You were thinking about yourself now.

Caroline paused to take a dainty bite of a cucumber sandwich, and you smiled through clenched teeth.

"I found her two years ago," Caroline finally replied. "She was seventeen when she had me, and she and my dad weren't capable of raising a baby. They ended up getting married eight years later, though, and they had two sons. My mom—my real mom, the one who raised me—has been so great about it. Some people might feel threatened, but she invited everyone to dinner. We've all gotten pretty close."

You masked your impatience. "But how did you track her down?" you rephrased, struggling to keep your tone light. You've wondered about your own birth mother, of course—especially since you were given to such a nightmare of an adoptive mother.

Caroline sipped her champagne—vintage Dom Pérignon; only the best for your brides—and leaned in closer.

"I hired a private detective. It actually wasn't that difficult."

It was easy to get the detective's name out of Caroline after she downed another glass of champagne. And the next day, you called the PI.

He was an older man named Tony Wagner who gave you his office address and asked you to bring him several documents: your social security card. Your birth certificate. Your driver's license.

You showed up for your appointment feeling apprehensive. He had thinning gray hair, a trim physique, and was dressed in a polo shirt and khakis. He could probably read the conflicting emotions on your face as you sat across from him in his cluttered office.

"You sure you want to dig all this up?" he asked.

You nodded, even though you suddenly felt very unsure.

"I ask because sometimes, people find out things they didn't want to know." His tone was a little gruff, but you could tell he had a good heart. Here he was, probably approaching seventy, working alone in a small, windowless office, trying to locate people who didn't want to be found. He didn't wear a wedding ring, and there were no pictures of kids or grandkids around. Maybe he needed the money, or maybe he just didn't have much else to do.

"Find out what kind of things?" you asked.

He leaned back in his chair, exhaling like he was trying to rid himself of the tension he carried.

"Once, I followed a husband who was cheating," Tony told you. "The wife insisted she wanted to know. But the other woman was her sister. It destroyed her."

A shadow fell across his face. It was clear the case haunted him.

"The thing is, it wasn't a big love affair. It only happened a couple times, and as soon as they were found out, they stopped. I always wonder what would've happened if I hadn't gotten the evidence. Maybe it would have run its course and he would've been faithful from then on."

You wanted to ask what happened to the wife, but something held you back. Maybe you didn't truly want to know.

Tony kept talking, like he was in confessional, seeking absolution for his sins.

"There was another case once, a guy in his thirties who wanted to know who his birth father was. Turns out the man was in jail for murder. That did a real number on him. The father kept calling him, wanting things. He was a master manipulator. It turned into a real mess."

Tony looked at you.

"Are you really sure?"

You thought about it. You were far less certain now, but a tiny part of you still held out hope that your birth mother would be lovely and welcoming. That you could finally have a positive family relationship.

You paid Tony's retainer and thanked him, then went back to work.

You thought it would take a while to hear from him.

But he called later that same day.

"They've been lying to you," he said.

CHAPTER TWENTY-SIX

MANDY

I'm jerked awake, my senses under assault. Light pierces my eyes, music pounds through the air, and an alien force is pinning down my limbs.

I thrash around and free myself from the sheet I'm twisted in. I squint and take in my surroundings. A shade is gliding up, revealing a wall of windows and the cardinal and violet hues of the sunrise. Beyoncé is singing about girls who run the world.

Someone got into Georgia's apartment and turned on the music and flicked the switch to raise the blinds. I'm no longer alone.

"Hey!" I shout as I leap out of bed. "Who's there?"

No answer.

I look around wildly for a weapon. I keep a baseball bat under my bed at home, but unfortunately my twin doesn't. I yank open the drawer of her nightstand, hoping to find a can of Mace but it's empty.

All I have to defend myself are my hands and feet. But I can fight well; I've done it before.

The bedroom door is wide open. I move to the side of it, my breaths coming fast and shallow. I spread out my feet so it will be harder for someone to knock me off balance and wait for the intruder's next move.

Nothing happens. It's hard to hear over the music, but I don't pick up sounds that indicate anyone is approaching.

Then the lyrics hit me: Beyoncé is singing about working hard, doing the nine-to-five, making her millions.

I think I know what's going on now.

But the only way to prove my theory is to test it. I leap out into the hallway and spin around, looking in all directions. No one is in sight. I walk into the living room, more casually now, peering into the open door of Georgia's office as I pass it.

The apartment is empty.

Apparently Georgia likes to wake up abruptly, like diving into a cold swimming pool. The music and blinds must be set on timers, maybe through a device like Nest.

My sister may look like a pampered socialite, but she's hard-core in some ways. She once competed in an ultramarathon, running fifty miles in a single day. She built her own business—a very successful one. And based on what I saw in her eyes when I met her, she has successfully manipulated the legal system to allow her to stay in a psych ward rather than jail. Maybe I shouldn't be surprised by her boot camp–style alarm clock.

I rub my eyes and peer at the clock over the microwave. It's 5:45 A.M. It takes discipline to get up this early when you don't have to— and to work as hard as Georgia does when you don't need to. People probably underestimate her all the time. That's something else we have in common.

People think I kept Sweetbay's to hold on to a piece of home, and they're right. The pilsner glasses I use are the same ones my mom and dad filled countless times. When my fingers work the cash register, they graze numbers worn from their touch. If it's slow, I pull out a stool tucked next to the ice maker where my father rested during breaks.

My patrons think my sentimental streak is sweet. But they don't see the thing I changed about my bar. I added a small safe just beneath the cash register. I keep a six-shot pistol in it, fully loaded. I took a course at a shooting range, and I break down and clean my gun myself. And when the occasional fight erupts at my bar, I don't hesitate to step in and help break it up. I'm a red belt in tae kwon do, and when my nose was broken in a sparring match last year, I would've kept fighting if the ref hadn't stopped the match because of all the blood.

A woman closing up a bar late at night could become a target, and I don't ever intend to be a victim. I've witnessed the devastation caused by sexual assault. It happened to my college roommate, Beth.

It was our junior year. Beth was heading out to a fraternity party at the invitation of a guy she had a big crush on. I helped her pick out her outfit: her favorite old jeans, because she didn't want to look like she was trying too hard, paired with my emerald-green halter top, which made her hazel eyes pop. I did her eyeliner because she was so nervous she couldn't draw a straight line.

"How do I look?" Beth asked just before she walked out the door.

"Beautiful but scared," I told her. I grabbed a bottle of lemon-flavored vodka from our minifridge and poured a shot. "Drink this."

She wrinkled her nose. "Really?"

Beth was innocent in some ways. She'd never touched alcohol before college, and she'd slept with only one guy. She usually sipped beer at parties, and I'd seen her tipsy just a couple of times.

I urged her to do the shot. Told her it would take the edge off.

I hate myself for that now.

She swallowed the vodka, her mouth puckering.

"Have fun," I told her. She threw her arms around me, and as I hugged her back, I caught a whiff of my perfume. Beth hadn't asked to borrow it because she didn't need to ask. We'd gotten close during freshman year and we'd roomed together ever since. We shared everything: clothes, inside jokes, class notes, and confidences. We were both only children who were used to being alone, and neither of us needed a big circle of friends. All we needed was each other.

Beth walked into the party and greeted her crush, who grabbed her hand and pulled her to a table where people were playing beer pong. Beth kept losing; that much she remembers. She had to chug beer after beer. But she can't recall what happened after that.

She awoke the next morning in the guy's bed, confused and aching, her jeans tangled around one of her ankles. He lived in a triple, and his roommates were in beds nearby. The room reeked of sour beer and sweat.

She crept out of the bedroom while her assailant slept on, a snore escaping his open mouth, a forearm slung over his eyes. She stumbled to the bathroom and threw up.

As she was leaving, she was seen by a few guys in the living room. They were slumped on couches, drinking Gatorade for their hangovers and laughing.

When they spotted Beth stumbling down the stairs in last night's clothes, their laughter grew more raucous.

"Walk of shame! Walk of shame!" one of them chanted, and the others joined in.

They followed her out the front door and yelled it from the porch, laughing and egging each other on, while Beth ran back to our room.

I'd gone to a different party the night before, coming home around midnight. I went to bed assuming Beth was having a good time. I didn't think to swing by the frat party. It was two lousy blocks away. If I'd bothered to check on her, maybe I could have saved her.

I woke up to the sound of Beth hyperventilating. I'll never forget the sound of her breathing. It had a ragged quality, like her lungs had been shredded.

She was curled up on the floor between our single beds. I wrapped my arms around her, thinking someone had died. I was right, in a way. The happy, easygoing person she had been was gone.

I urged Beth to report the rape, but she wouldn't. Instead, she fell into a spiral of shame and self-doubt. Did people know? she kept wondering. Had his roommates watched—maybe even cheered on her rapist? And oh, God, what if someone had taken pictures?

Once, when we went to the dining hall to get lunch, the guy—his name was Bradley—was at a table, his feet propped up on an empty chair, eating a burrito. Beth froze like a trapped animal. She made a small, heartbreaking sound. When I took her hand to pull her away, it was ice cold.

Rage swelled in my body. It took everything I had to not go after Bradley, to punish him for harming my friend. To make him hurt just as badly as he'd hurt her.

Instead, I walked Beth to an off-campus smoothie place and talked to her gently. She was no longer hungry. She didn't want to talk. All she wanted to do was curl up in bed.

She lost weight. Couldn't sleep. Started skipping classes.

It broke my heart to see her lying there, like a shadow of her happy, chatty former self. I stroked her hair, brought her soup, and told her over and over again that she'd done nothing wrong, that she was the victim of a terrible crime and deserved help.

But she moved home to Nebraska and finished the semester on-line. Then she transferred to a small school, and I never saw her again.

I tried, though. I texted and called, but she rarely answered. When she did, she was polite yet distant. She didn't seem to want to be connected to anything that reminded her of that time. Not even me.

But I couldn't stop being reminded of Beth. And I don't think I've ever stopped mourning her.

Every time I saw Bradley around campus, shirtless on a warm day as he played Frisbee on the quad or doing his stupid bro handshake with his buddies, my rage intensified.

I kept thinking about how terrified Beth was that he'd taken pictures or a video—that her assault would be never-ending, with images of it passed from guy to guy.

So one night, I sought out Bradley and we had a conversation. There *were* pictures. I made sure no one else would ever see them.

It was the least I could do for Beth.

Now I turn off the music blaring in Georgia's apartment and go back to bed. I lie there for an hour, unable to sleep, before I give up and head to her shower. I towel off and borrow her toiletries, then look in her closet. I'll have to wear my jeans again since hers are a size too small, but I can fit into one of her tops. I select a black V-neck with three-quarter sleeves and a delicate ruffle on the ends. I look at her Chanel combat boots, but there's no excuse for me to wear them, so I put on my own slightly battered black ankle boots, the ones I bought for 20 percent off.

Caroline won't be here for another couple of hours, so I've got plenty of time to pick up breakfast and a toothbrush and her family's Bible. I sling my bag over my shoulder and walk to the elevator.

An older woman with a little white dog wearing a plaid bow on its collar is just stepping out. She stops and stares at me. This is the most exclusive floor of a ritzy building. All the neighbors must recognize each other. She looks like she wants to interrogate me, but I merely step around her, into the elevator.

"Have a nice day," I say as the doors slide shut, erasing her from view.

A different concierge is at the front desk—an earnest-looking young woman with dark braids.

I don't hesitate. I approach her with a smile. "Hi, just wanted to introduce myself. I'm Amanda, and I'm working with Georgia Cartwright's lawyer."

She blinks from behind her glasses. "Nice to meet you. I'm Jordan."

"Gavin probably told you I'll be doing some work in Ms. Cartwright's apartment, so you'll see me coming and going."

Her eyes grow wide, but all she says is "Of course."

I feel a strange confidence. It's as if I belong here in the epicenter of my sister's world.

It wasn't so hard to step into her life after all.

CHAPTER TWENTY-SEVEN

GEORGIA

Tony, the private investigator, wanted to meet in person to give you, as he put it, "a piece of information." You had a packed day, as you always did back in your other life, and it was excruciating to spend two hours tasting and discussing cake flavors with a bride and her finicky groom, then negotiating a contract with a florist who kept trying to raise her prices. As soon as your last appointment ended, you rushed to the restaurant he'd named, arriving five minutes early.

Tony was already seated on a bar stool positioned to let him face the entrance, so he spotted you the moment you walked in and gave you a little wave. Even if he hadn't told you at your first meeting that he was retired law enforcement, you'd have guessed it. It isn't just a look; it's a vibe. You learned that when you dated the police chief's son. They always remain very still, and they sit in a way that allows them to monitor the entrances into a room.

Even when they're the ones delivering the bomb.

You slid onto the stool next to him, your stomach roiling.

Tony was drinking sweet tea, which would've struck you as a humorously incongruous note if you hadn't been so nervous.

"Drink?" he'd asked. "I had to quit years ago because I liked it too much, but don't let that stop you."

"Sure, um, a Heineken," you'd said, not trusting the wine at a pub that had sticky floors and posters with peeling corners on the wall.

He signaled the bartender and ordered your beer, then got straight to the point, which you appreciated.

"When I take on a new client, first thing I do is check all the documents. Paper trails, electronic trails—we all leave them, even when we don't know we're doing it. So that's what I started with for you. At the beginning of your path through life."

You'd nodded, feeling your nails bite into your palms. The question roared through your mind: *What did he find?*

The PI paused while the bartender brought over your drink, serving it up in the bottle instead of a glass. You took a sip, then began picking at the damp, sticky label.

"I pulled your birth certificate." Tony reached down for the battered brown briefcase tucked between his feet and opened it, pulling out a manila folder. He straightened up and looked you in the eye. It was impossible to read his expression, another facet of his training.

Then his words slammed into you: "Your *real* birth certificate."

Your hands shook as you reached for the folder. It suddenly hit you that you could regret opening this investigation. Maybe your mother died of some incurable genetic disease, one she passed down to you. Maybe your birth father is in prison, like Tony's other client. Those are only two of a thousand awful possibilities.

You weren't sure if you wanted to know. But you *had* to know.

You felt his eyes on your face as you opened the folder.

Inside was a birth certificate. It looked identical to the one you'd scanned and sent to the detective. Your eyes skimmed the first few lines—it listed your name, city of birth, and the exact time you were born. It was all information you already had.

You glanced up at him, puzzled.

"Keep looking," he told you. "You'll see it."

And then you did. A single word in a box toward the upper right of the form. In the birth certificate you have, the one you thought was real, the box is blank.

The word filling this one read: *Twin.*

You gaped at those four letters, trying to comprehend what they meant. Was there another *you* walking around—a woman with your face, your mannerisms, your voice?

You blinked hard as the word blurred, then came back into focus.

"Is she— Does she live around here?" you asked in a voice that didn't sound like your own.

"I haven't checked yet. Needed you to authorize it first." Tony stirred his tea, the spoon clinking against the side of the mug. "Could be a he, too."

You nodded slowly. For some reason, you'd instantly imagined her as identical to you. But of course Tony was right. Your twin could be a guy. Or she could be fraternal and look nothing like you.

You came to Tony to find out about your birth mother and father.

In an instant, the focus of your quest shifted.

You looked into Tony's eyes and knew he understood.

"I'll find your twin," he said.

CHAPTER TWENTY-EIGHT

MANDY

When I walk back into the apartment building a little after 9:30 A.M., a young woman is pacing in the lobby.

"Mandy?"

Even if I didn't recognize her voice or see the sparkling rock weighing down her ring finger, I'd know it was Caroline. Everything about her matches my image of a privileged bride-to-be.

I'm swallowing my last bite of an everything bagel with chive cream cheese—an un-bridal meal if there ever was one—so I just nod.

"I know I'm early, but I couldn't wait."

"No problem." I brush the seeds from my fingertips. "Let's go on up."

In the few minutes it takes us to journey to Georgia's door, I learn about Caroline's hopes for a slightly overcast day on her wedding— "It's actually better for the pictures"—and her frustration with people who don't have the decency to RSVP by the due date.

I unlock the door to Georgia's apartment and usher Caroline in. She finally falls silent, as if she's entering a hallowed space.

"It's weird," she says a moment later. "Georgia's probably never coming back here again. She went to a party one night and just like that"— Caroline snaps her fingers—"she turned into a different person."

"Sounds like you know her better than I do," I say. "Did she ever bring up Annabelle?"

"Um, can we start looking for the Bible while we talk?"

"Oh!" As if I've just remembered, I lift up the cloth bag I'm holding. "I found the receipt on Georgia's desk and picked it up at the bookbinder's this morning."

Caroline snatches the bag and pulls off the protective bubble wrap to uncover the old Bible. She examines it briefly before gently hugging it to her chest, then swaddling it back into the packaging.

"My mother would've died if we'd lost it," she says. "I've got to text her."

She pulls out her phone and taps out a message. I walk into the kitchen, calling behind me, "How about some coffee?" Now that I've got her here, I don't plan on letting her leave until I've wrung some information out of her.

Caroline turns down my offer, but she follows me and settles onto a stool. She looks around the apartment, taking everything in.

"Have you been here before?" I ask.

"No, but it looks just like I imagined it. Of course Georgia would live in a beautiful place."

I clock her stare as I grab a mug out of a high cupboard and pop a ruby-colored pod into the machine.

"I know it's weird to be using her things, but she did give me her keys and I've made coffee in her kitchen before, so . . . Anyway, Georgia never really talked about Annabelle to me. What about you? What do you think happened between them?"

Caroline furrows her brow. "I guess it's like they say. She'd always been jealous of Annabelle. I heard that's why the Cartwrights sent Georgia to boarding school, to get her away from her little sister because she was so cruel to her."

"Where'd you hear that?" I take the almond milk creamer out of the fridge and pour a splash into my coffee.

"One of my mom's friends told her. I think her cousin knows Honey Cartwright."

"Wow," I say, widening my eyes. I lean forward, resting my forearms on the island. When I tend bar, I end up playing therapist sometimes, and what I've learned is that people want to talk far more than they want to listen. Show you're a captive audience, and they'll tell you just about anything.

"What else?"

Caroline leans closer, too, mirroring my pose. Her voice is low, but there's an edge of thrill riding it. "I keep thinking about this: Georgia said it would be sweet if my goldendoodle Lulu was the ring bearer and a bridesmaid walked her down the aisle on a white silk leash. Georgia really loves dogs, so I asked if she had one. She told me she really wanted one growing up but wasn't allowed because Annabelle was allergic. Then, right after Georgia was sent to boarding school, Annabelle outgrew her allergies and *she* got a dog. Not just that, but Senator Dawson gave it to Annabelle as a birthday present because he and his wife are best friends with her parents, so everyone made this huge deal about it."

I take a sip of coffee. "I mean, that's a little weird, but it can happen. Kids outgrow allergies sometimes, right?"

"I guess. But I got the impression Georgia was still bitter about it."

"How so?"

"Just the way she talked about it. Like Annabelle had gotten the thing Georgia wanted most, and Georgia was the forgotten sister."

It's so hard to imagine Georgia feeling that way—she looks like the woman who inspires envy, not experiences it. But some people are invested in cultivating an image that is worlds away from the reality bubbling beneath.

"Did Georgia say anything else about Annabelle?"

"No, and I was curious because my sister gets on my last nerve sometimes. She's always been competitive with me, and get this, she got engaged recently and scheduled *her* engagement dinner for a week before my wedding." Caroline tosses her long, beachy waves in indignation.

"And you're upset by that," I say, still in therapist mode.

"Yeah. I wish I could ask Georgia about it. She'd know exactly what to do. She always had backup plans for her backup plans, you know? Nothing ever went wrong when Georgia was around. We've got this new wedding planner who's taking over, but she isn't as good as Georgia."

Once again, it's hard to reconcile the portrait Caroline is painting of my sister with the one generated by the media: an enraged, out-of-control killer who descended into madness. I wonder how many sides there are to Georgia.

"My best friend told me to skip the engagement dinner and say I'm busy wedding planning. I don't know, I'd feel like she's winning then."

I've probably gotten all the information I can out of Caroline. In her world, all conversational roads lead to her wedding.

"Don't skip the dinner," I say without even thinking about it. "Here's what you should do: Show up twenty minutes late. Let them get all the gushing about her engagement out of the way. Oh, and wear a gorgeous white dress. Make them remember *you're* the bride. Your sister is just the warm-up act. You're the star."

Caroline is staring at me, her eyes round.

I'm a little surprised myself. I don't know what came over me; this isn't the sort of thing I'd usually say.

Then Caroline smiles broadly.

"You know what? That's *exactly* what Georgia would say."

CHAPTER TWENTY-NINE

GEORGIA

You feel Josh's eyes on you as you pick up your lunch tray. His stare feels like a bug crawling over your skin.

He is sitting at the far end of the table with an empty place next to him. You consider your options, your mind whirling behind the listless affect you've cultivated. You could sit at the opposite end, next to Patty and as far away from Josh as possible. You'd be protected physically. But you'd have to endure the violation of his eyes roaming over you.

Josh catches your gaze and pats the chair next to him, inviting you to take it. Your pulse quickens as you berate yourself for allowing that fleeting moment of eye contact. Josh doesn't need any encouragement.

You walk quickly to the middle of the table and sit down next to a bald man who likes to do endless laps through the hallways.

When you lean a bit backward, Josh's view of you is blocked.

You eat a bite of bow-tie pasta with bland red sauce. The cafeteria never sends foods that require cutting to this floor; the only utensils provided are dull plastic sporks.

You lean forward to take another bite and see movement out of the corner of your eye. Josh is getting up.

You instantly realize your mistake. There's an empty seat next to you.

Josh is walking your way. He's going to change seats. You have a split second to decide what to do.

You stand up and walk to the trash can, letting the contents of your tray slide into the bin. You skipped breakfast and your stomach feels hollow. There won't be any food for hours, until dinnertime. But what choice do you have?

You can't go to your room or sit down again. You need to be able to move quickly.

So you stand in front of the nurses' station, staring out into the courtyard. You've never once seen a bird or bee or butterfly winging around there. It's like other living things know to avoid this place.

You keep watching Josh through the side of your eye. He isn't moving, either. He's just standing there, gaping at you.

You pull away your gaze, looking toward the table. That's when you notice Patty has stopped eating. She's watching Josh watch you.

"All done with lunch, Georgia?"

You start at the sound of a nurse's voice close to you.

"It's your shower day. Would you like to take it now?"

This is the first time you've been offered a shower. Suddenly you're desperate to climb beneath the spray of warm water, to scrub yourself clean. You feel as if you could scour your skin for an hour and still not get rid of the dank, medicinal aroma of this place that has seeped into your pores.

"Come with me," the nurse instructs you.

You follow her down the hallway and through a doorway. Behind it lies the shower. It's tiny, barely big enough for a person to turn around in, and the curtain is white plastic.

On the sink counter is a thin folded towel and a paper cup holding a bit of sludgy liquid.

"You can use this to wash your hair and body," the nurse tells you, handing you the cup. "I'll be right outside. The door needs to remain two inches open. You have ten minutes."

You stand there, staring at your hazy reflection in the unbreakable polycarbonate mirror. Your features are blurred, and your pale skin and light hair give you a ghostly effect. You lean forward, trying to get a clearer look. But the woman in the mirror yields nothing; it's as if she's in a snow globe.

Even though time seems to stand still in this place, it must be ticking by and you don't want to miss your chance to feel clean. You turn on the shower and take off your bright green top and pants and socks. There's no hook on the back of the door—you suppose a patient could fashion a way to hang themselves on one—so you balance your things on the sink. You reach a hand into the shower and test the temperature. It's lukewarm. You try to adjust the dial to make it hotter, but the temperature doesn't budge. Another security measure, probably.

You step into the spray of water, feeling it course down your hair and body. A swell of emotion rises in your throat, but you fight it back. If you start crying, you may not be able to stop.

You scoop the soap up in your fingertips. It doesn't have much of a scent. You rub it into your scalp, letting the soapy water stream down your skin.

Then you hear the door to the bathroom creak open.

The nurse said she'd stand outside. Why would she be coming in?

Unless it isn't her.

Your legs weaken, threatening to collapse under you. You're too petrified to peer out and see who it is. But you have to.

You pull back the thin white curtain a few inches.

Your heartbeat explodes.

Josh is there.

"Hi, pretty baby. Need me to wash your back?" His lips peel back, revealing that horrible yellow smile.

Where is the nurse? How did Josh get rid of her?

You are trapped in the worst possible place.

"I bet you miss having a man around. A girl who looks like you, you're used to being taken care of. Am I right?"

Josh pulls the bathroom door shut behind him, the one the nurse said needed to be kept two inches open.

He's just a few steps from you now, filling the bathroom with his menace, sucking out all the air.

You want to scream for help. But you can't. It's not because you're staying in character—right now, the risk of being found out is less than the risk of being at Josh's mercy—but because your vocal cords are frozen in fear.

The running water will mask any sounds Josh might make.

What will he do to you?

You have no weapons. This place has been designed to eliminate them.

Is it better to try to fight or succumb?

Josh reaches for the curtain and yanks it all the way open.

You cover your breasts and cross your legs and bend down, trying to keep him from seeing your body.

Then, behind Josh, the door flies open.

It isn't a nurse or aide.

It's Patty. She takes in the scene—you cowering in the shower, water still beating down on you, Josh holding back the curtain.

She opens her mouth and does the thing you can't.

She screams, long and loud, the noise sounding an alarm that brings footsteps running.

CHAPTER THIRTY

MANDY

It isn't until after Caroline leaves and I go to put the creamer back in the refrigerator that I notice it.

The invitations on the side of the fridge include one for an event tomorrow night. I slide the card out from beneath the magnet and study the thick gold script across the top of the coal-black invitation.

It's a black-tie fundraiser for ALS, with cocktails, appetizers, and a live auction, held in the ballroom of Charlotte Country Club.

There's a private website for the gala with a password printed at the bottom of the invitation.

It's easy to access it on my phone. It's even easier to find the box where I can type in my name and RSVP. I blink hard when I see the price of a single ticket is $500. That's far more than I spend on social activities in a month. But if I want to learn about Georgia, I need to travel deeper into her world.

At least that's what I tell myself. The truth is more complicated. I guess I also want the chance to live a little bit longer in Georgia's shoes.

Still, $500 is a lot of money.

Then I notice something else on the event's website: the names of the chairs and sponsors, and a link to the list of those who have already RSVP'd.

There's only one way I can justify sneaking into this event. I walk into Georgia's office and sit down at her desk. I slide open the top drawer and find a silver Montblanc pen in a velvet case and a stack of thick note cards embossed with Georgia's initials at the top. I touch my phone's screen, pulling up the guest list for those who have already RSVP'd to the charity gala.

Then I begin the slow process of cross-referencing those names against the ones in the guest book I took a picture of at the Cartwrights' house.

By the time I've finished, I have seven matching names written on one of Georgia's note cards—including Colby Dawson, the son of the US senator. According to the tabloids, Georgia briefly dated him, and she's known him all her life. Not only is he attending the fundraiser, but he's a co-chair of the event.

There's another co-chair whose name appears on my list from the funeral reception, a guy named Harrison. I google him, noting his prominent nose and teeth and his broad-shouldered physique. If I can't get to Colby directly, maybe I can get Harrison to introduce me.

I type my name and credit card number into the RSVP box and buy a ticket.

Even though I have a lot to do at home and it's a ninety-minute drive away, I'm not ready to hit the highway yet. I need to bring Georgia the things I packed for her. But I'm not going to drop them off with a nurse.

I want to see my sister again.

I look up the number for the hospital's psych ward and dial it, then walk around flicking off the lights in Georgia's apartment.

The protocol for setting up a visit with a resident on the locked ward is surprisingly easy. A nurse reminds me that I'll need to bring ID and go through a metal detector and hand-wand check before being allowed onto the floor.

"When would you like to come?"

"Twenty minutes?" I suggest.

"That should work well. The other patients will be starting group activity then. Georgia is taking her shower now, but she'll be finished and ready for a visit—"

Her voice cuts off as a woman's long, wailing scream sounds in the distance. I hear someone shouting, then a huge commotion—it sounds like a stampede erupting—before the phone abruptly goes dead.

An electric bolt sears through me. I don't realize I'm running until I'm halfway down the hall.

I don't know how I know this, but Georgia is in trouble.

I need to get to my sister.

CHAPTER THIRTY-ONE

GEORGIA

Rage sweeps across Josh's face as he realizes he's been caught.

He curses at Patty, spittle flying from his lips as the takedown team descends.

You cower behind the shower curtain, shivering, as Josh hurls himself through the doorway, his fists flying. You hear a violent scuffle and voices shouting, and for one terrifying moment, you wonder if Josh has somehow achieved superhuman strength and is winning the fight. If he'll be coming for you next.

Then it grows quiet.

You wait, holding your breath, water beating down on your back.

A huge aide passes in front of the open bathroom door, removing the plastic gloves he must have put on before injecting Josh with the syringes.

A patient's high-pitched voice asks, "Why was Josh so angry?"

"You don't need to worry about that," someone replies. "Everything's fine now."

You're still trying to catch your breath when the nurse who gave you the little cup of soap enters the room.

"All set?" she asks, handing you the towel. Her tone is brisk and matter-of-fact. As if nothing has happened.

But she's looking down at the floor, like she's guilty of something.

Maybe she walked away to take a phone call or go to the bathroom when she was supposed to be monitoring you. You can't bear to think of what would've happened if not for Patty.

"I'll wait outside while you dry off and change," the nurse says. "Your clean outfit is on the sink, and I'll take away your dirty things."

She isn't going to acknowledge what almost happened. For her, it's a minor crisis at work. For you, it has stripped away any final illusion that you might be safe here.

You quickly rub the rough towel over your skin and pull on the scrub pants and hospital gown as fast as you can. You're shaking, but not from cold.

"Would you like to rest in your room, or maybe do some art?" the nurse asks.

You want to be alone, to curl up in bed and shake, but what if Josh comes around again? It would be safer to try to find Patty and stay near her.

You walk toward the art room, trying to tamp down the turmoil swelling inside you. You pass the bald patient doing laps, and a woman having an argument with a nurse's aide about needing to go to Morocco right now. The pressure inside you feels unbearable; if it doesn't find release soon, you'll explode. If you opened your mouth, you're half certain a stream of acrid smoke would tunnel out.

But no one acts any differently toward you. The bald man who always does laps passes you again, smiling his odd half smile. Behind the plexiglass shield, the staff are talking and working on computers.

Then a nurse looks up from behind the plexiglass and spots you. She sets down the chart she's holding and exits the locked area. Nurses on this floor never carry anything when they move among the patients. No charts, pens, cups of hot coffee, or cell phones.

She steps in front of you, halting your path toward the art area. Maybe it's time to break down, to plead not guilty and take your chances in the system. But your mother will testify against you. So will others. You won't have a chance.

The nurse says, "I have a message for you from Mandy. She's on her way to see you."

You almost fall to the ground in relief.

You shuffle away before the nurse can detect the change in your affect.

You no longer have a twenty-four-hour watcher. You can try to get a message to Mandy without fear of it being intercepted and used against you. There will be cameras, of course, but the staff aren't lip-readers. Even so, you'll need to be very careful. Plan your words painstakingly.

Your sister is coming.

This changes everything.

CHAPTER THIRTY-TWO

MANDY

Everything about my visit to the hospital feels like a replica of the last time I was here: the metal detector, the escort by a nurse's aide to the top floor, the phone call, the two locked doors that funnel into the high-security unit. The aide even walks me to the same room where I first met Georgia.

But there's one massive difference.

I almost don't recognize Georgia when she appears in the doorway.

In the space of a few days, my sister has sunk deeper into her transformation. The deathly pallor of her complexion ages her a decade. She's painfully thin; the skin is stretched across her cheekbones, and her collarbone is prominent. Her hair is coarse and dry.

She looks like she belongs here now.

"What happened to you?" I whisper.

She doesn't reply. She doesn't appear to be injured; there are no bruises or scratches on her face and arms. Yet I'm certain the scream I heard on the phone involved my sister. Panic roared through my veins; my heart was pounding as I drove here. My body reacted as if *I* were the one feeling threatened.

I've read about this eerie phenomenon: When something traumatic happens to a twin—from a broken bone to a broken heart—the other twin sometimes feels it.

Now she shuffles toward me, her head lowered, not making eye contact, and takes the chair across from me. We're alone in the room now, though the nurses' station is across the hallway just past the open door.

An icy tingle slips down my spine as Georgia slowly lifts her head.

I see it instantly: the sharpness in her eyes that she seems to turn off and on like a light. Georgia is fully present now.

"I brought some of your clothes," I tell her. "I gave them to the aide who brought me up here."

She holds my gaze, and I watch the nuance of what I've said register. She knows I've been inside her apartment.

"Thank you," she whispers. Her voice sounds scratchy and uneven.

I can't pull my eyes away from her. Once again, the connection between us feels akin to static electricity. *I know you,* I think. *Maybe not the story of your first heartbreak, or your earliest memory, but I know you even more deeply than that. I recognize you on a cellular level.*

She drinks me in as I do her. I see her blink as she takes in my shirt with the ruffles at the ends of the sleeves.

"I hope you don't mind I borrowed it," I tell her. "I ended up staying over at your place."

She nods ever so slightly. "Good," she whispers.

I was right. Georgia wanted me to get into her apartment. But why?

A nurse pokes her head into the room. "How are we doing, ladies?" she asks brightly.

"Fine, thanks," I reply. Georgia doesn't answer; she's instantly back in character. Flat, disaffected. Wispy as a ghost.

The nurse moves on.

Georgia looks down at her feet. She reaches up to cover her mouth, but I can hear the faint words that seep through: "Don't trust anyone."

Does she think someone is eavesdropping on us in here? Or watching her as she talks?

"What do you want from me?" I ask.

"You borrowed my shirt, now borrow my socks," she whispers.

It's like she's speaking in code. Or maybe her mind is jumbled and fragmented. Perhaps it really did tell her to kill Annabelle.

She lifts her hand to her mouth again.

"And find Colby Dawson," she says. "But don't tell him you're my sister. Don't tell anyone."

The senator's son—the one I was hoping to see at the fundraiser tomorrow night. It's like Georgia's mind entwined with my own even before I came here, urging me to sneak into the gala.

"How long have you known about me?" I ask.

She thinks for a moment. "A month," she replies.

That stings. She had plenty of time to reach out to me. Why didn't she? On top of that thought comes another one: Would she have ever reached out if she didn't need my help?

A nurse's aide—this time a huge guy with tattoos—looks into the room and gives me a thumbs-up while he raises his eyebrows. I return the gesture: We're fine.

Georgia may not be on a twenty-four-hour watch any longer, but they're sure keeping close tabs on her. Or maybe they're doing that because she's with a visitor, another young woman around the same age as the sister Georgia stands accused of killing.

"Colby's lonely. Sensitive. Nothing like his father." In a few clipped sentences, Georgia has told me so much. Her words are like haiku. She must have thought this all out, preparing exactly what to say to me.

"I'm not a lawyer, I'm not a shrink," I tell her. "Why do you think I can help you?"

"You're my sister," she says. "And never forget it could be you in here."

I look around at the bare walls, the drab floor and ceiling. I hear a woman angrily yelling in the distance. The air feels heavy and thick. My chest tightens. I couldn't survive in here.

"What do you mean, it could be me?" I ask.

She waits a moment as yet another nurse passes by the door. Are they trying to eavesdrop on us? Now I feel unhinged. It must be this place; it does strange things to your mind.

"Who divided us up?" Georgia asks me. "Who decided which twin went where?"

I stare at her. I guess I'd assumed the authorities who handled the adoption had placed us with our respective families.

I watch as Georgia's eyes drift up to a tiny clear plastic dome in the ceiling. I'd assumed it was a light when I first saw it. Now I scrutinize it. There isn't a light fixture inside. But there's something else. I think it's a video camera.

Someone is probably watching us right now.

Is Georgia crazy, or is she the sanest person in this place?

"Be very careful," she whispers. "You have no idea how big this is."

CHAPTER THIRTY-THREE

GEORGIA

You watch Mandy leave, escorted by an aide. Several patients, including Patty and the woman with blond and pink hair, look at her as she passes through the hall. Mandy isn't quite to the first security door when the giant man with the keloid scar comes around the corner and spots her. He quickens his pace, trying to get to her.

But the aide who is escorting Mandy must hear the heavy footsteps. He moves behind Mandy, blocking the man from getting too close to her.

"Where are you going, Ramon?" the aide asks.

"I need to get some pineapple juice," the man replies.

Mandy stays behind the aide, her eyes growing big, watching it play out. She looks intrigued, not scared, which is good. You're depending on the fact that your sister is tough.

"I'll see if the kitchen has any," the aide says.

Ramon turns and walks away, but the second the aide moves to unlock the door, Ramon comes back, standing just a few feet behind my sister and the aide.

The aide isn't calling for backup. He doesn't seem intimidated, despite Ramon's size. Ramon must not be considered dangerous anymore.

"Come on, Ramon, you know you have to stay in here," the aide says.

"Oh, sure, I know," Ramon replies, as if he's surprised by the implication that he might be trying to escape.

"Take five steps back, please," the aide says. Ramon complies.

Mandy and the aide walk through the door. It closes behind them with a thud; then your sister is gone.

Tears prick your eyes. You need to distract your mind, something you've become practiced at. You walk toward the common space where art supplies are kept, thinking about what to draw to perpetuate the illusion that you belong here. You think about sketching Annabelle, but instead, you decide on a self-portrait. You'll make the two halves of your face asymmetrical.

When you get to the long, low table where patients eat and do art, it's empty. You choose a blank sheet of paper and some stubby crayons and sit down. Then you see Patty on the telephone just outside the nurse's station. She spots you and smiles, then quickly ends her call and comes over to the table.

You haven't seen her since she saved you. You want to hug her, to cry out your thanks, but you can't do any of that.

You begin to draw, your purple crayon creating an off-center oval.

"I like the color you chose," Patty says very softly, slipping into the seat beside you. It's as if she doesn't want to be overheard any more than you do.

You want to acknowledge her, but how? The watchers can't see you being fully present.

Finally you settle for briefly letting the back of your hand rest on Patty's. It could be seen as an accidental touch by anyone who spots it.

"I know you aren't talking right now, but I hope you don't mind if I do," Patty says. "Is that okay?" She waits a moment, and you feel the tension rising in your body. You are desperate for someone to talk to, someone who makes sense. Your brain is craving any kind of connection. Should you risk it?

You can't resist. You nod, a slow up-and-down movement of your head.

"Good, sweetie. I saw the way Josh was looking at you and it worried me," Patty tells you. "I used to work with a lot of men, and when I was younger, the culture was much worse than it is now. I was grabbed and harassed, and once, my boss came to my hotel room late at night and pounded on the door. So I know what it looks like when a guy is trouble. When Josh followed you to the shower, I followed him."

Her words bring back the terror you felt when you pulled back the curtain to peer out and spotted Josh. You begin to tremble. And then you feel it, the brush of Patty's hand against your own again.

"Don't be scared," she whispers. "I won't let him do anything to you."

Relief pours through you, warm and liquid. *Why do you care so much about me?* you want to ask.

Then Patty answers your unspoken question. "I had a younger sister who died," she says. "Darby. She was always troubled—she was the kind of kid who'd skip school or wind up with a boyfriend who was bad news—so I guess I got immune to her stirring things up. And when things got really bad, I was too busy at work to see it. Darby overdosed. I was the one who found her. I was too late to save her."

Patty swallows hard. "She had long reddish hair, like you."

Patty picks up a yellow crayon and begins to draw a crescent moon at the top of her page.

"I think about her all the time. Things I wish I'd said or done. We fought a lot when we were younger, but when we became adults, we grew close."

You're barely breathing, you're so intent on catching every word.

"Then, a few nights ago, I had too much to drink, and I realized my life is passing me by. It's like I've been on a train, and instead of looking up at the glorious scenery and talking to the interesting people around me, I've had my head down working. I put everything into my job. I never married or had a family. And now my parents are gone, and I failed my sister, and I'll never see her again. And I was in the kitchen and I saw a knife and I just . . . made an impulsive decision. And now I'm here."

Your crayon has stopped moving. You're desperate for Patty to keep talking. She is the only patient in here who seems cogent. And she cares about you. She saved you once. Maybe she can help you again.

Don't trust anyone. The warning you gave Mandy comes back to you.

But another patient, a middle-aged woman who attempted suicide, hardly seems like a risk.

"Do you miss your sister, too?" Patty asks.

You suck in a breath, startled by her question. No one has ever asked if you miss Annabelle. Maybe only another woman who had a complicated relationship with her sister can understand all the intense emotions you've felt toward Annabelle.

"Maybe you can answer me in another way," Patty suggests. "You could just draw a single line on your paper now to mean yes."

She will know you're fully present, despite the shell you've affected. But maybe that's a good thing. Patty wouldn't want to talk to or be around someone who isn't truly here.

You lift your crayon and draw a long, straight line from the top of the oval to the bottom of the page. If anyone is watching on the cameras, it could simply be the first strand of hair in your portrait.

Patty nods slowly.

"I'm sorry, Georgia," she whispers, and your chest constricts with sobs you can't release.

CHAPTER THIRTY-FOUR

MANDY

Georgia looked like a different person when I visited her yesterday. Tonight I'm the one who has undergone a transformation.

I stand in front of the full-length mirror in her walk-in closet, turning to glimpse myself from every angle.

I'm wearing one of my sister's dresses, a black floor-length Oscar de la Renta. It's composed of structured tiers of lace and tulle, and the bottom has a mermaid flare. I had to squeeze into Spanx to get it to zip up, and I'm wearing the highest heels in her closet because it's two inches longer on me than it would be on her.

My feet are already beginning to ache, but I barely notice them.

With my hair styled by Glamsquad and a makeup tutorial that I followed on YouTube, I hardly recognize myself.

I also discovered Georgia's jewelry drawer and chose a few delicate rings and diamond hoop earrings. I haven't finished organizing her closet, so her evening bags are still strewn in a corner on the floor. I pick out a small black clutch from the top of the pile.

The gala begins in thirty minutes, and I want to be on time.

I call up my Uber app and study the options. I can take a regular Uber for $14.95. Or I can take a luxury vehicle for four times the price.

I choose the Lincoln because money isn't a concern for me right now.

I've checked Georgia's sock drawer.

Hundred-dollar bills—$10,000 in total—were rolled up inside her socks.

I have no idea why Georgia would keep that kind of money around—maybe it's a rich-person thing—but she clearly wants me to use it if I need it. She wouldn't have told me to borrow her socks otherwise.

I tuck the lip gloss I borrowed into her clutch purse, then look down at my phone. The Uber is five minutes away.

When I walk to the elevator, I again pass the neighbor with the little white dog. This time, she nods at me approvingly. I guess I look like I fit in here now.

I walk out into the crisp, starry night as the black Lincoln pulls up. A family is strolling down the sidewalk, and the little girl stops and stares at me. The driver leaps out and hurries around to open the back door for me, the first time I've ever had an Uber driver do this. I climb in, making sure the mermaid swoosh of material around my ankles is safely inside before the driver shuts the door. Outside, the little girl is still staring at me.

Is this all it takes? I wonder. Maybe the image we project shapes who we become as decisively as our genetic blueprints. Because it isn't just the dress and makeup. I feel different on the inside, too. I'm exuding something I can't put my finger on, but it's akin to confidence. It's the thing that is making people stare at me. Then I realize I know what it is. I noticed it in the first pictures I saw of Georgia. It's charisma.

The Lincoln driver pulls up at the hotel at the stroke of 7 and a bellman hurries to open my door. I thank the driver and step out. My foot wobbles in the four-inch heels, but luckily I'm still holding on to the vehicle's door.

"Are you here for the ALS fundraiser?" the bellman asks.

"Yes."

"Right this way, miss." He leads me inside, holding the door for me. A woman at a table outside the party room greets me and gushes over my dress, then checks my name against the guest list.

"Enjoy!" she calls after me as I step inside.

The room has been transformed into a wonderland. Lush plants and flowers are draped everywhere, making it feel as if we're inside a greenhouse, and high round tables glow with the golden light of candles flickering inside votives. A band is playing a Rascal Flatts hit on the elevated stage, and bartenders in dark suits stand ready in front of bottles of premium liquors, with gleaming silver dishes full of cut limes and lemons and maraschino cherries.

I'm one of the first ones here. But not *the* first.

Because I see a group of about ten people raising champagne glasses in a toast in the center of the room. I recognize the guy with the prominent nose and teeth: Harrison. And clinking his glass with the others is Colby Dawson. The senator's son.

"Champagne, miss?"

I turn and accept a flute from the waiter.

Already people are beginning to stream in through the entrance. In another few minutes, this room will likely be filled.

It's now or never, I tell myself. I take a big swallow of champagne and walk toward Colby, but keep my head averted, as if I'm watching the musicians instead of where I'm going. He's starting to turn away from the group, which is good, because it means he's going to be walking toward me, too. Just before I get to him, I give a little lurch, as if I'm about to trip.

And I throw my drink onto his jacket.

"Oh no!" I gasp.

"It's okay," he tells me as a waiter rushes over with a napkin. Colby takes it and dabs his jacket.

"Can I get you another drink?" he asks.

"I feel like I should be getting you one," I tell him.

A waitress comes by with two fresh champagne flutes, and Colby trades our empty ones.

"I'm Colby," he says.

"Amanda." No one but my parents have ever called me that, but I like having another layer of protection over my true identity.

"Nice to meet you."

"I bet you say that to all the girls who throw drinks on you," I joke.

He looks surprised, then laughs. Instead of a comeback, he looks at me like he's waiting for me to continue the conversation. So I do.

"I'm new in town," I tell him. "Where are some fun places to go?"

"Oh—um . . . I mean, if you like to eat, Charlotte has the best restaurants."

I'm about to ask another question when a tall, rail-thin woman appears, clutching Colby's arm and shrieking a hello. She pulls him away, telling him he *has* to come say hi to someone named Hunter.

I watch helplessly as Colby moves away from me and my chance evaporates.

Then I square my shoulders. *No*, I think. Not tonight, not in this dress, not in this life.

I approach a bartender and ask for a pen. I take a cocktail napkin from his stack and write my name and number on it with the message *I'd love to see you again.*

Then I walk directly to Colby and hand it to him.

The thin woman is mid-story, her hand still clutching Colby's arm, and her eyes shoot daggers at me.

"You might want to have this in case we bump into each other again when I'm holding a drink," I tell Colby.

I see him look down and clock what I've written. A shy smile spreads across his face.

"Have a wonderful night," I tell the sour-faced woman. Then I float away, into the crowd.

CHAPTER THIRTY-FIVE

GEORGIA

Memories of Colby drift through your mind while you lie in bed, staring into the smoke-gray darkness.

You played Candy Land together as little kids: You both wanted to be the green gingerbread man pawn, but Colby let you have it and took blue instead. He had a gap between his front teeth that he tried to cover by putting his hand over his mouth whenever he spoke.

You played other games, too. Like hide-and-seek while your parents sat in the living room, drinking and talking, the smoke from the men's cigars turning the air acrid. Your parents spent a lot of time together, with the dads and moms pairing off along gender lines, which you and Colby figured was because none of them seemed to particularly like their spouse.

And one spring break, while you were still in elementary school, your two families took a ski trip to Aspen. You watched his father, who was then the junior US senator from North Carolina, berate Colby for being too scared to try a black diamond before skiing off and leaving his son hanging his head.

Colby was skinny and sensitive and awkward, the antithesis of an alpha male. He never fought back, even when his father cracked him across the face with the back of his hand because Colby refused to kill a buck on a hunting trip he was forced to attend as a twelve-year-old.

Colby was never the son his father wanted. And you were most definitely not the daughter your mother wanted.

You and Colby went out a few times, but the gossips got it wrong—he was a co-conspirator, not a love interest.

Besides, Colby's father didn't want him to date you. You were the troubled Cartwright sister who knocked little Annabelle down on the church stage during the Christmas pageant and jumped in front of her, reciting the line Annabelle had been practicing: "Good tidings for Merry Christmas, and a Happy New Year!"

Everyone made such a big deal about that. You were sent to your room without supper, even though it was Christmas Eve. Annabelle was barely hurt; she only had a little bump on her head. But you learned from that. You couldn't take on Annabelle directly. You needed to be more subtle.

The big surprise was that Senator Dawson didn't want Colby to date Annabelle, either. It took you a long time to figure out why. A union between two of the most powerful families in North Carolina would seem like a desirable thing. It didn't start to make sense until last Christmas Eve. Your parents had invited the Dawsons over for eggnog and singing around the piano, another tradition your families shared. A few other guests, all members of the same exclusive country club your parents frequented, came, too. Annabelle played, because naturally she was an accomplished pianist. Your parents didn't want you around any more than you wanted to be there, but they had to extend an invitation for appearances' sake: What would their neighbors think if they barred the door to one of their children on Christmas Eve? You decided to stick it to them by actually showing up. But when the first notes of "Deck the Halls" rang out, you slipped upstairs to the guest room your old bedroom had been converted into long ago. You lay down on the bed and wondered why you'd ever thought it would be a good idea to come here.

Annabelle's voice, faint yet bright as a silver bell, drifted into the room. She sang like an angel. Your sister's singing lulled you to sleep.

When you awoke a few hours later, your stomach rumbled from hunger. You crept downstairs and made your way past the empty living room.

You thought about going into the kitchen to make some pasta or a sandwich, but you didn't feel like putting in that much effort. So you turned toward the butler's pantry instead, the antechamber between the kitchen and dining room. The room was designed to muffle the clangs and conversation of the cooking staff and to give servers a place to stage dishes before serving them. There were always delicious snacks in the cabinets and on the counters lining the pantry, especially during the holidays—tins of sugared gingerbread, bowls of roasted almonds and cashews, platters of bright tangerines and red grapes.

You pushed open the swinging door a few inches and automatically began to feel for the light switch, just as you'd done countless times in the past when you'd snuck down here for a late-night snack.

But the room was already faintly glowing. A corner lamp was on, but turned down very low.

And the antechamber wasn't empty. Senator Dawson was there with Annabelle.

He was holding her upturned face in both of his hands, her cheeks in his palms, staring down at her. The expression on his face was rapturous.

Her eyes were closed, and she was smiling.

"You are so beautiful," you heard him whisper. As he began to lower his lips to hers, you silently eased out the door.

CHAPTER THIRTY-SIX

MANDY

After I walk away from Colby, I move toward Harrison. The room is filling, and men in tuxedos are carrying around some of the live auction items—a pair of diamond solitaire earrings, a box of luxury Cuban cigars, a golden retriever puppy.

I move past the group of squealing young women petting the puppy and reach Harrison.

"Excuse me, but you look so familiar," I begin. "Oh, I know where I've seen you. The funeral reception at the Cartwrights'."

He nods somberly. "It was a beautiful service."

"It really was," I agree. "How do you know the Cartwrights?"

"Our parents have been friends for ages."

That's how these circles work: the same schools, country clubs, restaurants, and vacation spots—the wealthiest of families trace established paths, intersecting and mingling, strengthening their social spiderwebs.

"How about you?" he asks.

"I was Annabelle's sorority sister." I lower my voice. "Did you know Georgia well?"

He blinks sharply, and I wonder if I've committed a faux pas by being so direct. The very rich don't tend to embrace outsiders without knowing their bona fides.

I press on, though. "I only met her once. It was obvious there was tension between her and Annabelle."

"That's an understatement." Harrison tosses back the rest of his scotch, and I see a muscle tighten in his jaw. "If Georgia's ex-boyfriend hadn't ordered a psychiatric hold, she'd be in jail where she belongs."

Her ex-boyfriend? I want to ask more, but Harrison excuses himself and steps away to get his drink refilled.

I mingle a bit longer, but don't chat with anyone useful. When the auction begins, I slip out.

As soon as I enter Georgia's apartment, I kick off her heels, flexing and curling my toes with relief.

Overall, tonight was a success. When Colby calls—it doesn't feel like an *if*—I'll suggest dinner. I'll find a way to work Georgia into the conversation. His perspective will be a valuable one.

I unzip the black dress and slip out of it, smoothing it onto its special padded hanger. I exhale as I roll down the Spanx that cinched my waist, then toss the garment into the laundry basket along with my strapless bra. The single glass of champagne I drank, along with nibbles of passed hors d'oeuvres—grilled oysters smothered in herbed butter, chilled shrimp with spicy cocktail sauce—didn't erase my appetite. I'd kill for a slice of hot, greasy pizza. Maybe this is how Georgia stays so thin.

I put on leggings and a T-shirt and then, since it's relatively early, decide to tackle the rest of Georgia's closet. I finish with the clothes still crumpled on the floor, then untangle the purses.

I pick up a hobo bag and hear the metallic sound of something hitting the floor. It could have fallen out of a purse, or maybe Georgia displays it in her closet.

I reach down and pick it up for a closer look.

I stagger backward, collapsing onto Georgia's bed, as if I've been punched in the solar plexus. All the air rushes out of my lungs.

My mind reels, trying to create a logical reason for Georgia to own this item. But I can't find one.

I've discovered eerie parallels between my sister and me before. But this one is different. It adds a whole new dimension to the secrets and lies swirling around me and my twin.

The pocket-sized St. Michael statue is an exact replica of the one my parents gave me on the day I was born, the one I keep on the high shelf of my bar next to their photo. I've heard the story so many times: They came to see me in the hospital hours after my birth, but couldn't take me home until a few days later because I had a touch of jaundice. They left me the statue with the message on its pouch—*Protect Me Always*—as a talisman.

The shape, the muted brass of the metal, the size—everything is identical.

My brain is desperately trying to make sense of it all. Because this doesn't compute. I've never known anyone who has the same statue and pouch as I do. And this one is timeworn, as is mine. It has the feel of something Georgia has owned her entire life.

The only explanation I can come up with is that my parents bought two statues. They gave one to me and another to Georgia. Twin statues for twin babies.

For thirty-two years, I didn't know about the existence of my sister.

But all along, my parents must have.

CHAPTER THIRTY-SEVEN

GEORGIA

The link between you and your twin feels weaker now. Is it because Mandy has traveled back to her own town, increasing the physical distance between you? Or has something else happened to diffuse your connection?

You stand outside in the courtyard, staring at the lonely tree, trying to summon what you've begun to think of as your twin soul frequency. But there's only the wind brushing across your face and a gnawing sense of emptiness.

Your time is running out. You learned today that a judge will hold a hearing for your case soon. You can be escorted to a special room that will be set up with a computer for the Zoom hearing, or you can let a mental health representative attend in your place.

Questions are exploding in your brain, but of course you can't voice them: Can the judge order you to be taken to jail? Is the judge in the pocket of your parents and Senator Dawson, like so many other people in town?

If Honey wants you executed, you'll be executed. Your father might try to dissuade her, but he won't be able to help you. Especially if Senator Dawson leans on the judge, which he will.

Senator Dawson has always had a taste for beautiful young women, and his wife, Dee Dee, is so used to looking the other way that her neck is permanently twisted. But no man should look at his best friend's daughter the way the senator did to Annabelle that night in the butler's pantry. This wasn't just the murder of a family friend; he actually seemed to be in love with Annabelle.

Which means the senator is thirsty for revenge.

The sun drifts behind a cloud. The wind picks up, stirring the leaves on the spindly tree. A patient sits at the low picnic table that's affixed to the cement beneath it, drumming her palms against the edge in a rhythmless melody. The man with the lopsided smile is looping around the circumference of the patio, driven by a hidden compulsion.

A sensation of hollowness engulfs you. It's different from any emotion you've ever experienced. It takes you a moment to identify it.

It's loneliness.

You've been independent your whole life. You didn't miss your family when you were sent to boarding school at fourteen—you were happy to be away from them. You've never had a boyfriend you wanted to stick around for longer than a year. You like living alone; having a roommate would be annoying.

But now you desperately miss Mandy.

You researched twins as soon as you learned of her existence. Suspended inside their private membrane, twins communicate long before they are born. They hug, they touch each other, and in one video, a male twin is seen reaching out to stroke his sister's face.

Twins also changed the course of modern medicine. In one famous case, premature twin girls who were born in a Massachusetts hospital were put into separate incubators, as was standard practice at the time. One began to die, her limbs turning grayish-blue as she gasped for air. A nurse who'd exhausted every other option finally put the second twin into her sister's incubator.

Something extraordinary happened.

The stronger twin put her arm around her smaller sister as they lay facing each other. Within minutes, the dying twin's blood oxygen levels improved. Her heart rate stabilized. She began to thrive.

They call it the Rescuing Hug.

Twins have saved each other's lives before. You need it to happen again.

CHAPTER THIRTY-EIGHT

MANDY

For the first time since I learned of Georgia's existence, I'm not thinking about her. My focus has shifted to other members of my family.

I stand behind the bar at Sweetbay's, checking supplies and unloading warm glasses from the dishwasher, but I'm preoccupied by memories of my parents. Ever since they died, I've ached to talk to them just one more time, but now the tenor of that conversation would change. *How much did you know about my twin?* I'd demand. *And what was your connection to the Cartwrights?*

Finding that duplicate religious figurine means I need to throw away all my assumptions. I've been trying to learn Georgia's life story. But I also need to look at my own.

"Miss?"

I nod at the customer who is holding up his empty pilsner glass, trying to get my attention. I fill it with Michelob and scoop some pretzels into a small wooden bowl, sliding both toward him.

"Worked here long?" he asks, crunching into a pretzel.

Normally I'm focused on customer service. Repeat business is the backbone of my bar, and most people like talking to the owner because it gives them a sense of community. I always take the time to learn customers' names and their preferred drink, just as my father did. Today I can't fake it.

"A few years." I smile noncommittally and turn around, busying myself by wiping down the counter. During a lull, while Scott finishes mixing dirty martinis for two women who are trying to flirt with him, I slip through the doorway into my office.

I exhale as I close the door and settle into the wooden chair with rolling wheels my father used, the one with the worn lumbar pillow my mother bought him to support his back. His desk was always tidy, but mine is covered in paperwork. The framed photographs he displayed are still next to my computer, though: one of our little family at Christmastime when I was about eight, another when I was in high school standing in front of my mother's espalier apple tree, and one of us at my college graduation.

I stare at the graduation picture, taking in my father's grin that reveals slightly crooked teeth, his dark suit, and his strong arms wrapped around my and my mother's shoulders. My mother wore a yellow dress, and her dark hair was curled. She always put up her hair with pink plastic rollers the night before special occasions.

It was just the three of us celebrating that day. My aunt Joan, who'd married a military guy, was living in Germany, and she and my father weren't close. And though my mother traveled to see her parents in Arizona once a year, she almost always went alone, so I didn't have much of a relationship with them. My parents didn't have many friends, either. I always figured that since my dad worked nights it was difficult for them to sustain a social life.

But now I'm eyeing my history with suspicion rather than trust.

I pick up the graduation photo I've seen thousands of times. I stare at my parents' faces, summoning a remembrance of that day.

When I found them in the audience after I'd walked across the stage to get my college diploma, they were wiping away tears. "You make us so proud, sweetheart," my father said. My mother just hugged me for the longest time. I think she was too choked up to speak.

All around us, my fellow graduates were celebrating with loud groups of siblings and aunts and cousins and grandparents. But it was just the three of us, like it had always been.

We went to a French restaurant for my graduation dinner. We'd eaten out before, but this was different. It wasn't the neighborhood pizza joint or the Thai restaurant we liked for takeout. It had a name I couldn't pronounce, and a leather-bound menu, and place settings with multiple forks and spoons.

I was completely out of my element. But my father wasn't.

He ordered a bottle of wine, and when the waiter offered him the cork, my father knew exactly how to sniff it and nod his approval. He swirled the sample of ruby liquid in his goblet, then took a small sip and held it on his tongue, considering, before swallowing and telling the waiter the vintage was delicious. When my mother excused herself to go to the restroom, my dad stood up from the table, something I'd never seen him do before. He asked my mother and me what we wanted for our first and main courses and ordered for us, flawlessly pronouncing "fromage." He knew which fork to use for salad, and he taught me how to arrange my silverware on my not-quite-empty plate to signal I was finished.

This was an alien world to me and my mother. But my father had clearly inhabited it before. It would be impossible to fake that kind of ease.

For a casual blue-collar guy, he had a deep familiarity with the trappings of elegance.

But that wasn't all: My parents didn't have a lot of extra cash. My mother dyed her hair in the bathtub and never paid for a manicure. She'd found her yellow dress at a discount store. But my dad's suit fit him so perfectly it seemed custom-tailored. He wore a crisp white shirt with French cuffs, and gold cuff links that I'd assumed were fake.

I'd never seen the suit until he pulled it out of his closet the day before my graduation and asked my mother to iron the shirt.

It didn't occur to me to ask where or why he'd gotten the fancy suit and cuff links. They weren't the sort of items he'd invest in because he planned to get a lot of use out of them.

My subconscious had held on to these details for a decade, as if patiently waiting for me to acknowledge them.

I look around the office again, trying to see everything anew.

My gaze lands on his tall metal file cabinet. My father kept meticulous records. He wasn't good with computers; he was always calling me when his desktop crashed or he needed help finding a file. But he kept a decades-old paper trail of maintenance bills, warrantees, county health certificates, tax records, and distributor bills.

My father died suddenly. He wouldn't have had time to clear away anything from his office that he didn't want me to see. I never came in here when I visited him at the bar; it was more comfortable to chat from a counter stool or in a booth together.

His files seem as good a place as any to start.

The top drawer of the metal cabinet squeaks as I open it, like it's protesting being disturbed. Some of the papers inside are so old they look brittle.

I begin to search, a sense of trepidation creeping down my spine.

CHAPTER THIRTY-NINE

GEORGIA

You used to live with your phone in hand; you were surrounded by the cyber noise of incoming text chimes, bright notes of musical alarms, whooshes of sent emails, and pop-up notifications. The abrupt dearth of the electronic soundtrack is jarring, like you've been transported from Times Square to the Sahara.

You fell asleep with your phone as a companion, too, ignoring all the warnings against blue light and REM disruption. You'd catch up on social media, tapping hearts on Instagram posts and scrolling through reels until your eyelids grew heavy.

Now, when the lights go out, you engage in a battle of wills with your mind.

You don't always win. Sometimes you think about Annabelle's last birthday, the one that ended with her crumpled on the floor as coppery-smelling blood seeped into her thick blond hair. Tonight, though, your mind skitters to a memory of a different birthday, Annabelle's thirtieth.

When you were younger, the excesses of her celebrations was one of the ways it was obvious she was the favored child. The gifts were more significant, and your parents' excitement was genuine.

You decided to attend her thirtieth because you were in a good place in life, with your thriving business and devoted boyfriend. You didn't plan to stay long. You'd swoop in, air-kiss her cheek, steal a bit of her thunder, and leave.

The party was held in the private room of a swanky Asian restaurant called O-Ku. Dozens of Annabelle's friends flitted about in their pink and lavender dresses while laughter rang out and champagne corks popped like gunshots. Your parents were there to fawn over their golden girl and pick up the tab.

You walked in on the arm of your model-handsome date, wearing a bright red dress, the only shade of that color you'd found that not only worked with your hair but enhanced it. You were embracing your role as the scarlet-letter daughter.

You made sure Annabelle and your parents saw you arrive, but you waited for them to come to you. You greeted them, feigning delight, and introduced them to your date, who shook your father's hand and declared himself honored to meet Honey.

Then Annabelle spun away to giggle with her girlfriends, and your mother decided to get another drink, dragging your father away. He glanced back at you, and you could swear you saw an actual emotion flicker across his face—regret, maybe?—before he gave a little shrug, as if he were helpless in the wake of Honey's determination.

Your family had no interest in spending time with you, even though you hadn't seen them in months.

It shouldn't have hurt; you thought you'd become immune to their slights. But hot tears pricked your eyes, and you realized you'd wrapped your arms around your stomach.

Coming to the party had been a mistake. You were about to leave when a booming voice sounded over the buzzing of the crowd: "I heard someone is having a birthday."

Senator Dawson stood in the doorway, his perfect white smile contrasting with his lightly tanned skin. His tall, powerfully built frame was clad in a bespoke suit with a rare and highly coveted accessory: the gleaming round pin that identified him as a member of the US Congress. His wife, Dee Dee, was beside him in a peach dress with a full skirt. His aide Reece DuPont, who accompanied the senator everywhere, stood behind him like a sentry.

"Is that . . ." your date whispered, and you nodded. The senator's star was rising. *The New York Times* had recently profiled him, calling him "the future of this country."

Then it happened.

Honey smoothed out her skirt as the senator and Dee Dee walked toward her, the senator leading the way. Honey's eyes were shiny, her face wreathed in delight. She smiled and began to lift up her arms, preparing for the senator's greeting of a warm hug, which would put her in the center of the spotlight.

But he walked right past her.

He had eyes only for Annabelle.

Tonight, with her lush curves wrapped in a white silk dress and the striking green eyes she'd inherited from Honey gleaming like emeralds, she looked better than she ever had.

The senator wrapped an arm around Annabelle's waist and leaned close to her, murmuring something into her ear that made her laugh.

You saw it: the tightening of Honey's and Dee Dee's faces as they watched.

They were used to being the most important women in the room, to commanding attention because of their great wealth and social prestige.

Now Annabelle had usurped them.

Dee Dee leaned in close to Honey and whispered something. Honey nodded grimly.

As Annabelle and the senator smiled at each other with his arm still around her waist, Honey and Dee Dee looked at Annabelle in a way they'd only looked at you before.

It was then you realized Honey and Dee Dee were capable of hating Annabelle, too.

CHAPTER FORTY

MANDY

I find the disruption in my father's pattern at 2 A.M.

I'm sitting cross-legged on the thin blue carpet of the office floor, holding his old tax returns, blinking at numbers that make no sense.

For most of his life, my father earned a salary that provided a comfortable but modest existence: food for us to eat and a mortgage on the little house where I grew up, but not a lot of extras. For vacations, we went camping, and new clothes were a rare splurge.

The outlier appeared thirty-two years ago—when I was born. My father's income rocketed up. He made as much in that single year as he had in the previous four combined. Then his earnings immediately dropped back down to their baseline level.

My hands begin to shake as I try to absorb my new reality. What did my father do for that kind of money?

But that isn't the only disturbing piece of evidence I've found. I've uncovered another staggering lie, one that sends a chill through my soul.

My father told me he worked as a bartender at Sweetbay's until he had saved enough to buy the bar. But his true employer in the years prior to my birth is recorded as a company I've never heard of: Pecan Tree Corp. in Charlotte.

He bought Sweetbay's shortly after I was born—during the same year his salary from Pecan Tree Corp. increased fourfold.

I google the company, but nothing turns up. It's like a ghost corporation.

What did my father do for them? And why did he leave his job, move with my mother from Charlotte to our smaller town ninety minutes away, and buy the bar?

His entire life erupted, then quickly reformed into a calm new pattern.

The nexus of it all had to be my birth—and Georgia's.

My mom and dad took me away while my twin remained in Charlotte with the Cartwright family. Both families buried the links between us, pretending only one daughter existed.

I drop my head into my hands, letting the tax returns flutter to the floor. It's hard to wrap my mind around the deceptions. My father once ran down the street after a customer who'd left a fifty-dollar tip in case it was a mistake. When I was six and stole a Snickers bar from a grocery store, my mother made me take it back and apologize to the manager. How could people with that code of honor perpetuate such staggering fabrications?

Did I ever truly know them?

A memory flutters into my mind: the three of us side by side on the couch, watching a Tom Hanks movie when I was a preteen. Monday night was our family movie night, because the bar was closed and we could all be home together. I made popcorn—"Not too much butter for your dad, his cholesterol is getting high," my mother said—and my father poured wine for my mom, popped the top of a Budweiser for himself, and got me a Sprite.

In the movie, Tom Hanks was alone on an island, struggling to survive.

"How long do you think you could last?" my father asked, bumping my shoulder with his.

"A year," I said.

"Without cherry Slurpees? I'd give you six weeks," he joked.

My mother swatted him with a pillow. "I'd make it a day," she said. "You could do it, though, Ray." My father was so handy and capable; he could build anything from a slingshot to a house.

"Maybe." He kissed me on the forehead, his five-o'clock shadow scratching my skin, then kissed my mother on the lips. "But I wouldn't ever want to without my girls."

I blink back tears. I *did* know them. There has to be a good reason why they didn't tell me. They weren't just my parents; they were my best friends.

A sharp metallic noise makes my head jerk up. It sounded like it came from the alley behind my bar. Maybe a trash can lid clattered off in the wind. Or maybe someone bumped into a can.

I stay perfectly still, concentrating hard to see if I can detect another sound. I'm the only one here. We closed up an hour ago and my staff left. Only two dim security lights are on in the bar area, and though I haven't yet set the alarm, the doors are locked. It seems unlikely someone mistakenly thought we were still open.

The next noise I hear fires adrenaline through my limbs.

I keep a bell hanging over the front and back doorknobs. During quiet stretches, the jangling lets us know someone is turning the knob to enter. During crowded, noisy times, you can't even hear it.

The back-door bell is jangling now. Someone is trying to get in.

I leap to my feet, running through the bar's shadows toward the small safe I keep on a shelf beneath the counter. I press my hand against the safe to digitally unlock it. When the door glides open, I pull out my six-shot.

I crouch down low, moving to the end of the bar closest to the back entrance. My breathing is shallow, and my finger is steady on the safety, ready to release it. I angle myself until I can see the top of the back door and keep my eyes trained on it, waiting for the intruder to burst in.

My senses heighten. I can hear the distant roar of a car's motor and smell the sharp tang of the cleaning solution that left my bar gleaming. My vision is adapting to the low light, allowing me to focus on the silver bell hanging from a thin leather strap on my back doorknob.

At any moment now, the door could fly open. But I'm not afraid. This is *my* bar. And I've had too much taken from me today.

I won't hesitate to shoot.

But the bell remains still, the echo of its chimes fading from my mind.

I wait until my legs threaten to cramp, then slowly stand up, my gun still in my outstretched hand.

If someone was peering through a window, they could have seen me dart behind the bar. Maybe that's why they stopped trying to get in.

I walk back into the office, holding my gun down at my side, and look at the files and papers covering the floor. There's a lot more I need to dig through, but my concentration is shattered. I'll come back in the morning, I decide.

I pick my iPhone off my desk and notice a text came in a little while ago. It's a security alert from Google. It seems like someone was trying to hack into my computer.

I've gotten these alerts occasionally before. They've never caused me any real worry because I have a strong password and two-step authentication on my devices. I typically just change my password as a precaution. But the timing feels concerning.

I tuck my phone into my bag and lock the door to my office. My car is in the parking lot behind my bar. It's the only vehicle in the lot. If someone is waiting for me, it won't be hard for them to figure out my path.

So I switch up my routine. I set the bar's alarm and exit out the front door.

The street is dark and quiet; no one else is around at this hour.

My gun feels steady in my hand as I sweep my head from left to right. I walk around the side of the building and take in the parking lot. My Honda is close to the back door, just as I left it. There's no one lurking around it.

I walk toward it quickly, my head on a swivel, bracing for the sound of rushing footsteps. But I'm alone.

When I reach my car, I check my backseat before I slip inside. I set my gun down on the passenger's seat and do a wide sweep around the parking lot, my headlights illuminating the dark corners. It's empty.

Could I have been imagining the jangle of the bell? I have two security cameras at my bar, but they're both inside. The footage won't tell me anything.

I shake off my doubts. I know what I heard.

I drive home, acutely aware of the dark sedan that pulls up next to me at a stoplight. I turn to stare at the driver. It's a middle-aged woman in the middle of a huge yawn. I keep my foot on the brake when the light turns, and she drives off ahead of me without ever looking my way.

Am I being paranoid? I wonder. A month ago, the jangling of the bell wouldn't have alarmed me this deeply. But ever since I met Georgia, everything has changed.

I keep hearing her whisper, *You have no idea how big this is.*

I reach my building and park in my usual spot. Only a few lights are on in the ten-story structure. I keep my gun down by my side as I quickly walk to my apartment, feeling grateful for the proximity of my neighbors.

I step inside and look around. Everything is as it should be. My laptop is on the kitchen counter where I left it.

I go into my bedroom and put my gun in my nightstand drawer, then sink down on my bed to take off my shoes. In the wake of the adrenaline that flooded my body, fatigue is suddenly crashing down on me. All I want to do is brush my teeth and change into a T-shirt and boxers and collapse into bed.

I'm pulling off my jeans when I hear the unmistakable noise.

Four quick high beeps.

Blood rushes between my ears. I'm instantly wide awake again.

The sound is coming from my kitchen. I know exactly what it is. I've heard it before.

My refrigerator door doesn't always catch, even when it looks closed.

After several minutes, the beeps send an alert, pausing and repeating until the door is shut.

If someone was thoroughly searching my apartment and peered in the refrigerator, they might have left before the beeps began. They wouldn't realize they'd left behind this clue.

I'm not being paranoid. Someone broke into my apartment to-night.

CHAPTER FORTY-ONE

GEORGIA

Group therapy feels less threatening today. The young, green therapist is still in charge, but Josh has been moved to another section of the ward, one typically used for prisoners who are transferred here from jail and need to be sequestered until they are stabilized. Occupants of that section are locked in one of four glass-fronted rooms, next to a sink with delousing shampoo, and a uniformed guard sits at a desk watching over it all. Josh will remain there until the doctors finish adjusting his medications.

You know all of this because you are now Patty's confidante.

She sits next to you at mealtimes, sharing her precious oranges and pears because she prefers bland food, and she joins you on the couch to watch HGTV, making an occasional funny or incisive comment. She chats while you stand outside in the courtyard, talking about her regrets of the past and her hopes for the future. She gives you so much, but asks nothing in return.

"Let's talk about some good memories," the therapist begins.

Patty is in the chair next to you. The bulky white gauze bandages on her wrists have been replaced by thinner ones. She looks livelier. Happier.

Which means she'll be leaving soon.

Patty is wearing her street clothes now, a pair of jeans with a high elastic waistband and a dark blue tunic. She looks as if she is ready to walk through that small wooden door again, back into the real world.

"Georgia?"

You start at the sound of your name. The therapist is looking at you.

"Can you share a pleasant memory? It could be as simple as looking up at a cloud drifting through the blue sky, or the taste of a chocolate chip cookie you ate."

He's leaning forward, an earnest expression on his face, asking you to reminisce about cookies when you could either be executed or spend the next few decades here without Patty. You feel like slapping him.

"She took my shirt!"

The pink-haired woman—you've learned her name is Lucy—who accused you of taking her glasses is now pointing at Patty.

"That's my shirt, you took it from my closet. Give it back!"

Lucy is getting all worked up, which happens a couple of times a day. Typically the nurses either let her ramble on or distract her, depending on how busy they are.

The therapist starts to talk, but Patty cuts him off.

"Lucy, I know you have a shirt exactly like this. We both have the same one. Yours is still in your closet. You have wonderful taste. I love this shirt, too!"

Lucy's mouth is hanging open, as if she's preparing to argue. But Patty's words seem to take the wind out of her. She closes her mouth and blinks.

"I know," she says. "I'm going to get a drink of water now." She stands and walks away.

The man with the keloid scar on his neck asks, "Does she really have the same shirt?"

Patty shrugs. "She thinks she does. It must be hard for Lucy to be in other people's reality when hers is so different. I guess I wanted to give her a break and join her where she is."

"That's exactly right." The therapist nods confidently, as if he's the one who engineered this dynamic. He changes the subject, and after another moment, Lucy returns.

But she doesn't reclaim her seat. Instead, she sits on the floor by Patty's feet.

"Lucy, wouldn't you be more comfortable in a chair?" the therapist asks.

Lucy shakes her head. "No. I like her."

"Is that okay with you, Patty?" the therapist asks.

You didn't realize how young Lucy really is. But she's probably only in her late twenties. Young enough to be Patty's daughter.

"Of course it is. I like Lucy, too." There's warmth in Patty's voice as she smiles down at Lucy.

It's the weirdest thing. You feel a tinge of jealousy; it's a physical sensation, akin to a darkness snaking through your body.

Just like how you always felt around Annabelle.

CHAPTER FORTY-TWO

MANDY

I awaken from an uneasy sleep, peeling open my eyes and looking around my bedroom. The chair I propped beneath my door is still in place. My window is open a couple of inches, just as I left it. I wanted the sound to carry in case I screamed in the night.

It's 9:42 A.M.—early, considering I didn't doze off until dawn.

Thoughts roar into my brain: My parents' deception. My fear that someone was trying to break into my bar. My certainty that someone *had* broken into my apartment.

But now, as I pull the cord to open my blinds and bright sunlight floods my bedroom, I begin to question my assumptions. I typically eat before I go to work, since I never know if I'll get a chance to have dinner on busy nights. So around 4 P.M. yesterday, I baked a frozen pizza and washed it down with a seltzer. I didn't finish the whole pie, so I wrapped the leftover slices in foil and tucked them into my refrigerator.

I can't remember how long I was in my apartment after that. I rinsed my plate and put it in my dishwasher, as is my habit because my sink is so small I can't let dishes pile up in it. I think I used the bathroom, but I'm not certain. I might have checked my reflection in the mirror and brushed my hair or rubbed in hand lotion. But I can't remember. Those tasks are so mundane and repetitive my mind didn't even register them.

It's possible I left less than four minutes after I put the pizza into the refrigerator. Maybe it was my fault the door didn't catch.

I climb out of bed and head for my refrigerator, opening the door and staring at the contents. Why would someone look in here? There's one precious item, but it's something that's valuable only to me: a sealed mason jar of apple butter my mother made shortly before she died. My mother hated picking the apples off her beloved espalier tree because they looked so pretty splayed across the fence, but when they began to turn soft every year, she gathered them and brought them inside and made batches of apple butter in her slow cooker, filling the air with the aroma of vanilla and cinnamon.

The last thing my mother ever gave me is right where I left it, in the middle of my top shelf. Nothing else seems amiss.

I head back to my bedroom and notice a new text on my phone: Hi Amanda, it's Colby from the ALS fundraiser. I'd love to take you to dinner. Any chance you're free one night this week?

I mentally run through the list of all the things I need to do, including sorting through the rest of my dad's paperwork for more clues. I'd planned to go to the bar early today to tackle that task.

But I can't miss this chance, and not just because of Georgia's whispered instructions. There's a connection between my parents and the Cartwright family. Colby is my best way in.

I write back: Love to. Tonight is actually best for me if that works for you?

Three dots appear quickly, as if he's been anxiously awaiting my response. That's perfect! What time should I pick you up?

There's no way I can agree to him picking me up. I'll be coming from Georgia's apartment, since I'll need to re-create a version of the woman Colby met at the gala the other night. Given that Colby and Georgia were lifelong friends who briefly dated, he knows where she lived.

I text back: Which restaurant? I'll meet you there.

He gives me the name and provides a link pinpointing the location and says he'll see me at 7 P.M.

By the time I show up at the restaurant to meet Colby, I'm frustrated and my back is sore from bending over paperwork all day. There wasn't anything else out of the ordinary in my father's tall metal cabinet or desk drawers. But my search meant I had to skip a few of my usual tasks to keep the bar running smoothly, including taking inventory and holding my weekly staff meeting.

I know my employees are wondering about my absences. So I told them a version of the truth: I have a date tonight. I pretended to throw a cup of water at Scott when he made theatrical kissing noises.

The restaurant Colby chose is called Teo. I arrive a few minutes early, wearing a pair of Georgia's knee-high black boots and jewelry and my own short black dress—I figure it's plain enough to pass as designer—but Colby is already waiting at a cozy booth for two by the window. It's a prime seat in this high-end place, where the tables are draped in heavy white cloths and classical music plays softly from hidden speakers. He stands as I approach, and I flash back to my father rising from the table at my graduation dinner.

I shrug off my bad mood. The woman Colby is expecting to meet is confident and friendly.

I smile brightly and greet him with a quick, friendly hug. I once read that smell is the sense linked most strongly to memory, which is why I'm wearing Georgia's Chanel perfume tonight. I hope when Colby inhales, she floats into his mind.

"I'm so glad you were free tonight," he says. "You look beautiful."

He stares at me for long enough that it makes me a bit uncomfortable.

I thank him and tell him the restaurant looks wonderful. After the waiter comes to take our orders and delivers our drinks, I tell Colby that I graduated from UNC Chapel Hill and left my marketing job after my parents died. But I have to muddle in some fibs, too: I don't reveal anything about my bar, instead implying that my parents' deaths were more recent and I'm taking a little time off to process everything.

"Your parents sound like wonderful people," Colby says.

I'm surprised by the tears that spring to my eyes. "They were," I say quietly. As hurt and angry as I am at them, I can't deny their goodness.

I take a sip of my icy-cold chenin blanc and force myself to lean into the segue that just presented itself.

"Are you close to your parents?"

Colby's shoulders slump.

"Not exactly. My father—do you know who he is?"

I've vowed to lie to Colby as little as possible. So I nod. "I do."

"I guess my last name is a clue." He gives a little laugh, then spears a piece of asparagus with more force than necessary. I notice his index finger sticks straight out, rather than curling around his fork with the rest of his fingers, and the knuckle is slightly misshapen. It looks like an old injury.

Colby probably has too many people in his life interested in his dad. I don't want him to think that's why I'm going out with him. I decide to go in a different direction.

"I've been so busy with everything going on I haven't had time to meet people recently," I say. "This is nice."

I hope Colby will reciprocate and talk about his dating history. I want to draw him out about Georgia.

But he doesn't take the bait. Instead, he points to the untouched grits on my plate. "You haven't tried the grits."

I wrinkle my nose. "I haven't had grits in years."

"Then what are you waiting for? They make them with sage butter here."

I scoop a tiny portion onto my fork and taste it. He reads my face: "No way! A Southern girl who doesn't like grits?"

"Guilty as charged," I laugh. "Feel free to have mine."

"You're only the second person I've met who—"

His words abruptly cease, like they've fallen off a cliff. His smile drops away, too.

And I know: He's thinking about Georgia.

I didn't have to apply her perfume or search for a segue to get him to think about my twin. All I had to do was be myself.

"Who was the other?" I struggle to keep my tone casual.

His eyes are faraway. I desperately wish I could plunge into the memory I'm sure he's lost in right now.

"She's a friend," he finally says.

"Did she grow up here?" I prompt. "Because you're right, it's hard to find a born-and-bred Southerner who doesn't eat grits."

For a moment, I think he's going to answer me. Vulnerable, trusting Colby is actually going to start talking to me about Georgia.

Then the worst possible thing happens: We're interrupted.

Colby reaches into his pocket and pulls out his buzzing cell phone. He looks down at the number.

"Oh no, I have to take this. I'm so sorry."

He answers and listens. Then his face fills with resignation. "How long until you're here?" He closes his eyes and shakes his head slightly. "Okay, okay. I get it."

He hangs up and twists his body so that he isn't facing the window. Then he asks me to do the same.

My brow wrinkles in confusion, but I comply.

"I'm sorry, but someone snapped a picture of us through the window. It's already online. One of the gossip sites just called my dad's office for a quote. They want to know who the brunette is with Colby Dawson."

"Why would the press care—" I cut myself off as it hits me. Colby's brief relationship with Georgia garnered headlines when she was arrested for Annabelle's murder. My appearance in Colby's life will give them a fresh angle to dredge up the salacious story.

"There might be more reporters out front now. One of my dad's guys is on his way here to get us out." He looks down at his plate. "I should've asked for a different table . . . I wasn't thinking."

"Hey, it isn't your fault." I start to reach out to touch his hand, then yank mine away. I don't want to give the photographer any more ammunition. "Look, I'm having a good time."

"Yeah?" Colby looks up, his eyes hopeful.

"Next time we'll go to a quieter place."

I'm trying to act unconcerned, but my heart is racing. I don't know how recognizable I am in the photo. Georgia warned me to stay invisible.

"Will you excuse me? I'm going to the ladies' room."

"Of course."

I put my napkin on the table and stand up, keeping my face averted from the window.

I cross the restaurant and find the sign indicating the bathrooms. I step inside and lock the door behind me, then pull out my phone and fire up a Google search. I find the gossip item quickly and zoom in on the picture.

I exhale. My hair is loose, and it's swinging forward and covering part of my profile. Colby is the main focus of the photo, not me. I can't imagine anyone would recognize me.

I put away my phone and check my reflection. I can't see a way to alter my appearance, so I'll keep my head down and trust that Senator Dawson's guy can get us out unnoticed.

I unlock the door and step out of the bathroom.

Then I freeze.

The blond man with owlish eyes I thought I saw in my bar, the one who introduced himself as Reece DuPont at Annabelle's funeral reception, is walking through the restaurant. His gait is unhurried and he isn't a physically imposing man, but there's something about him that makes me think it would be a bad idea to get on the wrong side of him.

Colby stands up and shakes his hand. Any second now, Colby's going to tell him I'm in the bathroom, and they'll turn and look my way.

My body reacts, spurring me into movement. There's only one other way out, but luckily I know exactly where it is: Bars and restaurants always have exits through the kitchen in case of fires. I pivot and push through the swinging double doors. Cooks and dishwashers turn to look at me, but I'm moving so fast no one has time to stop me.

I race out the back door into the cool night. A guy in a white chef's coat is leaning against the back of the restaurant, smoking.

"Escaping a bad date?" he asks, smiling.

"Something like that," I reply as I pull up my Uber app, setting my pickup location for two blocks away. Then I hurry in that direction, my feet protesting in Georgia's high-heeled boots.

On the way, I send Colby a text: I thought it would be easier for you to get out without me there as a distraction. I slipped away and I'm heading home. But I'd really love to see you again soon.

As bad as it would be to be spotted by the press again, something tells me it would be far worse if Reece DuPont saw me.

CHAPTER FORTY-THREE

GEORGIA

"You don't like grits? How come I never knew? That's practically a felony in Mecklenburg County!"

On that night almost two years ago, Colby was laughing. Colby hadn't had much to laugh about in life. A domineering father, two cruel older brothers, and a mother who was emotionally checked out equaled a dangerous formula for a sensitive, awkward kid.

People assumed the two of you were dating because you were spotted eating at a couple of restaurants and walking through a farmers' market sharing an umbrella on a drizzly Saturday morning.

But the gossip mill was wrong. You'd reconnected after Annabelle's birthday party at the Asian restaurant, but only as friends.

Colby wasn't in love with you. He'd harbored a crush on the *other* Cartwright sister for years.

You hadn't even noticed him at Annabelle's party. Colby wasn't the kind of guy the limelight favored; he'd been in a corner, nursing a bourbon and stealing looks at Annabelle.

Colby reached out to you a few days afterward, saying he'd love to catch up. But he had an underlying motive. He'd spotted it, too: the way Honey and Dee Dee looked at Annabelle—and the way the senator looked at Annabelle. It was a dangerous triangle.

You met at a restaurant where he ate all of his grits as well as yours. The two of you fell back into the rhythm you'd established as children. You were outsiders in your own families, finding solace in your shared exile.

By the time you'd emptied a bottle of wine, you'd revealed what you'd seen in the butler's pantry.

Then Colby told you a story that made your insides curl.

A year or so back, Colby had finally gotten up the courage to ask Annabelle out. He was taking her to a Mardi Gras–themed party thrown by one of his neighbors, complete with a rollicking jazz band and Cajun-inspired menu. Colby brought a sparkling green-and-purple headdress for Annabelle and a gold mask for himself. He wasn't sure if she realized it was a date because they'd been friends for so long. Annabelle could be a bit dense, or perhaps she was used to guys having crushes on her and enjoyed stringing them along. Either way, she seemed blithely accepting of his attention, smiling her big smile, chattering in that way everyone found charming as they drove to the party.

Colby knew he'd learn the truth about whether Annabelle liked him as a friend or was interested in more when he walked her to her door at the end of the night and tried to kiss her.

They never made it to the party, though.

He was driving with Annabelle in the passenger's seat when flashing blue-and-red lights appeared in his rearview mirror. He steered to the side of the road and waited for the sheriff's car to pass. But it didn't.

"License and registration, son," said the uniformed sheriff at his window, and Colby handed them over.

"Do you know why I pulled you over?" the sheriff asked.

"No, sir," Colby replied.

"One of your taillights is out."

Colby was surprised; his car was fairly new, and he had it serviced regularly. He promised the sheriff he'd have it fixed right away. He assumed he'd be sent on his way with a warning.

Instead, the sheriff leaned closer through the window.

"Have you been drinking tonight, son?"

Colby hesitated. He'd swallowed a shot of bourbon for courage before he'd left the house to pick up Annabelle. But just one, and he'd had a big lunch that day.

The sheriff didn't seem to like the hesitation. He told Colby to step out of the car and walk a straight line, heel to toe.

Colby aced the test.

When he finished, the sheriff was holding up a small Ziploc bag.

"This fell out of your pocket," he told Colby. "Want to tell me what it is?"

"It isn't mine," Colby protested, hot-cheeked with embarrassment as Annabelle witnessed everything from inside the car. He was about to be read his rights and put in the back of the sheriff's car and taken in for possession of marijuana while his dream girl watched.

But Colby was allowed to make a phone call first, in a departure from procedure. Colby knew he'd been offered this privilege only because the sheriff recognized his name.

Colby called the one man who could save him. He pleaded for help, embarrassed that Annabelle could hear his voice cracking: "It wasn't mine, Dad! It must have been on the road already . . . That's the only explanation I can think of."

The senator asked to speak to the sheriff, and Colby handed over the phone.

He waited, certain the sheriff would tell him it had all been a misunderstanding and wish him a good night. His father was a fervent supporter of law enforcement. It was the one time in his life that Colby felt grateful for his father's deep, intricate web of connections.

Instead, the sheriff listened for a moment, then said, "Yes, sir." Then he took out his handcuffs and arrested Colby.

You'd interrupted Colby's story at that point, aghast: "Your father told the sheriff to arrest you?"

Colby nodded, his shoulder slumping. You could see in his expression a reflection of all the other times his father had gutted him: the ski trip and the hunting trip, the times he'd turned his head while Colby's older brothers tormented him, the way he'd derided Colby's lack of athletic ability to whoever would listen.

But that wasn't the worst part. Not even close.

The sheriff then handed Colby's phone to Annabelle, telling her the senator wanted to speak to her. And while Colby was being taken to jail, the senator drove over to pick up Annabelle. Colby's car was left by the side of the road, where it was towed to an impound lot.

The senator took Annabelle to dinner, telling her she looked too pretty to be sitting at home all night alone. Colby was held in a cell until the next morning, when his mother came to spring him.

The charges against Colby disappeared. So did his chance with Annabelle. When he texted her to apologize and ask for a second chance, she came up with excuses until he stopped trying.

"What kind of father would do that?" Colby asked you.

You shook your head. You had no words.

"Sometimes I wonder if my dad set me up," Colby said. "The brake light being out, him being home and available—which he never was. Maybe he even got the sheriff to pretend to find the weed on me. When I saw my dad with Annabelle at her party, it felt like more than wondering. It feels like certainty. He didn't want me with Annabelle because he wanted her for himself."

It was a dark accusation.

What you didn't know at the time was Colby—gentle, soft-spoken Colby—possessed a streak of darkness himself. Maybe it was inherited from his father. Or maybe he'd just been pushed around too long, and finally snapped and pushed back.

CHAPTER FORTY-FOUR

MANDY

Colby's text lands on my phone just as my Uber driver pulls up: So sorry. Let's try again . . . another night this week?

I tap a heart on his message and text love to, let me check my schedule and get back to you before jumping into the backseat, glancing out the rear window as we drive off. There aren't many pedestrians around, and no one seems to be looking my way, but the back of my head tingles, as if someone's eyes are boring into it.

My imagination, I tell myself. But my body refuses to unclench. Once we reach Georgia's apartment, I take the precaution of changing up my routine, and I direct the Uber driver to the back entrance.

"Would you mind waiting until I'm inside before you drive away?" I ask.

"I've got a daughter," he tells me. "Don't worry, I'll make sure you get in safe."

My heart constricts. It's the sort of thing my father would have said.

Both my parents used to wait up for me whenever I was out late. They pretended they didn't, but the telltale sign was their bedroom light flickering off as I climbed the stairs to my room.

I've been so upset with them for the secrets they withheld. But now grief pinches me, causing my shoulders to roll forward and my back to hunch, as if I'm trying to make myself a smaller target for it. Memories flash through my mind: My mother singing "You Are My Sunshine" to me in the mornings to wake me up for school. My father teaching me how to change a flat tire, ignoring my complaints about how hard it was to get off the lug nuts. *Keep trying. You need to learn this. I don't want my daughter to ever be stuck on the side of a road alone at night.* And the two of them leaving my first apartment after they helped me move in, my mother's soft voice catching as she said good night, all of us knowing I'd never live at home again and things would never be quite the same.

I breathe through the pain as I unlock the security door. It's the strangest thing. I notice something I've glimpsed a dozen times before. It just hasn't fully registered until now. It's a mailbox key on Georgia's chain. I know exactly what the smaller key is for because I have one on my chain, too.

The police probably checked her mailbox immediately after Annabelle's murder. Still, I have nothing to lose by looking now. I easily find the rows of mailboxes behind a wall near the elevators. The apartment numbers are engraved at the top.

I slide the key into PH4 and turn it until I hear a click and the door opens, revealing a few catalogues and envelopes. I take them up to Georgia's apartment, and as soon as I'm through the door, I spread them out on the kitchen island. The clothing catalogues confirm what I already know: My sister has exquisite, expensive taste. The thin white envelopes are junk. But there's a small, lightly padded brown envelope, too. It's addressed to Georgia in blocky handwriting. There's no return address.

I start to tear it open, then hesitate. Georgia is a murder suspect, and her address is easy to find. The contents could be anything from a love note by a deranged "fan" to something gruesome or even deadly.

But the envelope is so small and light. And the postmark is dated the day Annabelle died—which means it was in transit before the murder occurred.

I rip it open, and a small rectangular object slides out. A thumb drive.

It could hold anything from documents to photographs to videos. I'm desperate to see the contents. But I can't, because Georgia's computer is gone.

I pick up the shiny, silver drive, turning it around in my fingers and watching it catch the light. The longer I look at it, the more certain I grow of one thing: There won't be any sleep for me until I see what's on it. I change into Georgia's sweats and a pair of her sneakers and head out again, this time to drive home as quickly as I safely can.

★ ★ ★

An hour and a half later, I turn off the highway into my neighborhood, thinking about how Charlotte is just far enough away that traveling back and forth is a hassle. Three hours round trip is a lot of road time—and that's without traffic. It's probably why I don't need all my fingers to count the times I've been to Charlotte in my life. A couple of concerts, once to see a friend from college, a few ball games, and once to visit the NASCAR Hall of Fame when I was dating a guy who was obsessed with racing.

I'm sure Georgia never visited my town, given there's no draw for someone who lives in a more sophisticated, vibrant city.

Then it hits me: Maybe that's the whole point.

I switch my radio off, stopping Kacey Musgraves mid-ballad so I can think more clearly. Maybe I've been chasing the wrong thread. Instead of trying to unravel what about our town had beckoned my parents to move here, maybe I need to look at what our town *didn't* offer. If my parents wanted to move far enough away from Charlotte that they'd be unlikely to bump into anyone from their past, but remain in the same general area, they'd probably pick a town just like the one they settled in. Especially if a small business was for sale and they had a sudden cash windfall to buy it.

It's late and very dark when I finally pull into my apartment's lot. I keep my hand on my gun as I make my way to the elevator.

Typically, the hallways of my building are filled with evidence of my neighbors' presence—muted voices on a television, the aroma of dinner casseroles baking, someone shushing a barking dog. Tonight it's utterly silent, as if I'm the only one in the whole building.

Before I unlock my front door, I check for the strand of hair I wet and stuck across the doorjamb. The hair hasn't fallen off—which it would have if someone had pushed open the door, according to a security hack I found on the internet.

I open my door and step inside, flicking on the lights. I hold perfectly still and listen for a long moment, but don't hear a thing. Still, I check every potential hiding place. I don't put my gun away until I'm satisfied I'm alone.

Am I being nuts or taking a wise precaution?

It makes my head swim that I'm not sure.

I double-lock my front door and head for my laptop on the kitchen counter. I slip the thumb drive into my computer and click to access the file. After a few seconds, a video begins to play. As the first image takes focus, I blink and rear back: The camera is panning across long wooden shelves that hold bottles of booze. I recognize the location instantly, but it's disorienting seeing something so familiar in a new context—the equivalent of running into your dentist at the grocery store.

Then the camera shifts, homing in on a new angle. My heart leaps into my throat. Of all the things I imagined seeing, I never anticipated this.

I'm looking into my own eyes. The subject of the video is me.

CHAPTER FORTY-FIVE

GEORGIA

Every day, every hour, sometimes every minute in this place requires a series of mental calculations. You eye potential steps you can take like they're stones across an angry river. You try to identify ones that seem to promise the sturdiest footing, a momentary reprieve from slipping and being swallowed by the dark, turbulent water.

Your current high-stakes challenge is determining whether it will be safer for you to attend the court hearing on your competency or have a representative stand in on your behalf.

Your fingers itch for a device. You haven't broken your reliance on having an answer always at your fingertips. You yearn to research what will happen at such a hearing, and what the odds are of an accused individual being found competent. It's agonizing knowing the information is just a few feet away in the nurses' station behind the wall of plexiglass, where computers and phones are kept.

It's probably safer to have a representative go, you finally decide. You have no idea what questions will be asked or what metrics will be employed to gauge your state of mind. The judge and psychiatrist are experts in this scenario. You're an amateur. They might trip you up, and you could be transported to a maximum-security jail in a matter of hours.

You aren't the first person to try to beat the system. Yesterday you overheard the nurses discuss the story of a man who murdered his wife in cold blood in Seattle. The man fled the scene and drove to the East Coast and voluntarily committed himself into a Washington, DC, unit, claiming he had intrusive thoughts of killing himself.

He thought he'd found a safe harbor. But it took the FBI only two days to track him down. They employed a sting operation, dressing like nurses and telling the man his blood pressure was so high he needed to be checked by a cardiologist on another floor of the hospital. They knew it would agitate the other patients to see a potentially violent arrest; they were biding their time.

The undercover agents led the man out through the series of locked doors, treating him solicitously. The minute the doors closed behind him, they tackled him to the floor and cuffed him. He's serving a life sentence now.

You almost threw up after you heard that story.

But there's another terrifying risk that could emerge from the hearing. You currently have the right to refuse medication. But if that right is taken away from you by a court order, you will be forced to take the drugs the nurses continue to offer you several times a day. They can't make you swallow pills. But they can—and will—inject medicine into your body through a needle. You've seen them do it a dozen times to others.

Your mind is your only weapon right now. But it's more finely honed than it has ever been. In this surreal place, you've found extreme mental clarity. Devoid of a constant barrage of input, your brain is reorganizing itself, allowing memories tucked in its long-term storage space to float into your consciousness, as crisply preserved as a flower pressed between the pages of a book.

Two more lines from your college psych paper float back to you: *Antipsychotics given to a mentally healthy individual can cause the same symptoms they are intended to relieve. They alter brain chemistry and can cause mania, impaired cognition, twitching, and extreme agitation.*

In other words, this place can make you insane.

There are no clocks in this facility, but sometimes, at night, you swear you hear one ticking in sync with your heartbeat. Time is everything to you now, because this will end soon. And it can only end in one of three ways: You stay in the locked ward until you go insane and die. You go to jail and die quickly. Or Mandy risks her own life to save you.

You have to call her, today, and show your hand. You can't whisper this information over the phone; there may be listeners. You need to tell Mandy that the PI you hired to find her worked another job for you recently.

You need to tell her what he discovered.

CHAPTER FORTY-SIX

MANDY

I stare at my computer screen, watching the video continue to play.

On the screen, I'm filling a glass with ice and squirting in fizzy soda before impaling a wedge of lemon onto its edge. I slide the soda toward the camera, smiling. Then I ask, "Need anything else?" The timestamp is 10:18 P.M. almost exactly a month ago.

I'm sure of one thing: It wasn't Georgia who ordered that drink. She would have stood out in my bar like a diamond on a dark surface.

She must have sent someone in to spy on me. While I remained oblivious, Georgia watched me until she needed me. My body feels tight and rigid, like it needs to release a violent explosion of energy. I wish I could grab my sister by her thin, sculped shoulders and roughly shake her. She sent someone to my town, to *my* bar, to violate my space.

The video stops playing. But there are two more on the thumb drive. I unclench my fists and click play on the second one.

It makes everything so much worse.

This one is of me in leggings and a T-shirt and jean jacket going into the indie bookstore on our town's main shopping street. The timestamp is 11:46 A.M., again about a month ago. The camera follows me inside. I see myself browsing the aisles, ducking in and out of the picture as the person tracking me slowly traces my path.

Then I reach for a book on the shelf of "staff-recommended" classics: *The Age of Innocence*. The one I couldn't believe Georgia was reading, too.

A dark mist descends in front of my eyes. She set me up. We didn't spontaneously pick the same book to read because of some eerie twin synergy. It was orchestrated.

The question roars through my mind: How long was Georgia having me followed, and what else did she see?

I take a few breaths, trying to think clearly through the adrenaline coursing through my brain. I bought that novel recently. It's possible Georgia told the truth when she said she'd only known of my existence for a month. But right now, I'm not inclined to believe anything she says. She also told me she didn't kill Annabelle. That could've been the biggest lie of all.

I pace around my apartment, yearning to put my fist through the drywall. Then I come back to the counter, gripping its hard edges with both hands while I look down at my laptop's screen. There's a third video. I'm almost afraid to play it—but not because I'm scared of what I might see. I'm scared of what I might do.

The anger engulfing me feels overpowering, like a rogue wave sweeping me up. I've felt like this a few times before, like when a guy in my bar was hitting his girlfriend in the face. I didn't hesitate; I jumped on top of my bar, leaned over, and dug my fingers into his eyes.

"Was it a case of life or death?" a police officer asked me after the guy had been taken away in an ambulance.

"Absolutely," I told the cops. But the truth is, it wasn't—at least not in that moment. He was hitting her with an open hand, not a fist. He didn't seem out of control; he probably would have stopped quickly. But he wouldn't have been adequately punished. He would have struck her and other women again and again, sometimes in locations where no one could intervene.

There was one other time in college when that kind of rage swept over me after my roommate, Beth, was assaulted at the fraternity party, but I don't let myself think about that night very often.

I open the cabinet above my fridge, standing on my tiptoes to reach the bottle of Maker's Mark. I take a big gulp straight from the bottle. It sears my throat and chest, but it helps. I know I'm going to need a lot more before I'll be able to sleep tonight, so I take down a glass and fill it with ice and pour a few fingers over it.

Then I start to plan.

First thing in the morning, I'll head back to the hospital. I'm sick of the drive already, but I have to see Georgia. It may be the last time I ever will, because if she doesn't answer my questions, I'm walking away for good.

Then I'll visit the Cartwrights. I've already got an idea for a cover story. By tomorrow afternoon, with help from my photo of the guest book signatures at Annabelle's funeral, it should be perfected.

When I call the nurses to tell them I'm coming in to visit Georgia, I'll ask if I can bring her a small gift. It isn't anything that can be used as a weapon. I'll ask them not to tell her. I'll say I'd like to surprise her.

I sip bourbon until I feel calm enough to watch the third video.

The focus of this one is an apartment building I don't recognize. It looks as luxurious as the one Georgia lives in, and although I can see the numbers on the front of the gray stone building—4402—there's no street name visible.

The video was taken at nighttime; it's dark out, but the entrance to the building is brightly lit. The timestamp of this one is 11:28 P.M., and it's dated a few weeks ago.

For a few seconds, nothing happens. Then a man hurries out the main door of the building, his head down low. The camera zooms in, swiveling to capture the man's movements. I lean in closer, noting his hair is silver and he's wearing a navy blue blazer over a blue-and-white-striped oxford shirt.

When he turns his head before crossing the street, I catch a full-on glimpse of his face. It's Senator Dawson.

The video stops playing after the senator gets into his black sedan and drives away.

I play it again, scrutinizing it for details I might have missed, but I can't make sense of why Georgia would have this particular video.

She'd better tell me tomorrow.

CHAPTER FORTY-SEVEN

GEORGIA

The call from Colby came a few weeks ago. You had on a face mask and were wrapped in a buttery-soft cashmere robe while you streamed a new series—luxuries you blithely took for granted back then.

"You won't believe this," Colby began, his breathing rough and ragged.

"Are you okay?" you asked, sitting straight up.

"We're at Stagioni's celebrating my parents' anniversary. Family dinner, the five of us at that round table my dad loves in the middle of the room because everyone can see him." Colby paused, and you could hear him take a long drink of something and swallow. "And he just walked out. He didn't even finish eating."

"Was there an argument?" You couldn't imagine the senator in that scenario. He was too vested in his image.

"Nope." Colby sipped and swallowed again. "He said it was a work crisis. A homeland security issue for the committee he heads. Of course no one can ask questions, because it's classified. He gave my mom a kiss on the cheek and hurried out the door—stopping, of course, to shake a couple hands. Gotta reel in those voters, right?"

Colby was drunk. You could hear the clang of silverware against china plates and the swell of conversation in the background. He was probably at the restaurant's bar.

"Is that what you're upset about?" you asked. "That he left your mom on their anniversary?"

Colby barked out a laugh. "If I was upset every time my father cut out from a family event, I would've been crying half my childhood. No, I saw his phone light up when the text came in. No one else was looking; his phone was lighting up all night. But this wasn't a work text."

"Who was it?"

You knew the answer a split second before he revealed it: "Annabelle."

"What did the text say?"

"I just caught the first few words: 'I need you.'"

You stood up and began to pace. "She texts and suddenly your dad leaves?"

"Like, thirty seconds after he saw her text."

Your mind whirled. He and Annabelle wouldn't risk being seen together out in public, especially not on the night of his wedding anniversary. He couldn't meet her at his place. He must be going to hers.

"How long ago was this?" you asked.

"I don't know, half an hour ago. We just finished up, and my brothers took my mom home. She drank the rest of her wine and my dad's. But she was all smiles—you know, appearances. That's the only thing that matters, Georgia!"

He was getting sloppy. You pulled off your sheet mask and slipped out of your robe. Someone had to make sure Colby got home safe.

"I need you to do two things right now," you said. "Drink a big glass of water. And don't talk to anyone or do anything until I get there."

You made a call and put it on speakerphone while you threw on clothes and brushed out your hair. It was almost 9 P.M.—hopefully not too late. You'd give anything to collect some dirt on Annabelle, the perfect daughter.

Tony Wagner answered on the second ring. By now, you'd gotten to know him a bit, since you'd sent him back into Mandy's bar to get a glass she'd used and send it in for DNA testing. You had to see the results in black and white. The lab responded by email within forty-eight hours, confirming that you and Mandy were full biological sisters.

Tony listened to what you wanted him to do—get his guys to cover all the entrances and exits of Annabelle's building. They needed to video everyone going in and out, and make sure the building was identifiable in the video. There had to be a date and timestamp.

"Last-minute, four guys to make sure all the angles are covered, possible overnight work? I know a lot of ex-cops who might be interested if you pay double." Tony gave you the exorbitant rate for the job.

It didn't matter what it cost. The video, which showed the senator leaving what was clearly Annabelle's apparent at 11:28 that night, was priceless.

CHAPTER FORTY-EIGHT

MANDY

Driving the same half loop to Charlotte gives me plenty of time to think—and for my roaring anger to distill into a white-hot coal.

I make one stop, at a CVS. I make one phone call, to my bartender Scott.

"Everything okay?" he asks as I speed along, going precisely eight miles above the limit since I've heard police only pull you over when you're ten miles over. "It's not like you to be gone so much."

I haven't taken a vacation in eighteen months. I work six nights a week. I start to bristle, then realize Scott isn't my enemy right now. He's asking as a friend.

"Yeah, I'm just going through some family stuff . . . It's complicated," I tell him.

"So the mystery man doesn't exist?"

I detect a hopeful note in his voice. I decide to ignore it. I've never thought about Scott that way, even though objectively he's an attractive guy. But another complication is the last thing I need.

"It's long story," I say. It isn't a lie: Everyone in my family is a mystery—my father, mother, and sister.

"Don't worry. Take care of yourself. I've got things under control tonight," Scott promises.

"Thanks." I'm about to hang up; then I remember.

"Hey, Scott? If I don't make it in tonight, make sure you lock up if you're closing alone. Crime is going up everywhere, so . . ."

I can feel his surprise come through the line. He wants to ask—but holds back. Maybe he's remembering I'm his boss first and friend second.

"Sure," he says. "See you later."

★　★　★

I park and lock my purse in the trunk. The unnerving routine—displaying my ID, walking through the metal detector, waiting at the guard's desk for my escort, removing my jewelry, and taking the elevator to the silent hallway—already feels less intimidating. Familiar, almost. It's strange how quickly the human brain can embrace alien circumstances.

But when the nurse visually scans me, looking for anything that could be used against me during an attack, I feel a stab of anxiety.

I'm going into a dangerous place, filled with people accused of horrible things. The last time I saw the man with the silvery scar on his face, he homed in on me. I can't let my anger stamp out that reality and weaken my guard.

Within no time, I'm stepping through the thick, narrow wooden door into the locked ward. Two male residents are sitting in the common area on a low couch. One is a preppy-looking guy with sun-streaked hair. He's talking while the other man, who has a short Afro, gazes into space, his eyes unfocused.

I catch snippets of the conversation as the aide leads me toward the meeting room.

"She tried to wait for me in Johannesburg, but I couldn't get my parents' plane that weekend," the preppy guy is saying.

He looks like he should be holding court at a frat party. I can't resist asking the aide why he's here.

The aide gives a furtive look around. He probably shouldn't tell me, but it must get boring here sometimes, and gossiping is a release.

"He's a stalker," the aide whispers. He names a wildly popular pop star, then tells me the man broke into the singer's Beverly Hills home, thinking she was speaking directly to him through her lyrics. He triggered a silent alarm and security found him before the young woman came home.

"His parents didn't want him in an LA hospital," the aide confides. "They're trying to keep the incident quiet. Not just because of her—they're Silicon Valley billionaires. So they got him in here."

I glance back at the blond guy. He's sitting with one ankle resting on the other knee, his orthodontist-perfect smile flashing.

"He doesn't look ill," I say. "You'd never know."

A lot of young women would flirt with him in bars or turn around to get a second look if they passed him on the street. He's a predator draped in the effective camouflage of appealing facial features and an athletic build.

But he slips out of my mind as the aide leads me to the meeting room and I take my usual chair. I stare at the doorway, waiting for my sister. The momentary distraction didn't diffuse my anger. My blood feels like it's boiling.

A moment later, Georgia appears as silently as a ghost. She wears the beige sweatshirt and dark blue sweatpants I brought in from her closet. She looks even thinner than last time, with dark circles ringing her eyes.

I don't have the slightest bit of sympathy for her.

I force myself to smile; I don't want her to know what I'm feeling.

"You're angry," she says quietly.

"And you're scared," I reply without thinking. As soon as I say it, I realize it's the truth. I can feel her fear.

"I brought you something," I say.

Her eyebrows lift a fraction of an inch, and I hold up the photograph I had printed off my phone at CVS this morning.

It's of me at my bar, smiling and sliding a soda toward whoever is holding the camera.

"Oh, Amanda," she says.

Hearing her say my name, her voice filled with compassion, takes my breath away. No one except my parents has ever called me Amanda in such a familiar way. It's like that version of my name was reserved for family. Like she understands those unspoken rules.

My voice isn't as steely as I'd like it to be when I wave the photo closer to her face.

"Why did you do it?" I ask. "Tell me the truth or I'm walking out and never coming back."

Then I see it, the change in her eyes. She understands what is at stake. She lifts her hand to cover her mouth's movements from the overhead camera. My sister is finally going to be real with me.

CHAPTER FORTY-NINE

GEORGIA

There is so much you need to tell Mandy. But first you ask a question: "How did you get that picture?"

Sparks practically shoot out of her eyes. "How did *you*?"

You've upset her deeply. This is good. It shows she cares.

She deserves the truth, but that's not why you give it to her. You need her to follow the lead you're offering. "Through a private investigator."

She takes that in, emotions tangling on her lovely face. "How did you even know about me in the first place?"

You can't let her derail this conversation. You gently steer her back on track, asking: "Did you see the other videos he took?"

You keep your head slightly bent and your hand rubbing your temple, as if you have a never-ending itch, to block anyone looking at the camera from reading your lips.

"Why?" Mandy asks.

She's not going to give up anything willingly. You tamp down on your impatience; if she walks out, you're done for.

"One showed you going into a bookstore and buying *The Age of Innocence*."

"And then *you* bought it." She's bristling.

"So we could share an experience. That's all it was."

A patient who Patty told you tried to burn down a shopping mall passes in front of the open doorway, then halts and stares at Mandy. She shuffles into the room, moving so slowly she could be underwater. An aide swoops in and redirects her back into the hallway.

"I've got another picture for you." Mandy displays it like a winning ace in a game of blackjack.

It's a photo of a couple who look to be in their late fifties. The man's arm is around the woman and they're both smiling. They have kind faces. They're strangers to you.

"Who are they?"

She folds her arms. "You mean to tell me you found out what I was reading but you didn't learn anything about my parents?"

"Only that they'd died . . . That was as far as the PI went."

"'Protect me always.'" She utters the phrase like a challenge.

You have no idea what she's talking about.

Her gaze darts to the doorway behind you. You shift your eyes and spot Opal, a nurse in burgundy scrubs, standing there. She's either new or was taking time off when you arrived; you've never seen her before today, when she introduced herself to the patients at breakfast. You would've remembered her by her hair. It must be waist-length because even though she has pulled it up, her bun is the size of a cantaloupe.

"How are we doing, ladies?" she asks.

"Fine." Mandy sounds annoyed.

Opal lingers in the doorway for several more agonizingly long seconds.

The minute she's gone, Mandy hisses: "Who gave you that statue of St. Michael?"

You blink hard. This isn't how today is supposed to go. Mandy is asking all the wrong questions.

You tell her the truth: You don't know. You can't remember a time when you didn't have it.

Mandy stares at your face as intently as if she's trying to see into your soul.

Then she leans forward. "Tell me something about Annabelle. It can't be common knowledge. Something only her closest friends would know."

You feel yourself blinking in surprise. "I don't—"

She cuts you off. "Bullshit. You're her sister. *Tell me.*"

You think about your other sister. Annabelle could be cruel; she colluded with your mother to make you feel like an outsider in your own family. True, she loved kids and did volunteer work—like most people, she was complex, with good and bad sides. You know these aren't the kinds of details Mandy wants, however.

"She didn't like chocolate," you say.

Mandy frowns.

"Very few people knew," you add quickly. "It would be rude to tell a hostess you don't enjoy her dessert or turn down a boyfriend's Valentine's Day gift."

Mandy nods slowly. "Was she a runner?"

"No, but wh—"

"One more."

"I don't know. She liked peach Bellinis, the sweeter, the better."

Your thoughts are all disorganized now; you can't remember the short speech you'd planned, so you whisper a warning. "They might be bugging your apartment by now. Your car, too. Be careful."

Mandy leans closer. "Who?"

"The people who want me dead."

Mandy still doesn't get it.

You supply the missing piece: "That last video . . . Senator Dawson was sleeping with Annabelle."

Her eyes widen. Does she understand now? No one becomes the most powerful person in the free world without creating a scorched-earth path to the Oval Office. People can do—*have* done—just about everything imaginable to achieve that kind of power. The Cartwright family is pouring millions into Senator Dawson's campaign and attracting big donors. If your parents knew of the affair and withdrew their support, they could back another candidate. The scandal combined with the loss of money might be enough to tip the scale in a tight race.

"Tony Wagner is the PI. He's local. Talk to him. He'll confirm it."

You can practically see your sister's mind churning.

"Who else knows?" Mandy asks.

"Only Colby."

She nods slowly.

If she's upset by what you've pulled her into, she doesn't show it. Maybe she doesn't yet realize you've put her life at risk to save your own.

CHAPTER FIFTY

MANDY

Georgia's revelations are growing wilder. But I can finally fact-check one.

As I walk toward the hospital parking lot, I google the PI. His number pops up as the first hit on my screen. One tap is all it takes to hear a ring. He picks up before the second one: "Wagner Investigations."

"Hi, I'm wondering if I could make an appointment with you to talk about a case," I begin.

"Sure. What's your name?" His voice is gruff and businesslike.

"Katie." He's going to recognize me the moment I step through his door since he recorded me serving him a drink a month ago, but I want the element of surprise on my side.

"What is it you need help with?"

I reach my Honda and unlock it. "It's complicated. Can we talk in person?"

"I'm in the office today. When do you want to come in?" I already like this guy's style, even though I feel violated by the videos he took of me. He's not pretending to be busier than he is to make clients think he's important.

"Are you in uptown?" I ask.

"Yeah, just off 277," he says.

I'm getting a little more familiar with the city; I know the general area.

"How about thirty minutes?" I slide onto my seat and close the door.

"Works for me. Need my address?"

"I've got it."

"I'm above the Chinese restaurant, so come in around the back. Take the stairs to the second floor, and I'm the first door on the right. You'll see the sign for Wagner Investigations. You don't want to go to the wrong door, trust me. There's this yoga woman next to me, and she's always ringing chimes and chanting."

I start my engine. "I'll see you soon."

"Bye, Katie No-Last-Name."

I tap his address into Waze and turn right out of the parking lot.

It's farther away than I expected; it takes me closer to forty minutes. When I turn off my car, I notice a new text on my phone. It's from Colby. Did you have a chance to check your schedule yet? I'd love to see you again soon.

I decide to reply later. I climb the back staircase and knock on the door with the sign for Wagner Investigations, and when there's no answer, I turn the knob and poke my head in. "Mr. Wagner?"

There's a small waiting room with two straight-backed chairs and a square table. I step in, causing a bell to ring from the strap around the door, the notes sounding a similar melody to the one that comes from Sweetbay's door. When the investigator doesn't immediately come out to greet me, I sit down by the ancient copy of *People* magazine splayed on the coffee table.

There's an interior door that must lead to Tony's office. He could be on a call, I think. I wait another few minutes, and when he doesn't appear, I stand up and walk over to the door, listening hard. I can't hear a thing. Maybe he gave up when I didn't appear at the appointed time. He could have gone out to grab a cup of coffee or early lunch.

But I wasn't *that* late.

And if he's got a bell, he's security conscious. He wouldn't have left without locking up.

I knock on the interior door. No answer. I test the knob. It's open. Trepidation swells inside me.

But the bright morning sun is coming in through the window in the reception room. There's another place of business right next door. I can hear cars honking just a few dozen yards away and smell the egg rolls being deep-fried a floor below.

I twist the knob and push the door open a few inches, and relief sweeps through me. Tony is asleep in his small, dimly lit office. His head is down on his desk and his eyes are closed.

"Mr. Wagner?" I say it once, then almost shout it a second time.

Terror crescendos through my veins.

He isn't asleep. I think he's dead.

I scrabble backward, a scream filling my throat.

I look around wildly, then realize if the murderer is nearby, it would be worse to be trapped in this small space. I burst through the waiting room and run next door. It's locked, so I pound on it. A woman with a colorful wrap around her hair opens it a moment later, her expression annoyed.

"I'm with a cli—"

"Call 9–1–1!" I scream, pushing past her into the room. I lock the door behind us, breathing hard.

The yoga teacher is staring at me, open-mouthed. Her client is sitting cross-legged on a mat, her fingertips pinched together.

"Do something!" I yell at them. Then I realize I'm holding my phone, so I call for police and an ambulance, giving them details with a voice that has begun to tremble along with my body.

Tony Wagner was alive less than an hour ago. He knew about the video showing evidence of the senator's late-night visit to Annabelle's apartment.

Georgia warned me my car might be bugged.

You have no idea how big this is.

Did my phone call to Tony get him killed?

CHAPTER FIFTY-ONE

GEORGIA

Patty is leaving today.

She sits next to you on the couch one last time while your throat constricts with the effort of holding back sobs.

The heavy darkness that suffocated her is lifting, she says. She wants to live. She is so grateful to have this second chance.

But in order to seize it, she needs to leave this place of sickness and malice.

"Maybe I can come back and visit you sometime," she tells you. The thinnest of bandages cover her wrists now. She is healing in every way.

The man who does constant laps passes by on his incessant journey to nowhere. The pink-haired woman is arguing with a nurse about wanting to get a mani-pedi. In the chair by the couch where you and Patty are sitting, the man with the thick raised scar is dozing, his chin dipping toward his chest.

"There's so much time for introspection in this place, and I've thought a lot about why I ended up here. Why all of us did," Patty says. "What I've concluded is this: Mental illness is a medical condition. Evil is a pernicious force. At times they intersect. That's what happened to most people in this ward. But not me. And not you either, Georgia. You're not evil. I can tell."

You soak in her words. What you would have given to have had a mother like her.

"If you want to call me, you can. I'll leave my cell number with the nurses," Patty says. Then she stands up. You do the same.

She reaches out and gently hugs you while you try to soak in her embrace. It feels like forever since you've been held. You're hungrier for human contact than you've ever been for food.

"Take care, Georgia."

You slowly walk back to your room, your head hanging low. You can't bear to see her leave.

The only thing keeping you going is the fact that Mandy could be meeting with Tony Wagner right now. Once she has his word that the video wasn't doctored, she can take it to the press. They'll pounce on the story, and it will have to create reasonable doubt that you're the only person with a motive to kill Annabelle. Maybe it will even be enough to get you out of here.

You turn the corner into the hallway that leads to your small, institutional, depressing bedroom. You stop short, your breath trapped in your lungs. Fear descends upon you, visceral and suffocating.

A man is walking toward you, wearing bright green paper pajamas, his silver scar gleaming like a tear running down his cheek.

Josh is back.

CHAPTER FIFTY-TWO

MANDY

"What time did you speak to Mr. Wagner on the phone?"

Officer Neilson's pen is poised over his small spiral notebook. With his blond buzz cut and round cheeks, he looks too young for his profession. His partner appears to be two decades older. He has hooded eyes and a downturned line for a mouth, like a falcon. He hasn't spoken a word.

I touch *Recents* on my call log and recite the time: "11:14 A.M."

"That's helpful. Can you take a screenshot and text it to this number?" He extends a business card.

"Of course." I comply, then tuck his card in my bag.

I've already told the officers I came to meet Tony Wagner for the first time as a new client. I recounted my movements, from my knock on the hallway door to my realization Tony wasn't sleeping to my frantic scramble to the yoga studio. I'm thankful I didn't touch Tony or his desk: My DNA won't be anywhere near his body.

My heart is still pounding. Even though police are around me, I'm so jittery I flinch at every unexpected noise.

Am I being unreasonable, or is my fear justified? Tony looked to be in his late sixties or early seventies. It isn't that unusual for men of that age to suffer heart attacks or strokes.

But Georgia told me they might have bugged my car—and I was getting in my car when I talked to Tony. If Georgia, Tony, Colby, and I are the only people who know of the affair between Annabelle and the senator, the first two of us have been effectively eliminated as witnesses.

Dizziness engulfs me. I blink hard, trying to bring the room back into focus.

"You okay?" The young officer is peering at me.

"Yeah. It was just a shock. Is he—definitely dead?" I ask.

The younger cop glances at the older one, who nods.

"I'm afraid so, ma'am," Officer Neilson says.

A high-pitched siren announces another approaching vehicle. There must be four or five here already, including an ambulance and several police cars. Through the thin walls, I hear someone next door snapping that he isn't done dusting for prints.

The yoga teacher brings me steaming tea in a chunky cup with no handle. I accept it gratefully, cupping it in my palms as I sip and taste ginger and cinnamon. Even though the room isn't cold, I can't seem to get warm.

"We'll be in touch if we have any more questions," the young officer tells me. He tucks his notebook in his pocket and turns to go.

Then the silent partner speaks.

"Why did you want to hire Mr. Wagner?"

My stomach plummets.

I can't lie. But if there's even a chance everything Georgia claims is true, I have to walk a tightrope.

"I'm having some issues with my sister," I say. "She makes up these crazy stories, and she's disrupting my life, and I wanted to check out some of the stuff she's told me so I can know whether or not to cut her off."

The young officer seems to tune out before I finish speaking. *Girl drama*, I can practically hear him think.

"Take care, miss," he says as he heads out the doorway, turning toward the crime scene.

The older cop stares at me for a long second, then follows him.

★ ★ ★

I feel as if I'm poised on the edge of a cliff, about to free-fall. All I have to do is lift my hand and knock on the door of the Cartwright house. But I'm terrified I'll make a mistake, and they'll discover my true identity.

I can't delay any longer. Eyes are already on me.

I've spotted no fewer than three cameras since I stepped onto the grounds, not to mention signs reading *Trespassers Will Be Prosecuted* and *No Solicitors*. There's also a Ring device on the front door, its unblinking round eye capturing and storing my image.

I have no doubt that if I hadn't gone to Georgia's apartment to cultivate a certain look—her Lilly Pulitzer flowered dress and kitten heels, my lips glossed pink, Tiffany jewelry gleaming on my earlobes and wrists, my hair sleek and shiny—someone would've intercepted me already.

I present as a wealthy Southern girl, one who would have been friends with Annabelle. It has become blazingly apparent to me that people make snap judgments based on appearance, forming an image of who you are before you utter a word. I'm counting on that to hold true.

I press the bell and melodic chimes sound inside the grand house. Unlike the story I told to the police, the tale I've prepared for the Cartwrights is 100 percent false. Until I understand what's going on, I feel safer hiding my identity.

The door opens, revealing a man in black slacks and a white shirt. His loafers are shiny, and his expression is neutral.

"Good morning, miss," he says, a question in his tone. He must be a butler. I didn't think those jobs still existed.

"Hello, I'm Katie Johnson." I smile sweetly.

I'm holding a massive bouquet of white flowers, which cost $200 from Georgia's sock stash.

"How may I help you?" the butler asks.

"I was a sorority sister of Annabelle's. I was here for the funeral reception, but I wanted to come again to pay my respects to the Cartwrights. I also wanted to let them know about a charity event we Tri Delts are planning in Annabelle's honor."

"Will you pardon me for a moment?"

It isn't really a question. He closes the door. I wait, my skin prickling. Time seems to expand, every second dragging by. Finally he returns and opens the door. I hold my breath and wait for the verdict.

"Mr. Cartwright isn't home, but Mrs. Cartwright is in the garden. She isn't up for a long visit, however."

And just like that, I'm in.

I step across the threshold into the grand foyer. It seems even bigger now that it isn't filled with people. With stunning artwork popping on the walls and gleaming marble floors, it's like being in a museum. Did Georgia ever get used to living in a place like this? I wonder.

He leads me down a wide hallway, and I catch glimpses of the rooms we pass: A library in walnut wood with maroon walls, a sitting room done in robin's-egg blue, a second living room that holds a Steinway. Several doors are closed, and I wonder if one of them leads to the main dining room, where Annabelle's body was found.

When we finally reach the back of the house, the butler opens a massive glass door and I step outside. If I thought the interior of the house was breathtaking, the gardens elevate it to another level. Explosions of red and yellow dahlias, purple marigolds, and blue zinnias fill wide flower beds, while flowering bushes and mature trees line the borders.

He leads me to the right, around a thick azalea bursting with orange flowers.

"Mrs. Cartwright, I've brought you Katie Johnson."

She's kneeling by a bed filled with roses, a wide-brimmed hat shielding her face from the sun, gardening gloves on her hands. Even though she's digging in dirt, she's dressed in yellow capri pants and a white blouse. She looks beautiful; her hair and makeup are done, and her hat frames her soft oval face.

"Mrs. Cartwright, I'm so sorry for your loss," I begin.

"Thank you, dear." She stands up slowly and I see the cracks in her genteel facade. Mud is smeared on the left knee of her pants, and there's another streak of it on her forehead, like she wiped away perspiration with the back of her dirty glove. The whites of her eyes are threaded with red spiderweb lines.

"These are for you." I extend the bouquet.

She tilts down her head and inhales. "Lilies. Annabelle's favorite."

It's a stroke of luck. I replicated the blooms I remembered from Annabelle's funeral. Hopefully it'll add authenticity to my story.

"David, will you put these in water?" she asks.

The butler takes them. "I'll be back in a few minutes."

As soon as he turns, I begin: "I wanted to let you know that a few of us sisters from Tri Delt—me and Clara and Sidney—are planning a 5K charity run in Annabelle's honor." The names are ones I photographed from the guest book, and a little social media sleuthing gave me their connection to Annabelle.

Mrs. Cartwright's brows rise slightly. "Oh? Isn't that nice."

"I know Annabelle wasn't a runner, but we will have some special touches in her memory. One of the sisters suggested everyone gather for mimosas and chocolates at the end of the race. But I told them Annabelle would prefer macaroons and Bellinis."

As I'm speaking, I reach into my purse and pull out a slim folder. Mrs. Cartwright is nodding, a sad smile twisting her lips.

"And the proceeds will go to the church, to fund children's programs."

I open my folder and let the photograph of my parents that was inside flutter to the ground.

I don't make a move to reach for the object. After a beat, Mrs. Cartwright bends down to pick it up, as I hoped she would. But she barely glances at it as she hands it to me.

"Here you are, dear."

I need her to see the faces of my parents. It's the whole reason I'm here.

"Thank you," I say. "I'm gathering sponsors for the race. This couple said they were going to donate the prosecco for the peach Bellinis we're serving after the run."

I know it sounds strange—why would I be carrying around a picture of sponsors?—but it works. When I don't take back the photo, she looks down at it long enough that I'm certain my parents' faces register.

My gut clenches. This is it: the moment when the decades-thick shell of secrecy could crack open. When Honey looks up with shock flooding her face, I'll demand to know how our families are connected.

Honey looks up. And there's nothing in her expression but a bland geniality.

"The 5K sounds like a wonderful idea. Please let me know how I can help."

My whole body deflates. I can't believe it. She doesn't know them. If she has never met my parents, then who engineered the separate adoptions of me and Georgia? There has to be a connection; the matching statues proved it.

I see David round the corner of the house, coming to take me away.

I tuck the photograph back in my folder. Honey is staring at me, and I realize I never gave her a response.

"We don't need anything from you but your blessing," I tell her. "Thank you again for seeing me."

David looks down at my feet. I realize I'm standing in dirt and Georgia's Chloé heels are filthy.

"We can walk around this way," he says. "The grounds are lovely at this time of year."

It's a polite way of saying he doesn't want me tracking dirt through the house.

"Of course," I reply. It doesn't matter. I went to all this effort to come here, and I ran into a dead end. I have no idea what to do next.

My shoulders slump as I follow David around the corner of the house, into the side yard.

The breath whooshes out of my lungs. My feet stop moving as I gape.

There's a long row of apple trees spread out against a massive wooden fence. It's like something out of an enchanted forest. The trees are meticulously pruned, and the branches create an intricate pattern as they grow flat against the fence. The wall must be fifty feet long and half as high, and the trees stretch from end to end, red apples adorning the branches like ornaments.

"They're called espaliers," Brooks tells me. "The trees have to be trained to grow that way. Beautiful, aren't they? They've been here for decades."

My mouth is too dry to answer.

I know exactly what the trees are called. My mother told me about them when she planted the apple tree she trained to grow flat against a fence in our backyard, saying she was inspired because she once saw the gardens of a grand house with a row of such distinctive espaliers.

My mother *was* here long ago. The trees are like fingerprints tracing directly back to her.

CHAPTER FIFTY-THREE

GEORGIA

You were always the bad sister. You screamed at Annabelle, you cussed her out, you hit her, you *despised* her. Everyone knew that.

But nobody understood the context.

The role of the angel at the Christmas pageant was yours first. You'd learned your line and were about to get your costume. Then Honey told the church youth leader Annabelle was heartbroken she wasn't the angel, and couldn't they find another spot for you? Annabelle stood next to Honey, wiping away crocodile tears while real ones welled up in your eyes. The youth leader glanced at you, her expression stricken. But she was young and nervous, and there was no way she could stand up to the force that was Honey.

During the Christmas Eve performance, you took back your role. But Annabelle still got all the attention.

Annabelle didn't deserve to be an angel. But neither did you.

★ ★ ★

Annabelle grew worse when she was a teenager. You'd befriended a boy named Charlie whose father owned a car-repair shop in town. He was a shy, smart guy who helped his dad after school and always had oil-stained fingernails. On your fourteenth birthday, he biked several miles to your house to give you a bouquet of flowers.

Annabelle made it to the front door a few steps ahead of you and opened it.

"Carnations?" she scoffed, her mean laugh bubbling out, while Charlie's cheeks flushed as deep a pink as the flowers.

After Charlie left, you slapped her across the cheek, hard enough to make a satisfying smacking sound. She fell backward onto the couch, and you leapt at her, yanking her hair and screaming curse words at her. Then a housekeeper ran into the room, crying out for Honey, while Annabelle sobbed dramatically.

The next day, Honey announced you were being sent to boarding school. Instead of shipping you off alone, Stephen accompanied you. He worked on his laptop for most of the trip, but as you sat next to him, you experienced a sense of peace you'd never felt around Honey or Annabelle.

You were given a tour by the overly solicitous head of school, who was probably hoping for a generous donation along with your tuition payment, then deposited in your dorm room, surrounded by suitcases and boxes. "I hope you'll be happy here," Stephen said. He looked like he wanted to add more, but the words seemed stuck in his throat. He stretched out his arms, but you pretended not to notice.

He was a victim, too, but he'd made the choice to hand over his power to Honey. He could've fought her on your behalf, but he was too weak. That was why you left him hugging the empty air.

As it turned out, living away from home wasn't a punishment. It was a relief.

Once you were away from the constant comparisons and competitions you could never win, you were able to view Annabelle dispassionately. You came to realize it wasn't completely her fault she acted horribly toward you. That was Honey's influence; she wanted to shape Annabelle into her own image.

And Honey was diabolical.

Now, as you sit on the hard couch staring at the slightly blurry images behind the plexiglass covering the television, you find your-self pulling up another memory, this one from when you were in elementary school. It began when the landline phone rang one Sat-urday morning. You picked up the receiver in the living room and were about to say, *Cartwright residence, Georgia speaking*, as you'd been trained to do. But Honey answered a split second before you.

"Dee Dee, darling," she trilled when she heard her best friend's voice.

You lifted the bottom of the phone away from your mouth so they couldn't hear you breathing, but kept the top glued to your ear as you eavesdropped. You liked gathering information. Sometimes it gave you a little edge at home, a way to even a playing field that was per-petually lopsided.

The senator's wife told Honey she needed to talk, right away, in person. *Privately.*

"We can have sweet tea on the back porch," Honey said.

"Better make it gin and tonics," Dee Dee had replied.

You were tucked beneath the porch twenty minutes before she arrived, lying on your tummy on the cool dirt. There was plenty of room in the crawl space for a kid, and you liked the way the lattice spliced your view of the yard into little diamonds.

Your vision was compromised, but you could hear everything.

Dee Dee broke down almost immediately, sobbing as she revealed she was terrified the senator was falling in love with a beautiful young widow he'd met at the country club. He'd taken to spending the night away from home, which he'd never done before.

"What if this isn't just another fling and he leaves me?" she'd cried. "What would become of me?"

You couldn't see Honey's face, but her tone was hard as steel. Honey got angry a lot, but this seemed deeper. You could practically feel her rage. "That's not going to happen. You've been with Michael for twenty years. You married him when he wasn't even a state sena-tor! That little tramp isn't going to replace you."

"What are we going to do?"

"Teach her a lesson."

That's when you learned Honey and Dee Dee were essentially murderesses. They plotted to assassinate the woman's character. They crafted a story that the young widow was a former prostitute who'd met her husband when he was her client. It wasn't true. But who could disprove it? The husband was dead. The woman had moved here from Boston to be with him, leaving her friends and family behind. She had no allies, probably because she was pretty enough to be a threat to all the other woman in their circle.

The Charlotte society rumor mill was perpetually hungry, and it greedily swept up this new bit of fuel.

The widow was shunned at the country club. Not invited to parties and galas. Other women became too busy to meet her for lunch. Whenever she entered a room, people grew hushed and stared, then broke into laughter.

It took only a few months for the widow to sell her home at a loss and flee town. By then the rumor mill was feasting on the fact that she'd turned into a heavy drinker.

Honey and Dee Dee had driven her off. Destroyed her as effectively as if they'd torn her from limb to limb. And they were utterly delighted.

What you intuited even as a child was the realization that it wasn't the affair that devastated Dee Dee. What shattered her was the risk of losing the title Mrs. Michael Dawson.

And what you learned about your mother was that she would stop at nothing to secure her own place in society. If the senator tossed aside Dee Dee for a younger woman, who was to say your father wouldn't do the same?

The mind-numbing TV show blends into the next program. It features a group of people slowly hiking into the Grand Canyon, packs on their backs as they descend on a narrow, rock-strewn path. You stare at the colorful layers of strata the TV hikers pass—light green, buff, gray, violet—and let your mind drift to the night of Annabelle's last birthday party, the final one she'd ever have.

Dee Dee arrived early to help your mother with the arrangements. She criticized the way the napkins were folded and told the servers the silverware needed to be repolished. The years hadn't been kind to Dee Dee, and she'd turned as tough and bitter as an overcooked piece of meat. It wasn't easy being married to a man like Michael Dawson, and it showed. Dee Dee's face was puffy from years of alcohol abuse, and her voice dripped with poison.

You desperately wish you could remember the order of what happened toward the end of the night. The Dawsons were among the last guests; they'd retired to the library with your parents for brandy and cigars and conversation. You were in the dining room with Annabelle, arguing; then you went to the bathroom on your way to leave.

You passed the senator on your way out of the bathroom. He acknowledged you with a brief nod.

Where was he coming from? Did he slip into the dining room when you left it? The flush of the toilet and rush of water out of the sink taps while you washed your hands would have masked the sound of conversations or footsteps.

You're still concentrating hard on the images stored in your memory from that night when Peter, the tallest nurse, approaches with a somber expression.

Your stomach clenches as you wait for him to reach you.

"We found something in your room during morning sweeps," Peter says.

You hope your face doesn't betray anything.

"How did you get that piece of wire, Georgia?" he asks. "Did you pull it off the fence in the courtyard?"

You recite a nursery rhyme in your head, then count backward from twenty, doing everything you can think of to hide the effect his words have on you. Your mouth grows dry. It's hard to swallow. They found the wire in your room. How?

Peter squats down so your faces are close together. "What were you going to do with it, Georgia?"

It's safer not to say a word. It has been ever since you arrived here.

You see the new nurse, Opal, watching you from a few feet away. She shakes her head, her giant gray bun moving from side to side.

"I'm going to have to talk to the doctors about this," Peter says. "They're not going to be happy."

CHAPTER FIFTY-FOUR

MANDY

I walk down the long private drive and make my way to Queens Street, not caring that I'm scuffing the delicate fabric of Georgia's shoes against rocks or that sweat is dampening the nape of my neck. I'm so tantalizingly close to the missing piece of the puzzle. It's infuriating.

I stumble against a loose stone, then kick it hard, wincing as my ankle twists. The words I'm itching to yell at my parents swell up in my throat, feeling like they're strangling me. I want to demand to know why they hid so much from me. Yet I still ache for them to hug me and reassure me everything will be okay.

I didn't fight much with my mom and dad, even as a teenager. One of our few arguments came the summer I was fourteen, a few weeks after my best friend, Melissa, moved to California so her father could start his new job. Mel and I had been inseparable since elementary school—giggling through weekend-long sleepovers, getting our ears pierced together, and joining the same soccer team.

"You know, you two don't have to do everything together," my mother would say, only half teasing. "You're allowed to have other friends."

But I didn't need anyone else. Why would I?

Then Mel was gone.

I couldn't sleep that too-warm June night. The summer stretched ahead of me, endless and empty. My mother kept urging me to make new friends, like it was easy. She didn't understand how hard it was to break into established cliques, especially for a teenage girl who felt awkward in groups.

After a few hours of lying awake, I decided to go to Mel's house. It was only a few blocks away; I'd walked and run and ridden my bike there a million times. I tiptoed past my parents' bedroom and crept downstairs. I slipped out the back, easing the screen door shut so it wouldn't slap against the frame. Mel's home was empty; the new owners hadn't yet moved in. Her bike was missing from its usual spot on the front porch, and the yard swing was gone. The begonias in the window planters were brown and withered, and no lights were on. Her house looked as hollow and forlorn as I felt.

I walked around to the backyard and climbed the steps to the tree-house her dad had built. Secretly I was hoping Mel had left me a note, or maybe dug a message into the soft wood walls. But there were only our initials, carved into the wood like a scar from years before.

I lay down on the floor and cried myself to sleep. I didn't awaken until the sun was strong overhead.

I was a block from home when I saw the police cars converged on our street. My mother was sitting on our front steps, her head in her hands. I ran to her, shouting, "What's wrong?"

When she looked up at me, I saw raw terror splashed across her face.

She'd awoken right after I'd snuck out—a mother's instinct, more finely calibrated than an echocardiogram machine, sending a warning rippling through her slumbering brain that there'd been a disruption in the rhythms of her home. She'd checked on me and saw my empty bed.

I'd left the back door unlocked because I thought I'd be right back.

When she saw the unlatched door, she screamed for my father, and he came running. They searched the house, garage, and yard, calling my name. There was no sign of me. They knew I had nowhere to go.

Wild thoughts tore through their minds: Had someone crept inside and kidnapped me? Maybe my birth mother, who'd somehow tracked me down, or a strange man who'd caught sight of me in the convenience store where I often walked to buy snacks?

My dad spent the rest of the night searching the streets, his car headlights illuminating shadowy cul-de-sacs. When he got the news I was safe, he came running into the house in a T-shirt and pajama bottoms and sneakers, his hair sticking up, his eyes wild. He hugged me so hard it felt like I was being crushed, his heart beating so powerfully I could feel it against my own skin.

Later, as we sat on the couch together, my mother stroked my hair and asked a simple question: "Why didn't you wake us?"

"I tried to," I began. "But you wouldn't wake up."

"Mandy." My father's voice held a warning. "We're not angry with you. But we will be if you lie to us. Whatever it is, we can get through it as long as you're honest."

I bowed my head. "You wouldn't have let me go," I finally whispered.

That day, I promised to never lie to them. Technically, I've upheld my word. It doesn't mean I've always told them the full truth—I never told them the circumstances surrounding my roommate Beth's departure from college, or everything that happened afterward—but I've tried to be as honest as possible.

You were the liars! I want to scream now. *You lied to me about the most important thing!*

My chest is heaving as I reach the bottom of the Cartwrights' hill, and sweat is gathering beneath my armpits. I wrench my focus away from my emotions, concentrating on the facts in my possession.

My mother visited the Cartwright home long ago. In what capacity?

She told me she'd worked as a waitress until my dad bought Sweetbay's. I no longer trust that's true. But it's been a long day, and I'm hot and thirsty. It can't hurt to check out a local place and show her picture around.

I pull up the location of all the bars and restaurants within a few miles of the Cartwright estate. There's a fancy French bistro, an even fancier seafood place, a few chain coffee shops, an all-you-can-eat buffet restaurant, and a joint called The Penguin that has been serving award-winning fried okra and fried pickles since 1982, according to the website. That's the place calling to me.

I order an Uber since I left my car outside Tony Wagner's office. I don't want to take even the slimmest chance someone can track my movements.

When the Uber pulls up, I climb into the backseat, grateful the driver is playing country music instead of soliciting conversation. My outfit is probably all wrong for the bar, so I do what I can during the four-minute drive. I take off Georgia's jewelry and tuck it into her purse, tousle my hair, and wipe off my pink lip gloss with a tissue.

I use my iPhone's camera as a mirror. I don't look like me, but I don't look like a Southern sorority girl, either. I'm somewhere in the middle, slipping between identities, like a glitching video game character.

"Miss?"

I look up from my phone and see we're in front of the bar. A heavy weariness seeps through me. Today I saw a dead man, one I spoke to on the phone only minutes before he ceased to exist. It feels almost like a dream, or a memory from long ago. Adrenaline has propelled me through the past few hours, but it's ebbing now, leaving a bone-deep fatigue in its wake.

I force myself to step out of the Uber into early-evening air that feels thick and warm. I push through the door to the bar.

The first thing that hits me is the sight of a long, gleaming wooden bar, the swell of conversation, and the tangy, slightly sour aroma of beer.

It feels like Sweetbay's. Like home.

For a split second, I can almost see my dad pulling amber-colored drafts behind the counter and my mother wiping a table, a smile breaking across her face as she looks up and spots me. My mom did that every single time she saw me: She smiled like she was opening a present and seeing the gift she'd always wanted inside.

There's one empty stool in the middle of the long wooden bar. I claim it, grateful to sit down. The two guys next to me are hunched over drafts. They glance over, checking me out, but I avoid eye contact. They're around my age. They won't be any help to me.

The fifty-something bartender walks the length of the bar, pausing to grab someone's crumpled napkin and toss it in the trash can. She stops in front of me. "What can I get you, hon?"

I have to drive home, so I reluctantly decide against whisky.

"A Sam Adams would be great."

"Coming right up."

She pulls it, leaving a good inch of foam, then sets it in front of me. I take a long sip of the ice-cold beer, feeling my body unclench a fraction. Then I pull my folder out of my purse and open it to the picture of my parents.

I don't often feel lonely. But here in this bar, with nothing to do but look at their faces, an ache suffuses me. Losing my parents left a hole in my heart, one that might scab over but will never heal.

I close the folder and lay the picture of my parents on top. But I turn it around so that my parents will be facing the bartender. I wait for the bartender to make her way back to me.

Before she does, another text from Colby lands on my phone: Looking forward to seeing you soon! When are you free?

If I didn't need information from him, I'd ghost him. He's too aggressive for a guy I've only met twice. But I simply text back: Tomorrow night?

His reply lands instantly: Yes!

I don't read the rest of his message because the waitress is approaching. I muster a smile.

"Anything else, hon?"

I slide the photo closer to her. "Actually, I have a quick question. I'm trying to find my mom. I was adopted."

She looks at me, and I get the sense she's an empath and can tell I'm feeling hurt, tired, and depleted.

She looks down at the picture. "This is her?"

I nod.

I watch as the studies it closely, taking in my mother's long, wavy brown hair draped over her shoulder and her flowered dress.

Remember her, I silently plead.

But when the bartender looks up, I read only sympathy on her face.

"I don't know her."

"Can you look again?" I plead. "Maybe her hair was shorter then . . . this picture is ten years old. I think she knew the Cartwright family a long time ago. Like maybe thirty years."

She bends back down. Stares for a moment.

"I'm sorry."

Tears stings my eyes. I know she sees them when she looks up. She thinks I'm a young woman searching for my mother. She wants to help me, I can tell.

"Tell you what." She reaches under the counter and pulls out a phone. She taps on it, then holds it above the photograph and snaps a picture of it. "I'll ask around."

She asks for my number. My mind feels sluggish, and it's hard to know what to do. Is it safe to give it out?

I can't decide. So I do it.

CHAPTER FIFTY-FIVE

GEORGIA

"I know you're faking."

Opal, the new aide, stands in your bedroom, speaking so softly no one passing by will be able to overhear.

"Lying is a sin against God and man."

You remain perfectly still, sitting on the edge of your bed, staring down at the bony curves of your kneecaps.

"You're used to faking, aren't you? You act like you're gabbing on your phone so you can ignore the homeless guy begging you for a dollar. You flirt with men, then pretend you have a boyfriend and leave them all hot and horny. Not such a pretty girl now, though, are you? Looking a little rough."

Opal's voice is a venomous hiss. Her eyes are flinty and hard.

"Things are so soft in here for you people. Pick what you want to eat. Take a nap or paint a picture, whatever you feel like. Don't clean up after yourselves, just sit back and let us do it for you. And you get all this because you've sinned."

You've read about this particular kind of health care worker. They're drawn to the vulnerable, but not to help. They disguise their need to hurt and dominate. At their most extreme, they're called Angels of Death.

She approaches with a small paper cup, the kind that holds the sludgy liquid you use to wash yourself. But it isn't your shower day; you won't have another one until tomorrow.

"Prove you're not pretending, then. Take these."

Terror spikes through your veins as you look down at the pink and gray pills.

Because of the wire they found by your bed, you're back on a one-to-one. Opal is your watcher. The security camera is above, capturing the scene and transmitting it to a screen in the nurses' station. But there are dozens of cameras on this floor, all feeding to the screens. The nurses and aides are busy. How closely do they really monitor those cameras?

"You're going to swallow these now. If you don't, I might inject you tonight while you sleep. Maybe I'll even give you a little something extra."

If you take the pills, how many hours or days will it be until your mind is irrevocably altered?

Your chest is so tight it's hard to breathe.

The crushing stress and constant fear have worn away your outer layers, leaving you raw and exposed. You are an inch away from screaming.

"Look at your fancy painted fingernails. Probably cost more than I make in a whole day here." Opal rattles the pills in the cup. "Ten seconds. Then I'll do it for you."

Opal may be as off-kilter as any of the patients.

You could pretend to swallow but keep the pills tucked against your upper gums, way in the back of your mouth. But you've seen how the nurses check mouths, instructing patients to stick out their tongues and tilt back their heads.

"Nine."

Opal has just reached four when Peter walks into your room.

Your body goes limp with relief.

"Hey, just wanted to— What's this?" He's staring at the paper cup.

"Isn't it time for her medicine?" Opal's voice is flat with disappointment.

"She isn't on meds yet," Peter says. "Her competence hearing was just scheduled." He flicks his eyes to you. "That's what I was coming in to say. Her lawyer's on his way in to talk about it."

"So no meds for her yet?" Opal puts the slightest emphasis on the word *yet*.

"No."

Peter frowns, and you can see the flicker of worry dart through his mind. His subconscious is telling him there's something off about this encounter. But he won't let himself realize it until further down the line—when a few patients are hurt or injured. Even then, with the potential threat of lawsuits, Opal may just be let go instead of punished, free to float to another hospital or nursing home.

"When is her lawyer coming?" Opal asks. It's as if she's trying to find out how much time she has to terrorize you.

"He's on his way in now. So Georgia, you get to eat lunch early. Why don't you come into the dining room?"

Your legs feel too wobbly to stand up, but after a moment, you steady yourself and rise. Opal follows you as you walk to the dining area, her footsteps echoing behind you like an executioner's.

CHAPTER FIFTY-SIX

MANDY

"Mandy? You okay?" Scott's voice yanks me out of my thoughts.

It's almost closing time at Sweetbay's. The kitchen has been cleaned and swept, the dishwashers are churning, and only two stragglers are parked on bar stools.

"I'm good. Why don't you head out?" I smile at Scott.

After I left The Penguin, I took an Uber back to Tony Wagner's office complex and got my car. A police cruiser was in the parking lot, and I spotted an officer checking out everyone who passed by. I wanted to ask if they'd learned whether Tony's death was from natural causes, but I knew attracting more attention to myself wouldn't be wise.

The whole drive home, my battered mind tried to absorb everything I'd seen and heard. I knew I needed to protect the thumb drive, especially if it's the only copy that exists. So I downloaded the videos onto my phone, then stopped at the bank where I keep a safe-deposit box.

Inside the box is a slim envelope holding a few Polaroid pictures. No one but me knows about them; I've never shown them to a soul. I keep them locked up here for Beth. I locked the thumb drive in with them.

Right now I can't gauge if it's more vital to pursue the questions swirling around my sister's life, or dig more deeply into those around mine. And I can't shake the fear that if Georgia is right and someone put a tracker on my car, they'll know exactly where I am tonight.

One of the two men remaining at my bar puts the phone he's been scrolling into his pocket, signs the bill Scott left by his drink, and walks out.

The other guy keeps nursing his beer. He isn't peering at his phone or trying to talk to us. He's just staring into space, like he's thinking deeply about something.

I take a closer look. I haven't seen him at my bar before. He's in his early fifties, with steel-gray hair cut military-short. He's got the physique of a boxer, and he's wearing a wrinkled blue T-shirt with a pink pelican pattern and a gleaming gold Rolex. It feels like an odd juxtaposition of details.

A month ago, I wouldn't have thought twice about him. He looks up and meets my eyes, and I quickly turn away, wiping down an already clean counter. I feel a prickling between my shoulder blades, a physiological warning that I'm being watched.

I whip around, expecting to catch the guy staring at me, but I see Scott standing there instead.

"I was thinking about what you said the other day."

I raise my eyebrows in a question.

"The crime in the area. It's not a good idea for you to close up alone. I'm staying until you leave."

"You don't have to—" I begin. But the warm relief pouring through me makes me realize how much I want him to.

Scott said this loudly enough for the guy to hear. Deliberately? I wonder. Maybe he also thinks there's something sketchy about the guy.

Or maybe I'm experiencing paranoia.

A moment later, the guy swallows the remaining two inches of beer in his glass and sets it down. He leaves without a word.

Instead of rinsing out the glass and turning off the lights, Scott reaches for a bottle of Johnnie Walker and fills two glasses with ice.

He pours a generous splash of the amber-colored liquid into each. "These are on me. You look like you could use a drink."

I take a sip. The welcome burn fills my throat and chest, warming me in places I didn't know I was cold.

"You're right," I tell him. "But they're not on you."

"We'll argue about that later. C'mere." Scott leads the way to a two-top. I follow and claim the chair across from him.

"What's really going on?" he asks.

"What do you mean?" I ask.

"Mandy, come on. You forgot about six things tonight. You jumped out of your skin when Clarissa dropped a tray. And you just look . . . sad."

I want to confide in Scott. It would be such a relief to unload on someone, to get a fresh perspective. But if even a fraction of what Georgia is telling me is true, I could be putting Scott in danger.

Before I can say anything, my phone rings. I glance down at it. The number is unfamiliar, but the area code is Charlotte.

"Excuse me a sec?" I ask Scott. He nods.

I pick up and say hello.

"Hey, hon. That picture you showed me of the woman you think is your mom?" The voice of the bartender I spoke to earlier today at The Penguin comes over the line. I can hear the clatter of dishes in the background; she must be closing up, too.

"Yes?" My heart starts pounding.

"I asked around. No one knew her."

"Oh." Disappointment sears through my voice.

"Hold on, now. *Him*, he's a different story. One of my old-timers recognized him, but he'd grown out his hair and shaved off the mustache he used to have. Said he came in here most Sunday nights, but a long, long time ago. He used to work for the Cartwrights. How does your mother know him?"

Pecan Tree Corp. It must be one of the many companies the Cartwrights own. My parents lied to me about that, too.

"Hon? Still there?"

I blurt out: "I think they were friends."

"Well, if she's hooked up with him, that's trouble."

Everything shudders to a stop. I whisper, "What are you talking about?"

"Word is he disappeared one day. Silver, jewelry—he took whatever he could from the Cartwrights and fled town."

I can feel my heart breaking.

Because maybe that's where the extra money came from the year I was born. My father stole it from the Cartwrights. Maybe he shaved his mustache and let his hair grow longer so the Cartwrights wouldn't recognize him.

"Thank you," I manage to whisper.

"No problem. I hope your mother got rid of him."

I hang up and drop my head into my hands. Maybe my father stole more than silver and jewelry. What if he stole me, too?

CHAPTER FIFTY-SEVEN

GEORGIA

Milt Daniels, the public defender assigned to represent you, is young, clearly overworked, and almost certainly underpaid. The first time you met him, you noticed he bit his fingernails and his white oxford shirt had a frayed collar. Today he's in a blue shirt, but his nails still look raw and ragged.

"Georgia, I'll be honest with you," he says from the cement-heavy chair set a few feet away from yours. "It's not looking good."

Opal hovers in the doorway, her heavy hair pulled into her ever-present bun.

"You have no history of mental illness. But you do have a history of animosity toward Annabelle, and the prosecution is building a strong list of witnesses who will testify to it."

He leans forward, putting his elbows on his knees. A stubby pen that's half the length of a standard one is gripped in one hand and a miniature legal pad that holds only a few sheets of paper is in the other. Everything is a deadly weapon here, even the innocuous objects that used to populate your surroundings.

"Your aunt Beverly will testify that when you were thirteen, you pushed Annabelle off a dock into Lake Norman in the early spring, when the water temperature was dangerously low. She was fully clothed and she panicked. She might have drowned."

He looks up at you. You say nothing. Annabelle was a crybaby back then.

"Your cousin Grace will testify that you repeatedly told her you wished Annabelle was dead."

You told that to many more people than Grace.

If your lawyer thinks this is going to get you to open up, he couldn't be more wrong. All your life you've heard about how awful you've been to Annabelle, the pretty, sweet, *perfect* daughter. The only one Honey and Stephen ever wanted.

"Georgia, help me out here. You were found at the scene of the crime with your sister's blood on your dress. I can't find anyone else who might have had motive to kill her."

Should you tell him?

He looks eager and innocent, with his big brown eyes and shock of bangs that keep falling into his face. He pushes them back so frequently with his index finger that the movement seems as compulsive as a tic.

"The nurses found a length of wire in your room, Georgia. That makes things worse for you. They can testify about it, and say you might have been planning to use it on someone."

You could just speak the words—*Annabelle was having an affair with Senator Dawson*—and watch his eyes bulge out. He'd scramble to create a new narrative to superimpose over the existing one. Multiple people could have motive: the senator, his wife, Dee Dee, Colby or one of the Dawsons' other sons, or Reece DuPont, the guy the senator calls his right-hand man, whose round blue eyes always seemed to see beneath your clothes as they slithered over you.

Your lawyer could call Mandy and get the video, then release it to the media, deflecting the attention swirling around you and spinning it onto this new scandal.

Or the opposite could happen.

Milt Daniels could take in your words, and his expression could grow wary and remote. He could leave as quickly as possible, eager to report what you've revealed.

If he is in the pocket of Senator Dawson—like so many other people in town—that's what he'd do. The senator would reward him handsomely, perhaps with a swift track to a prime position in the US attorney general's office.

"Your competency hearing is in seventy-two hours. If you're found mentally incapable of standing trial, you'll be forcibly medicated under the direction of your psychiatrist to restore your capability. If you are found capable of standing trial, the prosecution will seek the death penalty."

The corners of Opal's mouth curl up. A private smile, intended for you alone.

CHAPTER FIFTY-EIGHT

MANDY

When the waitress from The Penguin hangs up, I sink back into my chair, feeling numb. I can't believe it. My dad was not just a liar but a thief.

"I take it that wasn't good news." Scott's voice cuts through my thoughts. I lift my head and bring my glass to my lips and practically inhale the rest of my scotch.

"Not so much."

"I'm a good listener." Scott waggles an eyebrow. "Occupational hazard."

He's trying to cajole me out of my mood. I appreciate his effort, but he has no idea what I'm going through. This isn't a bad breakup or a clash with an obnoxious boss.

"Give me a second. I have to check something." I pull up Google on my phone and type in different combinations of search terms—*Cartwright*, *twins*, *stolen baby*, my father's name and my mother's—but get no results. If my parents had stolen me from the Cartwrights, there would have been massive media attention, I reassure myself.

Scott takes my glass and walks to the bar sink, tossing out the ice. I watch as he moves behind the counter in his faded jeans and black

T-shirt with the Sweetbay's logo on the chest. He scoops in fresh ice and tops it off with another three fingers of scotch.

"Maybe take it a little more slowly this time," he tells me when he returns to the table, setting the glass down in front of me.

A car horn blares outside and I flinch. Scott's eyes narrow. "After you finish that, I'm driving you home."

I start to protest, but he shakes his head. "Not this late, after two strong drinks, when you're already a little shaky."

He's right. And I haven't eaten since—I squint and try to remember. Coffee and a banana this morning. My stomach has been too knotted to accept food.

Scott's gaze feels too intimate, so I flick my eyes away. When I first took over here after my dad passed, Scott had already been bartending for about six months. The day after my mother's funeral, I was about to climb onto the counter to display the photograph of them on the high shelf when Scott approached, asking if he could help. He took the photo from my hands as reverently as if it were a sacred object and stretched up his arms and positioned it so it was almost as if my parents were watching over their old bar.

"What did you really think of my parents?" I blurt. "Tell me the truth, even if it isn't positive."

"Your parents?" Scott's wooden chair creaks as he leans back. "Your mom was a total sweetheart. She never had a bad word to say about anyone. She was a real *mom*, you know? The kind everybody wants."

I nod because it's true. My mother listened to me—really listened, even when I was a kid—and French-braided my hair and taught me to bake cakes from scratch.

"And your dad . . ." Scott's voice trails off for a moment. He clears his throat. "I learned more from him than I did from my own dad, which isn't saying much. But still. Your father . . ."

He pauses, seeming to search for the right words.

"Did he tell you what happened right after he hired me?"

I shake my head.

"I fucked up, Mandy. I stole from the till during my first week. Not much—just forty bucks. I did it all the time at my old job, and I guess the habit stuck when I started here. But your dad knew. I don't know how, but he did. He called me into his office and I knew he was going to fire me. Anyone would've, you know? Then he asked if I was in trouble. If I needed a loan. If there was anything—" Scott's voice breaks. "If there was anything he could do to help me."

Scott bows his head.

"He said if I put back the money, he'd give me another chance and never tell anyone. So when you ask me what I thought about your dad? What I still think about him?"

I hold my breath.

"He showed me the kind of man I want to be."

My throat thickens. Silent tears leak from my eyes. This is exactly what I needed tonight: someone to counterbalance the awful words I just heard about my dad.

"Hey." Scott reaches over and pulls a napkin out of the holder, then passes it to me. His empty hand rests on the table, outstretched toward mine, like he's yearning to touch me.

So I surrender to it. I entwine my fingers through his and keep holding on while I stand up and walk around the table. I wait until he rises; then I lean into him, pressing my body against his long, lean warmth. After a second, he bends his head and kisses me.

I lose myself in the kiss, running my hands over Scott's broad shoulders, feeling his tongue, tasting of scotch, slip into my mouth.

Scott pulls away and breathes my name into my ear.

I look up at him. "Can you take me home now?"

Disappointment crashes over his face. I don't let myself think about the twisted reasons I'm doing this, including the fact that after seeing Tony's body, I'm scared to be alone in case Georgia is right and my movements are being monitored. I just say, "Let's have another drink at my place since you're staying over."

CHAPTER FIFTY-NINE

GEORGIA

It's group activity time, and today it's taking place outside. The sun is warming the back of your head and shoulders, a gentle breeze stirs the air, and music plays from a tiny speaker a nurse holds. The song is upbeat; it's supposed to make you feel good.

But all you can think about is hatred.

You've been the subject of hot bursts of hatred a couple of times before—once after you clipped a guy's new Mercedes in traffic, another time when a girl in college lost it on you after her ex-boyfriend asked you to a formal. But you've come to the realization that quiet loathing can be even worse because it's harder to identify or have validated. It rides in under the camouflage of politeness, or hides inside hollow words, while its invisible animosity tears you apart like acid.

Honey was an expert in loathing you.

When you were eight and had your tonsils taken out over your school's winter break, Honey and Stephen and Annabelle flew to Australia for Christmas. You stayed home with a babysitter, eating popsicles and taking Children's Motrin, while Annabelle petted baby koalas and snorkeled with dolphins. "It's too bad you had to rest and heal!" your mother lamented for the benefit of the babysitter. "We'll do an extra special trip next time!" They did—without you again.

After you were sent to boarding school, you were always a holiday holdover because your spring breaks didn't align with Annabelle's. Your family flew to St. Barts or went skiing in Vail while you ate Easter dinner with the quiet, vaguely creepy family of the English teacher who had long, spindly fingers and liked to recite Shakespeare.

Those were just a few of the unspoken messages pressed into you like a bruise upon a bruise: *We don't want you. You're not one of us.*

Sometimes the slights felt deliberate. Other times they were careless. Take the last family Christmas photo you ever posed for: You were sixteen, and home for Thanksgiving, one of the few times you'd left school for a holiday. You slept in that morning, then went for a long run, finding solace in the snap of twigs under your feet and the cold air drawing into your lungs.

Six miles later, you'd completed your loop and were walking toward the front door when it burst open. Honey and Annabelle stood there in sleek red dresses, their hair and makeup flawless.

"I thought you were the photographer!" Honey said. "Hurry, put on something red. We're doing our holiday photo."

You barely had time to rinse the sweat off your body and swipe on some mascara.

Annabelle and Honey looked gorgeous in the picture sent out to hundreds of your parents' closest friends. You were squinting, and your face was almost the same beet color as your dress.

A scuttling noise makes you look down. A dry leaf is blowing across the concrete floor of the outdoor space. It'll be trapped here, bandied about by the wind, until someone's foot crushes it.

"Someone's got a visitor coming." Opal's voice jars you. "Better wipe that expression off your ugly face. No one likes a disagreeable woman."

A visitor is coming to see you? Your lawyer already came today. Mandy always calls first.

You're desperate to know who it could be. Opal seems to sense this.

"You'll just have to wait and see," she gloats. "Come inside now."

You follow her to the meeting room with two chairs and take the one farthest from the door, as always.

You hear the heavy tread of footsteps as your visitor approaches.

Then he appears in the doorway.

It takes everything you have not to gasp.

CHAPTER SIXTY

MANDY

Regrets slam into my mind as the bright morning sun hits my eyes.

I had sex with Scott last night—twice. He's in bed beside me right now, his warm, heavy leg draped over my hips. As if my life needed another complication.

Like the universe can hear my thoughts, my phone pings. I gingerly pull it off my nightstand and read the text. It's from Colby: Can't wait to see you tonight, beautiful.

Colby is acting way too familiar. It's creepy.

"Mmm," Scott mumbles as he wraps his arm around me, pulling me in closer.

"Bathroom," I whisper, slipping out from under him.

Last night's alcohol and lack of sleep have wreaked havoc on me. My face looks pale and drawn, and my hair is tangled.

I jump into the shower and scrub myself down, rinsing Scott's scent off my skin.

I'm lathering my hair with shampoo when my shower door opens.

Scott's standing there, naked. I cringe when I see the marks my fingernails left on his shoulders. "Room for two?"

I know the response I give him isn't what he wants: "I'll be right out!"

I quickly rinse the suds from my hair and don't bother with conditioner. I turn off the water and step out, twisting up my hair in a towel and slipping on my terry cloth robe.

"Didn't mean to rush you," Scott says.

I can't meet his eyes.

"No, no, it's good. I just have to go to Charlotte this afternoon and I need to get a few things done at the bar first."

I grab a wide-toothed comb out of my vanity and start digging the knots out of my hair.

"I'll shower at home then." Scott's voice is flat. He goes into my bedroom, and I hear the rustling sound of him pulling on his clothes.

I've not only hurt him, I've messed things up at work.

I close my eyes and see an image of Scott staring at me tenderly as he moved on top of me.

I turn around, an apology rising in my throat. Before I can speak, I hear my front door shutting.

★   ★   ★

I'm still thinking about Scott at twilight as I sit by a window in a coffee shop, waiting for Colby. Dress casually—tonight's going to be great! Colby texted this afternoon. Then, less than an hour later: Bring a sweater in case it gets cold. Can't wait to see you!

I'm feeling claustrophobic. If I didn't desperately need to find out what Colby knows, I'd cancel. His texts are over the top.

I'm wearing jeans, ballet flats, and a white linen shirt—all belonging to Georgia. I can actually fit into her pants now that stress has peeled a few pounds from my body. I folded her fuchsia cashmere sweater into one of her big shoulder bags. All told, my outfit probably costs over $1,000, which equals casual in Georgia's world.

It's a good thing I'm there early. Fifteen minutes before we're scheduled to meet, Colby comes hurrying down the sidewalk, holding a bouquet of roses.

I step outside to meet him, then stop short when I glimpse his face.

"What happened?" I blurt.

"Long story." He sweeps me into a long hug. "Wow, you look even better than I remembered!"

I thank him for the flowers, trying to conceal my discomfort at his lavish bouquet, and he leads me to his Lexus, which is parked half a block down. I keep glancing at him out of the corner of my eye. There's a bruise the size of a plum on his jawline, and the area around it looks painfully swollen.

"Where are we heading?" I ask, laying the roses on my lap while I fasten my seat belt.

"It's a surprise." We drive through the city, onto a two-lane road lined with horse pastures and big homes and the occasional farmers' market or antiques store. The sun is beginning to sink when Colby turns onto a bumpy gravel path. We travel another fifty yards, then reach a small parking lot.

He cuts the engine and a sense of unease floods over me. No restaurants or even other people are in sight.

"Shall we?" he asks. He walks around to open my door, then goes to the trunk and pulls out a picnic basket and blanket. I follow Colby down a trail to a small, grassy area overlooking a creek. In the daytime, it would be a beautiful spot. At twilight, it feels a little spooky.

Colby spreads out a blanket and tells me to make myself comfortable, then opens the huge picnic basket. It's a fancy contraption with sides that bend down and out. Inside are special holders for two wineglasses, a bottle of wine, votive candles, and two covered platters. Colby uncorks the wine with a silver corkscrew from yet another compartment and fills the glasses.

"To a beautiful night and an even more beautiful woman." He clinks his glass against mine, his index finger sticking out slightly again. Maybe he broke it playing sports when he was young.

There's something off about Colby. I want to get whatever information I can out of him and get home.

I take a big sip of wine. "It's so peaceful here."

"And no paparazzi to interrupt us." He shifts closer to me. I can tell he's about to try to kiss me, so I lean back.

"Hey," I say. "I'm not ready for that yet." But at least he's given me a segue. "I just got out of a long relationship," I lie. "And I guess my heart was broken. He cheated on me with a friend of mine."

I need to get Colby to admit what he knows about his dad and Annabelle. His testimony would go a long way toward freeing Georgia.

"Sorry that happened to you. I never understand why people cheat," Colby said. "Me, I'm a one-woman man."

"Yeah, I guess my ex-boyfriend learned it from his father. His father always had young girlfriends on the side."

Colby's mouth tightens. "Women who do that are trash." It doesn't escape my notice that he put all the blame on the women, and none on the man.

It's like there are two sides to Colby—the awkward, gentle guy and the one who is simmering with a quiet anger.

I decide to change the subject. I put my hand over my stomach and force a laugh. "My stomach's growling. I guess I'm hungry."

Colby reaches into the basket and brings out the top plate, which is filled with fruits, cheeses, and crackers. We eat for a moment in silence. I'm not hungry, but I force down some fresh strawberries and sliced peaches.

The light is fading away, and Colby's face is harder to read in the shadows. The bruise on his jaw isn't nearly as noticeable now.

"So what happened to your face?" I ask again.

"My brother Kyle happened."

"He hit you?" I ask. "Why?"

"He's never needed a reason. At least this time it isn't permanent." He lifts his index finger, the one that I've noticed doesn't bend. "He broke this middle joint when I was ten. It never healed properly."

"That's horrible." I feel my temper rising. There's nothing I despise more than a bully. "Kyle hit you for no reason? You weren't arguing?"

Colby shrugs. "Maybe in his mind he had a reason. Kyle's a lot like my father."

The world around us is still and quiet, except for the chirping of a lone cricket. I ask the question gently, wanting to lull Colby into revealing a confidence. "What do you mean, he's like your dad?"

Colby sips his wine. He's not looking at me; his eyes are narrowed, like he is lost in an angry memory.

Then he says, "The most dangerous place to be in the world is between my father and something he wants."

CHAPTER SIXTY-ONE

GEORGIA

Kyle Dawson stands in the doorway looking like he owns the place. His hands are casually tucked into the pockets of his dark pants, and his crisp shirt is buttoned up to his strong-looking neck. They probably made him take off his tie before he came in, but he still has on his suit jacket.

"Georgia, it's good to see you."

You never liked being around Kyle under the best of circumstances. He always has an agenda, but you've never been sure if he possesses a heart.

The big male nurse who escorted him gestures for Kyle to sit. Kyle smiles and complies. It's the same charming smile his father can switch on or off as easily as a light.

"I can take it from here, but I appreciate your help," Kyle tells the male nurse.

Opal is in the doorway, gaping at Kyle. She's got to be twenty years older than him, but she's not the first woman to fall sway to his athletic, six-foot-two frame and piercing blue eyes.

The male nurse leaves, and Kyle runs his gaze over you, letting it linger on your tangled hair and sweatshirt with a juice stain dribbled down the front. A smirk tugs at the corners of his lips.

He leans forward, putting his elbows on his knees. You brace yourself. Kyle isn't here on a mercy mission. He wants to twist the knife. He likes watching people suffer; you've seen him inflict plenty of pain on Colby as well as other boys on the lacrosse or football field.

"Let's cut the bullshit, Georgia. I know you understand every word I say."

You don't give him anything, not even a flicker of an eye.

"I was there the night Colby called you from Stagioni's to tell you my dad went to Annabelle's."

You rear back slightly. His triumphant expression tells you he clocked your involuntary movement.

"Colby's an idiot. I could tell he was twisted about something when my dad left. So I told Bryce to take home my mom, and I stood two feet behind Colby while he called you. That moron never knew I was there."

This is bad. Very bad. Because if Kyle knows that Colby knows—

You can't even complete the thought before he speaks. Kyle is one step ahead of you. Guys like him always are.

"Blood is thicker than water. You think my brother's going to sacrifice our father to help *you*?"

You're frozen, like a small animal trapped in a corner by a bird of prey.

"I saw Colby this morning. He isn't going to talk." Kyle gives a little chuckle, seemingly lost in a private memory.

"I guess you two have that in common," he continues. "Here's what you're going to do. You need to plead guilty. My family doesn't want this mess dragged out at trial. And neither do you, because you won't win. My dad had a conversation with the district attorney."

You knew Senator Dawson would be calling in favors. He'll have plenty to dispense when he reaches the pinnacle of power.

"In two days, you're going to be found competent to stand trial. If you plead guilty, you'll get twenty years. If you don't, you're going to die. We'll see to that."

He leans closer. You can smell his minty breath and see the glow of his lightly tanned skin. How can someone so handsome and fresh be so rotten at his core?

"Everyone has dark secrets. Even my brother. It was pathetic how quickly Colby folded when I reminded him about that."

Forty-eight hours, then it will all be over.

Opal is in the doorway, but Kyle is speaking too quietly for her to hear. Even if she did know what was going on, she wouldn't help you. She'd rejoice.

"Twenty years, maybe some time off for good behavior, then you get out of jail and move somewhere else. Given the alternative, it's a sweet deal. Don't ever think you can win. You can't even imagine the forces that are lined up against you."

He stands up abruptly, looking down at you from his dominant position. You keep your eyes averted, desperately hoping he gets out soon. His presence is a crushing weight on your rib cage.

"Take care, Georgia," he says loudly enough for Opal to hear.

You watch as he gives her a full-on smile. "I admire you for doing this job," he says. "It can't be easy."

"Oh, it's not so bad." Opal's cheeks are flushed, and her voice has risen an octave.

Kyle isn't just protecting his father. He's protecting his own ambition, too. Sons of presidents have followed in their fathers' footsteps before. Kyle has never made any secret of the fact that he wants to be the co-architect of his family's political dynasty.

Something occurs to you as you watch Kyle disappear down the hallway. His comment about Colby's dark secret must be about the girl Colby fixated on in college. There was a rumor of stalking, and a restraining order. Nothing could be substantiated, though, because all the allegations disappeared.

But given this, and how obsessed Colby seemed with Annabelle, you need to reconsider his story of the night he got pulled over by the sheriff and his father swooped in and stole his date.

Maybe the senator wasn't trying to seduce Annabelle, at least not at first. Maybe he was trying to protect her.

CHAPTER SIXTY-TWO

MANDY

My cell phone rings just as Colby is refilling my glass of wine over my protest that I don't want another drink.

I glance down at caller ID and my heart skips a beat. It's coming from the hospital.

It could be a nurse or doctor, but I know it's my sister. The certainty swells within me, seeming to originate deep within my cells. I can *feel* the desperate pull of my twin.

"Will you excuse me?" I say to Colby. "It's a friend calling, and she's going through a rough time."

He doesn't look pleased. "I hope it doesn't take too long."

I stand up and answer the call, walking a few feet away from him. "Mandy?"

Her voice is feather-light. I imagine her standing in the hospital with the phone cord stretched through the small window in the nurses' station. Her head is ducked down, and her body curled around the phone so no one can see her lips moving. The vision is so real it's almost as if she is here with me.

"Don't talk to Colby. It's too late. They got to him."

I look over my shoulder. Colby is illuminated by the two candles that send shadows flickering across his face.

"I'm with him now."

"Where are you?"

"In the middle of a nowhere having a picnic."

"Get out of there." The urgency in her tone pulls me up.

"Why?"

"Look, Colby isn't a bad guy—he just . . ."

"He *what*, Georgia?"

"He gets these fixations on women. I don't want that to happen to you."

I think about the barrage of messages and the bouquet of roses. "You may be a little late."

She exhales. "The private investigator—did he corroborate the video? You can go to the press. Maybe we don't need Colby. Come see me tomorrow, okay? We can make a plan."

"Tony Wagner is dead."

She falls silent and I repeat her name. There's nothing but the faint sound of her quick, shallow breaths.

"Oh no," she whispers. "I'm so sorry." Then the line goes dead.

I walk back to Colby. He's taken advantage of my absence to shift even closer to my spot on the blanket. I've either got to sit practically on his lap or on the grass.

"Round two coming up." Colby pulls another platter from the picnic basket, this one filled with a sandwich on a baguette, deviled eggs, and sliced heirloom tomatoes.

I notice there's a second bottle of wine in the basket. I can't sit here for another hour or two, dodging his attempts at intimacy. If Colby's going to be a dead end, I need to spend my time following other leads.

"I'm sorry," I say. "I ate so much already . . . I don't have much of an appetite left."

"We can just sit awhile. You'll get hungry again."

Then a thought occurs to me. I don't have to follow Georgia's directives. I can ask questions of my own.

"I have to confess something," I tell him. "I was reading an article about that terrible crime, the Cartwright murder?"

"What about it?"

"The sister who was charged with it . . . the article said you'd dated her."

He reaches into the basket and pulls out a serrated knife and small cutting board. He lays the baguette on the board and saws off a small piece.

"We didn't date," he finally says. "Our families were close. You probably read that. We were friends since childhood, though we went years without spending much time together because she was always at boarding school."

"Still, it must be so strange to have someone you know accused of murder."

"I'm used to being around screwed-up people. I have been all my life."

I lean close to him and rest my hand on his forearm. "Do you think she did it?"

He shrugs and starts to move his hand to cover mine. A split second before my hand is trapped, I pull it out, pretending I was reaching for the piece of sandwich he just cut.

"The evidence seems pretty clear. A few of us saw Annabelle when they loaded her onto the stretcher . . ."

He swallows hard. His face grows pale.

"The right side of her face—that's clearly where she was hit. Only someone who's left-handed would swing a heavy weapon from that direction."

I nod, thinking about how I always lead with my left, whether I'm dragging a big suitcase by its handle or plucking a tissue out of a box.

"Georgia's great, but she always had a cold streak," Colby continues.

"What do you mean?"

"Once, when we were little kids, we were playing hide-and-seek in the basement of my parents' house. My brother Kyle was the seeker, and the three of us were trying to find a place to hide. Georgia told Annabelle to hide in the clothes dryer."

I take a bite of my sandwich and nod encouragingly at him.

"Annabelle gets in and Georgia closes the door. Then she turns the dryer *on*."

I envision Annabelle tumbling around in the tiny, hot space. A child would have to be deeply disturbed to do something like that to a younger sibling.

"What happened?"

"Luckily Annabelle kicked the door open. She was scared but not hurt."

"Her parents must've been furious."

Colby reaches for the knife and cuts another section of sandwich.

"They would've been if they'd known. But Georgia told Annabelle she'd put her in the dryer again and duct-tape it shut if she told."

CHAPTER SIXTY-THREE

GEORGIA

The constant shuffle of the bald man's footsteps is a countdown now, a reminder that time is running out.

You watch him come into view, round the corner and disappear, then reappear a couple of minutes later. Again and again and again. Your thoughts spin in constant loops, too.

Twenty years in jail—if you survive, which you won't—or medication that will render you insane. Which choice is less horrifying?

"Somebody's popular," Opal barks, her lips inches away from your ear. "Guess who's coming to see you now?"

She's taken to sneaking up on you ever since yesterday, when you hung up on Mandy and went to your room to lie on your bed, despairing. You were curled in the fetal position when Opal leaned in close and shouted into your ear, "Are you awake?"

You flinched, which was all she needed. Ever since, she's used every chance to blast her voice at you.

Did the senator's people kill Tony Wagner? Maybe they made it look like a heart attack or suicide. No one will question the coroner's findings too closely. Tony was a heavy smoker, and his nose and cheeks were lined with tiny purple veins from his years of alcoholism.

You'd asked Mandy to come see you today. Even if she's angry you threw her into Colby's path, she has to understand both of your lives are now at risk.

You need a Hail Mary play. Mandy is smart and tough. She can help you create one.

You drag yourself out of bed. You're too listless to comb your hair or change the clothes you slept in. Your eyes are having trouble focusing; it's as if your body is shutting down, preparing for the inevitable.

"Move it," Opal hisses as she leads you to the familiar room with two heavy chairs. Opal lingers a few feet behind your chair, her warm, heavy breaths landing on the top of your head.

Footsteps approach. They're lighter than yesterday's. It's a woman coming to see you; it must be Mandy.

Then your visitor steps through the doorway, her kind face creased with worry.

"Georgia? I was so worried about you . . . I had to come back."

It's Patty. She's wearing a dark pantsuit and low heels, and there's color in her cheeks. It's like she was two-dimensional before, and she's bloomed now that she's living back in the real world.

She takes the seat across from you. You can tell from her expression she recognizes your despair.

She glances at Opal. "Can we have a bit of privacy?"

Opal smiles smugly. "She's my one-to-one. I need to be here."

Patty assesses her. She's a businesswoman now, not an emotionally broken being. You're viewing her in a completely different light. You can envision her running a bank or holding court in a boardroom. She's not used to answering to people, you suddenly realize. She's used to *giving* the orders.

"I'm sorry, I didn't get your name?"

"Opal."

"Well, Opal, I understand that you need to observe Georgia, but you do not need to overhear our conversation, nor will you. So please step into the doorway. Unless you'd rather I get your supervisor?"

Opal's mouth puckers like she's bitten into a lemon. But she moves away.

Patty smiles at you, warmth flooding back into her expression. It thaws the ice around you a bit.

"I can't stay long, sweetie. I just wanted to tell you not to give up. Once you're out of here and feeling better, you won't believe how beautiful life can be. The things I took for granted—the sound of rain at night, or the feel of my cat purring against me—are so precious to me now. It *will* get better, Georgia. I promise."

She's trying to lift your spirits, but she doesn't understand.

"Is there anything you need?" she asks. "A change of clothes, or some food you're craving?"

A prickle of bright energy runs through your body as you consider the opportunity she just offered you. It's a risk, but one you have to take. What's the alternative?

You lean closer to her. "I need you to get the silver bookend tested for my fingerprints," you whisper. "Find a way to do it independently, without the police or my lawyer involved."

Patty's face is like a caricature of surprise. It's the first time she's heard you speak.

Your fingerprints aren't on the bookend. The shopkeeper put it in a box and wrapped it for you. Will it be enough to create reasonable doubt?

Patty's eyes flick up to Opal. Then she leans closer to you.

"I don't understand. What's going on, Georgia?"

You plunge in, your stomach dropping like you're leaping off a cliff. "Annabelle and Senator Dawson were having an affair. It was going on for a while, I think."

Patty's voice is incredulous: "What are you saying? Do you think he killed Annabelle?"

"Yes. Or maybe someone close to him."

She leans back and exhales. "My God."

"Do you believe me?" you ask desperately.

She looks you square in the eye. "I do," she says simply.

And the world blooms for you, too. You are acutely aware of everything around you: the gentle puff of cool air blowing from the vent above your head and the sweet smell of Patty's shampoo. Your favorite old sweatshirt, the one Mandy brought you, so soft and light against your skin. Hope expands in your chest. The world will be so beautiful to you now, if you just get another chance to live in it.

"I've known about their affair for a while," Patty whispers.

Your body jerks back as your eyes pop wide open. Her words make no sense.

"He saw Annabelle as often as he could. She was the only person he would ever rearrange his schedule for."

A shrieking noise erupts in your head. It's as if Patty has pulled off a mask, letting you see the cold marble surface beneath.

This can't be happening. Is it? Or have you already gone insane?

"If Annabelle went on a date, he made me find out all about the guy before the guy even rang the bell to pick Annabelle up. I think the good senator was a bit obsessed with your little sister. Maybe that's where Colby gets it from." Patty gives a little laugh.

Your mouth is bone-dry. Your fingers grip the edge of your chair. "You work for him," you whisper.

"Bingo." She smiles. "But you won't find me on any official payroll."

You grow faint and dark spots cloud your vision. You've read about people like Patty. They fly beneath the radar, doing the sort of dirty work that can't be traced to the politician it benefits.

She stretches her arms over her head, like she's luxuriating from waking up from a long nap.

"Do you know what it's like to have power over the most powerful person in the world? I will soon. It was worth cutting my wrists. I made sure to call 9–1–1 before I did it, and I didn't cut too deeply. These scars? They're my battle wounds. They'll remind the president every single day of what I did for him."

Bile rises in your throat. You have to get out. But Patty is between you and the door.

"I had to know what you knew, Georgia. And you caved so very easily." She's smiling. "One last thing. You say your fingerprints aren't on the murder weapon. I can assure you they are, Georgia. Do you actually think I'd miss a detail like that? So plead guilty or get the death penalty. The choice is yours. But that's the only choice you get to have for a long, long time."

CHAPTER SIXTY-FOUR

MANDY

Ever since our date last night, Colby has rung me incessantly. My phone shows eight missed calls and texts.

When my phone shrills yet again, distracting me and nearly causing me to run a red light, I snatch it up, ready to blast him.

But it's Georgia. "Where are you?" she asks.

"Heading to work."

"No!" she whispers. "Don't go to work."

Am I supposed to take orders from a woman who threatened to kill Annabelle when she was a little girl? I want to crack my phone down on the dashboard, but something in her tone stills my hand.

"A former patient came to visit me today. She works for the senator." Georgia's thready whisper raises goose bumps on my arms. She sounds almost like a ghost.

"What are you talking about?"

"Did you see her when you were here? Middle-aged, dark hair. She had gauze on her wrists."

The image comes to me. "Yeah, I saw her once when I was leaving."

I can practically hear Georgia's mind whirring. "That means she saw you. She could've made a phone call while you were here. Told them you were at the hospital visiting me and to track you. Have you had any indication someone is watching you?"

The late-night jingle of the bell on my bar's door. The computer warning. Those refrigerator beeps. Maybe someone didn't break into my apartment to *take* something. Maybe they left something behind— like a tiny camera.

I don't know what to say anymore. I don't even know what's real. I choke out the word: "Maybe."

"Don't go home, either. I think they know about you, Mandy. Do you have any idea how much danger you're in?"

The vision of Tony Wagner's body flashes before my eyes. "Where the hell am I supposed to go then?"

"A hotel—but use cash and a fake name. Or if you know anyone who has a house where you can crash, but not a close friend. You can't imagine how much information they'll be able to pull up on you. They'll know when you lost your first tooth, your social security number, whether you have a drinking problem or an STD. These people are ruthless."

My mind spins through possibilities. Then it comes to me: I can stay in Georgia's apartment. I haven't been there since the possible break-in at my apartment, and the only time I drove there in my car, I parked a couple of blocks away in an aboveground lot.

"Hang on a sec," I tell Georgia. I yank my wheel to the right, pulling into a parking lot for a strip mall with a twenty-four-hour grocery store. I find a spot and jump out, locking my car. I dart into the grocery story, then slip out a side entrance and speed-walk toward the other end of the mall.

"What's happening?" she whispers.

"I ditched my car."

"Good."

"Where are you going to stay tonight?"

"A hotel," I lie. I still don't trust Georgia completely.

"Now all we need is a plan." She's still talking, but my attention is commanded by the storefront window I pass. I step into the electronics store and tell Georgia to hold on. It only takes a minute to buy a burner phone. Something tells me I might need one.

"Once they've done away with me, you'll be the only one left who knows about the affair," Georgia says in the same eerie whisper. "Do you really think they're going to let you just walk away?"

"What if I call a reporter? I have that video downloaded on my phone."

"No reputable reporter would run that story. And if a tabloid did, the senator's office could claim the video was digitally altered and no one would take it seriously. They're going to be ten steps ahead of us."

"So where does that leave us?" I ask.

"We've got two days," Georgia says.

"Until?"

"Until you're the only one left."

Two days. And my mind is blank. "What are we going to do?"

She hesitates. "You're not going to like it."

My spine stiffens. "*What*, Georgia?"

"You need to get to Senator Dawson. You've got forty-eight hours to get him to admit he was sleeping with Annabelle."

CHAPTER SIXTY-FIVE

GEORGIA

Your entire life has been filled with luxury, but in the end, what you'll miss most are the simple things, like early-morning clouds spun into cotton candy by the rising sun.

The mental health representative sitting across from you has a row of permanent lines etched in her forehead, like a series of ocean waves. "I will represent you to the best of my ability," she tells you.

A cozy Sunday afternoon nap on your couch. A warm bath with lavender essential oils. The hopeful sound of early-morning birdsong.

"They found a piece of wire hidden by the top of your bed. If you were planning to hurt yourself, can you nod?"

Mandy has to get to Dawson, but that's a near-impossible task. Mandy might be able to hold her own at her bar, but there's no way she can take down a sitting US senator.

"Were you planning to try to hurt someone else with the wire, Georgia?"

A granite wall is tilting toward you, precariously close to crashing down and eliminating you. You need to prepare. It's probably better to go to jail. If you reach out to Patty and convince her you won't ever talk, maybe they'll let you live. Other inmates could have it in for you, but you made it this far here. Maybe you'll be one of the lucky ones. Twenty years from now, you'll be too old to have children, your business will be dead, and you'll have lost your apartment and your friends—but that's better than losing your mind.

"Take care, Georgia." The mental health representative stands up and walks away.

You sit lost in thought on the couch in the community room for a long stretch of time. Then the odor of vinegar assails your nose. Josh has materialized and is looking down at you. "So pretty . . ." he mumbles.

Medication has dulled his outer layer, but the core of a predator is intact. He sits down next to you. You look toward the nurses' station, hoping someone is seeing this. But they're all busy. You're on your own.

Josh's hand creeps out and lands on your thigh.

Your eyes dart to the hallways, then back to the nurses' station. No one is coming to help you. Opal is supposed to be watching you, but she's talking to the mental health representative.

Josh's hand slides higher up your thigh.

Something inside you snaps.

You put your hand on his and dig in your nails, hard. He yelps, and a nurse looks up, then exits through the plexiglass door and comes hurrying over.

"Josh, you need to move."

He stands up and follows the nurse, holding his injured hand to his chest.

He glares back at you, and instead of shirking or averting your eyes, you stand up. What does it matter anymore if the staff is onto you? Your time is almost up.

You follow him until he reaches his room. You almost wish he'd turn and try to fight you.

You're becoming a stranger to yourself.

CHAPTER SIXTY-SIX

MANDY

Scott's curt reply lands on my cell phone in response to my text asking him to cover for me tonight: Sure.

When I get back to my regular life—*if* I get back to it—I'll try to make amends with him.

I don't feel safe using Ubers anymore, but my burner phone lets me book a cab anonymously. I ask the driver to drop me off a few blocks away from Georgia's place.

I take the back exit to the building and don't let down my guard until I'm inside Georgia's apartment and have checked every possible hiding place. Then I put my six-shot back in my purse and double-lock the door.

I sit in silence in Georgia's office for a few minutes, thinking through my sister's idea. It has too many holes in it to count. But I may have come up with another way. I don't know if it's a better or worse plan, but I need to do something and do it fast.

I'm through with hiding and sneaking around, trying to find out the truth. Every single person in this tangled, sordid mess seems like a twisted liar—including my twin, who dragged me into it and complicated my memories of my parents.

Anger is tearing through me, the kind I felt in my bar when that woman was being hit, and when I found out what Beth's date had done to her in the fraternity house.

I jab out a two-sentence text on my burner phone, using the phone number Georgia gave me the last time we talked. Then I stand up and look in the full-length mirror on the door of her closet. I'm not dressing like a wealthy ex–sorority girl today, pretending to be someone I'm not. I'm going in as myself: My hair is up in a ponytail and I'm not wearing any makeup. I'm in jeans and a simple shirt. My cross-body purse carries my keys, two phones, and gun.

I start to head out, then turn around and tuck one more item in my bag.

I call for a cab and go into the lobby to wait, sitting on a couch in full view of anyone who might be passing by.

I'm done hiding. This needs to end today.

CHAPTER SIXTY-SEVEN

GEORGIA

Families love to tell stories about themselves—yours did, anyway. Most were about adorable things Annabelle did as a toddler, like call dessert "bazzurt." Honey loved recounting the tale of how she won the title of Miss North Carolina. Then there was the story about the time you tried to kill Annabelle by shoving her stroller into traffic.

That oft-repeated tale fostered bad blood between you and Annabelle from a very young age.

Family lore—which spread to Honey's circle of cohorts and beyond—went like this: Honey, along with a nanny, was taking you and Annabelle on an errand. You were walking because you were too high-energy to sit. Annabelle was in the fancy Bugaboo stroller, the kind celebrities favored. While everyone waited for the light to change to cross the street, you released the stroller's brake and gave it a push. The nanny yanked the stroller back just before Annabelle was hit by a car.

Evidence of your pathological envy, even as a small child.

It's your very first memory.

If Honey hadn't repeated the story so often, it wouldn't have wedged deeply into Annabelle's mind. But that origin story was what ultimately brought you and Annabelle closer together toward the very end of her life.

You'd barely spent any time together in two decades, ever since you'd left for boarding school. You certainly didn't meet for mani-pedis or call each other to chat. You texted on the rarest of occasions. The last one you'd received from her came months earlier, a flat, two-word message: happy birthday.

So when your phone rang one afternoon, you were shocked to see her name flash on the screen. You answered, assuming something monumental had happened.

"I was just with my friend Taylor," she blurted in a high, tremulous voice. "We were shopping, and her baby was in the stroller. Then, when we were waiting to cross the street, the stroller began to roll forward, even though Taylor put on the brake. I saw her do it."

You sank down onto your couch, holding the phone close to your ear.

"The baby is fine, but she could've been hit by a car. Taylor completely freaked out. And this older woman who saw it happen told her to sue the manufacturer—she said stroller brakes have this long history of being faulty. We looked it up and it's true. All kinds of companies have issued recalls because of it. Even Bugaboo, a long time ago."

You closed your eyes as hot tears filled them. You understood what Annabelle was asking.

The sights and sensations of that long-ago day came rushing back to you—the heat of the sun on your bare arms, huge cars whizzing by, the stroller beginning to roll. The panic tightening your chest. Your little hands stretching up and closing around the handle.

You released the words you'd held inside for so long they'd atrophied into a hard, painful knot in the center of your heart: "I was trying to save you."

The only sound you could hear for a long moment was Annabelle breathing.

Then she said, "I remember you telling that once to Mom. I must
have been five or six. She told you if you kept lying about it, you'd go
to hell. Who says that kind of thing to a little kid?"

You gave a bitter laugh. "If that was the worst thing Honey ever
did or said to me, I'd consider myself lucky."

You and Annabelle talked for a solid hour. The next day, you met
for your first sisters' lunch.

Yes, you told her to hide in the dryer. But Kyle Dawson turned it
on. Then Kyle told Annabelle you did it and said, if she told anyone,
you'd threatened to duct-tape the dryer shut next time. Annabelle
and Colby stared at you, wide-eyed, while you stood by silently. You
were too scared of Kyle to rebut him.

You pushed Annabelle into the lake because she was being bitchy
to you that day. The water was only a couple of feet high; it didn't
even reach her chest.

Siblings who fight and shout that they wish the other one would
die? You're far from the first sisters to do that.

Family stories are like the old game of telephone. As they get
passed along, details blur and change. Embellishments are added.

But everything was seen by Honey through the lens of you as the
villain and Annabelle as the victim.

That singular phone call created an opening in the membrane
surrounding your old world with Annabelle, one filled with mutual
distrust and antipathy.

It was why you came to her thirty-second birthday party. You
wanted to celebrate her and your new, fledging relationship.

In those final days together, you and Annabelle had other conversations. Rewrote old scripts. Flipped the lens Honey had built for you
both to see through.

"It was like she pitted us against each other," Annabelle said one
night. "I'm so sorry I was so awful to you . . . I'm ashamed. I hope
you can forgive me someday."

Her words seemed to ring through your apartment, tearing apart the remnants of that bitter old world and allowing light and warmth to flood the new one.

This is how close you became in that short amount of time: Annabelle was the only person you ever told about Mandy.

CHAPTER SIXTY-EIGHT

MANDY

I walk up the steps of the Cartwrights' grand front porch and ring the bell, waiting for David the butler to answer.

When the door opens, I can't help gasping.

A different man is standing there, staring at me with his bulging blue eyes. It's Reece DuPont.

His expression hardens as he takes me in.

"How can I help you?" he asks in a tone that's anything but solicitous.

"Hi, Reece." He blinks, and I feel a stab of satisfaction that I caught him by surprise by addressing him by name. "I need to see Honey."

"Come in." He stands back, opening the door to the cavernous hallway.

For a split second, I'm seized with the urge to turn and run. But if everything Georgia says is true, they'll find me.

I walk inside and Reece closes the door behind me. The house is utterly silent other than the echo of our footsteps as he leads me down the hallway and opens the door to the library. It's filled with dark paneled wall-to-ceiling bookshelves, making the space feel smaller than it really is. One thing I register right away: There's a skylight overhead, but no windows. No one on the outside can see what might unfold in here. A bouquet of lilies on the coffee table fills the air with a powdery, sickly-sweet aroma.

There's also only one door to the room.

Reece gestures for me to sit. I choose the chair that puts me closest to the door, just like I always do in the locked ward.

"Coffee?" he offers.

"This isn't a social call." There's no way I'm drinking anything this man gives me. Honey must've told him about my text. He had to have scrambled to get here before me. Either that or he's been ahead of me all along.

He assesses the remaining seats, then closes the heavy wooden door and takes the chair directly across from me.

"Would you like to tell me what this is all about?"

I want to shift away from him. But he'd probably view that as a victory. So I lean forward, matching his stare.

"The only person I'm talking to is Honey."

"You do realize she is a mother in mourning."

"I'm pretty sure she'll want to hear this. If she doesn't, I can find someone else who will."

In a quick, fluid motion Reece stands up and I suppress a flinch.

"A friend is coming to pick me up in thirty minutes," I lie. "If I don't walk out of here to meet her, she's going to the police."

He smirks, and I remember something else. The Cartwrights are close friends with the chief of police. They can probably make arrests happen with a snap of their fingers, just like Senator Dawson can.

I brace myself for what Reece might do next, but he simply opens the library door and walks out.

I stand, waiting for whatever comes. But nothing happens for several minutes.

He's probably sweating me, like a cop does to a suspect. He doesn't know how much I know.

I think back to how he opened the door and stood there, almost like it was *his* house. Honey's husband travels a lot. Could Reece have been here even before I texted? And if so, what exactly is Honey's relationship with Reece?

After another few minutes that feel like an eternity, the door opens and Honey stands there, her hair swept back and her face stony.

She doesn't look like a mourning parent. She looks livid. Reece is behind her, his expression so calm it's more unsettling than her rage.

"Did you send me that text?" she demands.

I nod. My text read: I have some important information about Annabelle and Senator Dawson's relationship. I'll be at your house within the hour to discuss it.

Maybe she's wondering how I got her private cell number, the one Georgia gave me at the end of our last phone call. Or maybe she already knows.

"There's something I need to show you," I tell her.

"Who are you?" she demands.

Confusion floods me. I was here only days ago, with her in the garden.

"You don't know who this is?" Reece asks. "She was at Annabelle's memorial service."

"I've never seen her before in my life."

When I was here, I looked a little different—my hair was down, I had on makeup, and I was dressed in the image I wanted to project. But that was just window dressing. Does she truly not recognize me?

I feel myself gaping, caught off guard. Then Honey steps closer, squinting. "Wait a minute. You're Annabelle's sorority sister."

Maybe she needs glasses and is too vain to wear them.

I press on. "I need to show you something." I reach into the bag strapped across me. My hand moves past the reassuringly cold metal of my gun, then closes around my cell phone. I pull it out.

I have to look down to navigate to the video Tony Wagner sent, which makes me uneasy. I quickly press play and hold it up.

Honey moves even closer, just out of arm's reach. I can smell her strong perfume and something else: the sour echo of wine on her breath. My heart pounds as the video begins to play.

"That's Annabelle's apartment," she says.

"Keep watching."

I see her eyes widen as she takes in Senator Dawson.

"He left Annabelle's apartment late on the night of his last wedding anniversary. Other people know about this. They were having an affair. It was going on for a long time right under your nose."

You wait for the shock to dawn in Honey's eyes, for her to start shrieking and turn on Reece, demanding that he summon the senator and Stephen. Annabelle's father will be apoplectic upon learning his best friend was sleeping with his young daughter. Everything is about to explode.

But Honey does the last thing you expect. She throws back her head and laughs.

"You stupid girl."

CHAPTER SIXTY-NINE

GEORGIA

"You have a twin sister?" Annabelle's expression was stunned as she gaped at you.

You were curled up on the couch in her apartment's living room, your feet tucked beneath you, a nearly empty bottle of sauvignon blanc on the coffee table. The clock had long since passed midnight.

"Have you talked to her?" Annabelle asked.

"Not yet." You confided how conflicted you felt because of how difficult family relationships have always been for you. You feared reaching out to Mandy would bring a new turbulence into the steady life you'd fought so hard to build.

Annabelle got it, of course. Only another sister would recognize the complications of your potential new relationship.

You told Annabelle about your fascination with the things you and Mandy had in common—the uncanny traits you shared. You even showed her the video of Mandy serving a drink, pointing out her left-handedness and double ear piercings.

"She raises one eyebrow when she asks a question!" Annabelle squealed. "That's so *you*!"

"Really?"

"Georgia, you've done that ever since you were little!"

You told Annabelle about your chatty bride Caroline, who described how she tracked down her birth mother through a private investigator. You explained that she gave you the name of the investigator, Tony Wagner, who tapped a government source to dig up your true birth certificate. You revealed how simple it was to get a DNA test done after Tony collected a water glass Mandy drank from at her bar and you provided him with a sample of your own. A day after Tony sent in the samples, the lab sent an email confirming your sisterhood.

"She looks a bit like you—but not in an obvious way," Annabelle said, staring at the screen. "I guess it's all those little things that add up. What was it like to find out about her?"

You struggled to put the sensation into words. "Have you ever been walking somewhere and passed a mirror and felt this electric jolt of recognition right before you realize it's actually *your* reflection? It was sort of like that when I watched this video. Like I knew her already, somehow."

You both grew quiet. Annabelle seemed lost in her own world for a moment. Then she took a deep breath and leaned toward you, like she was about to say something important. But her elbow grazed her wineglass on the coffee table, knocking it over. By the time you'd cleaned up the wine splatters, the moment had passed.

You knew, deep inside, she was about to confess her affair with Senator Dawson. You'd shared an enormous confidence with her, and she wanted to do the same.

But it was very late, and you'd have plenty of time for that conversation in the future, so you didn't press her.

Forty-eight hours later, Annabelle was dead.

CHAPTER SEVENTY

MANDY

Honey's laughter is far more disturbing than if she were screaming in rage. It sounds unhinged, like she has tipped into mania.

I fumble to regroup.

"You already knew about their affair? Well, soon everyone else will, too. This is all about to come crashing down. Think of how ugly it'll be—Georgia hired a private investigator to spy on Annabelle sleeping with Senator Dawson."

Reece DuPont steps closer to me, but at an angle, so he's between me and the door. I'm trapped. I put my phone in my purse so my hands are free, and I leave my purse unclasped. It'd take me only seconds to grab my gun and aim it at them, I reassure myself.

"Clearly there's a price for your silence," he says. "What is it you want?"

"Two things. The first is for Georgia to be set free. She didn't kill Annabelle."

"Oh, for God's sakes. Of course she did! Georgia was a monster from the start." Honey walks over to the bar set up in a corner of the room and reaches for a crystal-cut glass. She pours herself a glass of something amber-colored from a matching decanter and takes a deep drink. "How dare you come in with your threats of blackmail? You probably created that video. You can do anything these days with AI."

I shift, putting my back closer to the wall, my eyes darting between her and Reece. He feels like the bigger threat. But Honey is a wild card.

"And the second thing you want?" Reece prompts.

Why is he running the show? I wonder. Could he and Honey be having an affair? It feels more and more possible, given his proprietary attitude. My head begins to swim.

"What is the second thing you want?" Reece asks again.

It wasn't supposed to go this way. I'm supposed to be in control; it was going to be Honey asking me questions, desperate for information.

"I'm Amanda Ravenel. I'm Georgia's *other* sister."

A crashing sound explodes through the air. My head whips toward Honey. She dropped her glass, and the crystal is shattered across the dark wood floor.

She's staring at me like I'm a ghost.

Reece is watching Honey watch me. A startled expression crosses his face before he smooths it away.

"Why are you here?" Honey whispers. "You were never supposed to come back."

Honey did know my parents; I'm certain of it now. Maybe she didn't recognize them in the photo I showed her because her vision is weakening, or because their appearances had changed, similar to why she didn't recognize me at first. She assumed they were strangers because of how I portrayed them. We make snap judgments about people all the time, and miss seeing them as they truly are.

"It will be simple for me to prove beyond a doubt that I'm Georgia's twin, and I can assure you it won't just be the tabloids running that story. It'll be everywhere."

"What do you want from me?" Honey rasps. Her face is pale, and her skin seems to have collapsed; it's like she has aged a decade.

"Answers. My father worked for Pecan Tree Corp. What did my father do?"

I can almost see her wondering if she should lie.

"If you don't tell me the truth, I'm walking out of here right now."

"Ray was our butler," she says quickly. "He ran the household. Pecan Tree Corp. is one of the companies we own and we pay all our employees through it for tax reasons."

The fancy suit he wore at my graduation. His knowledge of fine wines and elegance. Now it makes sense.

"Did my mother work here, too?" I ask.

Honey shakes her head. "She had a job in town. Waitressing, I think."

"Why'd you pay my dad so much that last year, right around the time Georgia and I were born?"

Honey's eyes seem to sear through me. Hatred blazes in them.

"He took you away," Honey says. "That's what we paid him to do."

CHAPTER SEVENTY-ONE

GEORGIA

On the night of Annabelle's birthday party, the weather was so perfect it was as if Honey had made Stephen pay extra for it. A light breeze stirred the clear, pleasantly warm air as the setting sun splashed the sky with shades of tangerine and rose. Honey had gone all out to celebrate Annabelle, as usual, hiring a top caterer to stock a lavish buffet and a local celebrity DJ to keep the music flowing. Hundreds of votive candles scattered throughout the house and backyard tent bathed everyone in a golden light.

You were adept at gauging the cost of celebrations, and you put this one at sixty grand—and that was before Annabelle opened her gift of sapphire-and-diamond earrings.

You'd made a last-minute decision to attend when your relationship with Annabelle turned around. You didn't have much time to shop for a gift, but one thing you'd discovered you and Annabelle had in common was a love of reading.

After you dropped off your bride Caroline's family Bible at the specialty bookbinder to repair the tear in the cover, you popped into the boutique next door and found a pair of heavy silver bookends in the shape of her initials. After a stop at your apartment so you could file away the receipt in Caroline's white binder and change into your backless silver dress, you headed to the party at your parents' estate, the place that had never truly been your home.

"Good evening," David the butler said stiffly as he opened the door to you. Clearly he still thought you were the enemy.

You greeted him and entered the house, nodding to Dee Dee Dawson, who was holding court in the living room with a group of sycophants. She pretended not to notice you.

Dee Dee looked like a woman on the verge. Her voice was too loud; her affect was brittle. A lock of hair had freed itself from her chignon and snaked down the back of her neck. For the first time, you felt a twinge of pity for her. She'd sold her soul a long time ago in exchange for a privileged lifestyle.

Then you saw Annabelle. Never before had you and she greeted each other with any warmth. This time, she ran to you and wrapped her arms around you tightly.

"Happy birthday," you said, putting her gift down on the dining room buffet with the others.

At that moment, you heard someone calling your name. You turned and saw Honey and Stephen approaching.

"Georgia, perfect timing. We need a photo!" Honey cried. This was a surprise. Honey wanted to include you?

Then Honey handed you her iPhone. Of course. You were the photographer, not the family member.

But this time, Annabelle spoke up. "What are you doing, Mom? I want Georgia in the picture."

"Well, who's going to take it then?"

Honey's voice was syrupy, but her expression was steel.

"We have plenty of the three of us." Annabelle took the phone from your hand and gave it to Honey. Then she walked over and put her arm around your waist. She'd just crossed enemy lines, you thought.

When Honey grudgingly snapped the picture, your smile was genuine. You thought you caught Stephen's lips curve up, too.

The arrival of another set of guests distracted everyone, and you slipped away to get a much-needed glass of Sancerre.

Snippets from that evening are seared into your mind, like a video montage: The senator twirling Annabelle on the dance floor to the Bruno Mars song "Just the Way You Are" while Dee Dee stared at them and rapidly emptied her glass of gin and tonic. Colby was watching, too, his expression darkening. Dee Dee stepping forward—maybe to cut in?—as Honey hurried over to Dee Dee's side, distracting her by whispering into her ear.

You'd give anything to know what Honey said.

You were mentally coming up with possibilities when you felt a tap on your shoulder. It was Alden, the son of the chief of police, whom you'd dated a while back.

"For old times' sake?" He held out his hand in an invitation for a dance.

You felt the warmth of his strong body close to yours, and listened to him singing along to the music. Alden had a good voice, deep and tender.

When the song ended and you broke apart, you lifted your hand to his cheek and looked into his eyes. Maybe it was the recent softening of your heart, or perhaps it was just the wine that made you so unfiltered.

"You deserve someone really great," you whispered. "It was never you . . . It's me. I don't know how to love someone." Maybe that part of you had been broken long ago when your family taught you that you were unlovable.

You pulled away before he could respond and stepped off the dance floor, planning to head home.

But Annabelle intercepted you.

"Don't leave yet. I need to talk to you."

She glanced behind her. Senator Dawson had rejoined his family. He was standing next to Dee Dee. Colby was with them, too. So was Kyle. They all seemed to be watching the senator stare at Annabelle.

The way he was looking at her sent a chill sweeping down your spine. It was a proprietary stare, as if, despite all the friends and family here to celebrate her, Annabelle was his and his alone.

Annabelle turned her head and caught sight of the Dawsons, too.

"Not here," she murmured, squeezing your arm so hard it hurt. "Let's go inside."

CHAPTER SEVENTY-TWO

MANDY

He took you away. That's what we paid him to do.

Honey's hideous revelation rings in my ears. It's like I've been sucker punched; I can't catch my breath.

"Why?" I finally gasp.

"Because I wanted one baby, not three."

My mind swims as I struggle to make sense of her words. She seems to grow impatient with me, stalking to the bar to pour herself a fresh drink. The remains of her first one are still on the floor, but she just steps over the puddle studded with shattered crystal.

I hold the most important cards, I remind myself. It helps me regain my voice.

"I'm going to need a better explanation."

"Reece, will you give us a moment?" Honey asks.

He steps out of the room, closing the door behind him.

Honey tosses back a big gulp of her drink and exhales. "My husband couldn't get me pregnant, so we decided to do a private adoption. Then, a few months before the young lady gave birth, I discovered I'd gotten pregnant against all odds."

I notice the way she puts the infertility blame squarely on her husband and refers to my and Georgia's birth mother as "the young lady." Honey is as cold as the ice clinking in her crystal glass. I can't imagine how horrible it must've been for Georgia to grow up under her watch.

"Then—surprise!—two babies were born. Technology wasn't as sophisticated back then, and no one realized she was having twins."

Honey swallows more of her drink. The alcohol seems to have a calming effect on her; her composure returns.

"Ray—your dad—desperately wanted a baby; I could see the longing in his eyes that first night, when Stephen and I brought you and Georgia home. You had colic and you screamed your head off. I was losing my mind, but Ray just stepped in and took over. I've never met a man with so much patience. He walked with you for hours and hours, that night and the next, even though he was off duty. He was the only one you'd take a bottle from, too."

"So you just . . . *gave* me to him?" Like she was casting off an ill-fitting item of clothing, I think.

"It was a kindness, don't you see? Ray and his wife—what was her name?"

"Cynthia," I say quietly, feeling my cheeks burn. "My mother's name was Cynthia."

"Yes, he and Cynthia desperately wanted a child but had given up hope of being able to have one, he told me. You even had dark hair, like he did. Georgia had light hair, like me. It felt destined."

She separated us by picking the most desirable baby, like she was plucking the ripest apple from one of her espalier trees.

"Why did you pay him off if they wanted me so badly?"

Honey's eyes dart toward the door. Mine follow her gaze. I think I hear a noise just outside it, but I'm not sure. The emotions roiling in me are dulling my senses.

Is Reece leaning against the door, ready to burst inside? I may be outnumbered, but I have evidence in my safe-deposit box, I remind myself. Plus, I have a gun.

"We handled all the legal papers, but they couldn't stay around here, not when they suddenly had a new baby. People would ask questions.

We gave him a generous bonus so they could take you somewhere else."

I can't imagine any universe in which Honey would spontaneously be generous.

"You didn't want anyone to know you got rid of an extra baby who was inconvenient," I challenge. "You paid him off to keep him quiet. Did you make them sign something? That's why my parents never told me about my twin."

Honey's eyes narrow. "If they didn't tell you, then who did?"

I'm not going to let her steer this conversation. "You told everyone my father stole from you. Jewelry, silver—you made that up so you'd have an excuse for why he disappeared."

She shrugs. "He got what he wanted and I didn't hear him complaining."

I keep pummeling her with questions.

"I have a video showing Senator Dawson leaving Annabelle's apartment late on the night of his wedding anniversary. Maybe you don't care. But don't you think it'll raise questions, especially since bank records will show that Georgia paid for the investigation?"

I'm bluffing; Georgia might have paid cash, for all I know. But Honey doesn't react. She merely refills her drink. I can't begin to imagine how much alcohol is already coursing through her body, but she seems sober. Which means she drinks quite a lot.

"Show it to whomever you want. No one will believe it's true. Like I said, people can doctor anything these days."

She's so blithe it catches me flat-footed. Where's her outrage and maternal protectiveness?

"It'll be enough to open an investigation," I blurt. "Maybe a good investigator can find a strand of the senator's hair on Annabelle's comforter or in her shower drain. They can match the DNA to him and prove the senator was in an intimate place."

Honey suddenly grows very still. She carefully sets down her drink.

The atmosphere in the room just shifted. The hairs on the back of my neck rise.

"I'd like to show you something," Honey says.

She walks to one of the bookshelves and selects a thick, maroon-covered volume at her eye level. It looks like a legal tome. I watch while she opens it.

Something is off; my sixth sense is screaming at me to get out of here.

Then I see it.

It isn't a thick legal book. It's a hiding place for the gun now in Honey's hand. She's aiming it directly at me.

CHAPTER SEVENTY-THREE

GEORGIA

On the night of Annabelle's last birthday party, you argued with her. That wasn't new; you'd fought countless times before. But this time, the tenor of your discussion was different.

"I'm so sick of how Honey treats you!" she yelled. "It's disgusting!"

Annabelle was finally seeing old dynamics in a fresh light—the family photograph meant to exclude you; the excesses of her party versus the ones your parents never threw for you; the way Honey introduced her to a new neighbor as "my daughter," as if there were only the one.

"I'm going to confront her. And if she doesn't start being kinder to you, she's going to lose me, too," Annabelle snapped.

You felt a forgotten old flicker ignite inside you. It was the stirrings of hope. No matter how old you were, it still hurt to have your mother show she didn't love you. You extinguished the flicker before you spoke so your voice would remain steady.

"Don't bother. She's your mother, not mine."

"That's bullshit! You deserve better!"

Annabelle's outrage was probably partially fueled by shame for the way she'd colluded with Honey. But back then, she was a child, just doing what was expected of her. You weren't bitter about it anymore. Besides, whenever she'd come at you, you'd given it right back to her.

"It's going to make things worse for me if you get everyone riled up," you'd shot back. "Just leave it alone."

She'd stared at you for a long moment, breathing hard. In a gentler voice, she said, "Okay. If that's what you want."

"Look, it's late and we've both had a few drinks," you began.

A chime sounded on Annabelle's phone then, the same bright note that alerted you whenever you had a new text or email from a sender you'd flagged as important. She looked down at the screen and her body language shifted. Became more rigid and alert. You could tell she was distracted. The message on her phone was far more pressing than anything else to her.

"Let's talk tomorrow, okay?" she suggested. "How about brunch?"

"You're going to be too hungover for that," you told her, trying to lighten the mood. "Let's have dinner. Come to my place. I'll order us something yummy."

"See you then." She started to hug you goodbye, then said, "Wait, I didn't open your gift yet."

"It isn't anything much . . ." you began, but she was tearing through the wrapping paper and opening the lid of the box to look at the bookends.

She lifted out the *A*, admiring the hammered silver. "They're so beautiful," she murmured. "Like a work of art."

"Happy birthday, sis," you replied. It was the first time you'd called her that. A big smile erupted across her face.

She hugged you and whispered something into your ear that took your breath away. You couldn't respond because you were on the verge of tears.

Then Annabelle glanced down at her phone again. You could tell she was eager to get back to the message. It had knocked everything else out of the forefront of her mind.

You walked down the hallway to the powder room, where you took a few minutes to steady yourself, splashing cold water on your face and blowing your nose.

You had to retrace your steps past the dining room to reach the front door. Your silver purse was in your hand, and you were count-ing the moments until you could slip off your heels in an Uber.

The dining room was empty; Annabelle must've left.

Then your peripheral vision registered something odd. Your head jerked around reflexively.

You were staring at the soles of Annabelle's bare feet sticking out at an angle into the open doorway.

"Annabelle?" you cried out, your voice high and strangled.

You hurried into the room. She was lying down, motionless. Her shoes were off, like she'd been knocked out of them.

You nearly slipped in the fresh blood puddling around her head as you rushed to her side. Had she passed out? Fallen and hit her head? There was a gaping wound on her right temple.

She stared up at you with empty eyes. A few minutes ago, your sister had been vibrant and whole. Now Annabelle was dead.

Time shuddered to a stop. You opened your mouth to scream for help.

But Honey beat you to it, her voice rising to a shriek as she rushed to Annabelle's side: "Georgia, what have you done!"

Then Honey launched herself at you, clawing at you and scream-ing in rage.

CHAPTER SEVENTY-FOUR

MANDY

I've held a gun before, but I've never stared into the small round eye of a pistol's muzzle.

"What are you doing?" I gasp.

"Every good Southern woman keeps a gun around just in case," Honey tells me. "You never know when an intruder is going to come into your home under false pretenses."

"I'm not—" I start to protest, then fall silent. I gave a false identity to Honey and her butler the last time I came here. They won't even have to lie about it.

"Did you know North Carolina is a stand-your-ground state?" she asks.

She isn't posing a question. She's giving me justification for what she's about to do.

I feel it build up in me, the dark, bottomless rage that sweeps over me from time to time. If I had a chance of being faster than a bullet, I'd leap through the space between us and rip off Honey's head.

It's a struggle to stand still and let her claim control. Adrenaline is coursing through my body—the fight-or-flight response—and I've never been one to run. My entire body is straining to attack her.

"You think the senator was fucking my daughter?" The words sound especially coarse coated in Honey's genteel drawl.

"I don't care." I enunciate all three syllables. "All I want is for Georgia to get a fair trial."

"Michael Dawson is a dear friend of our family. He loved Annabelle, but not like that."

My eyes dart around the room, gauging time and distance. There's nothing within reach I can throw at Honey. I can't duck beneath furniture because she'll see me. I can't get through the door before a bullet hits me. If I scramble for my gun, she'll fire before I can aim at her.

There's no escape.

"Why are you doing this?" I ask. "You said yourself no one would believe the video."

"You pushed me too far," she replies. "You never should've come here."

I should be terrified. But rage is tamping out all my other emotions. Honey threw me away when I was a helpless baby. She kept me from my twin. She made my parents lie to me for my entire life.

Honey feels like the nexus of all evil.

Something is nagging at my subconscious, cutting through the edge of my fury and commanding me to pay attention. My mention of a DNA test for the senator incited Honey. That was the only thing that set her off. Why would she want to kill me over that particular detail?

Honey releases the safety. The clicking sound seems to reverberate between my ears.

My vision tunnels as she lowers the gun another inch, aiming for the center mass of my body. I have no idea if she's a good shot. I'm less than six feet away from her. Maybe if she misses, I'll have a chance.

"Want to know a secret?" she whispers, stepping closer to me. She's not going to miss.

My blood runs cold. She looks deranged. Mascara is smeared beneath one of her eyes, and her lips are thin and hard.

"I'm going to sleep well tonight," she whispers.

In the instant before Honey pulls the trigger, time slows to a crawl. I inhale the cloying scent of the lilies filling the air. I'm aware of the dark glitter of Honey's eyes.

And I see her hand steady on the gun.

Her *left* hand.

The missing puzzle pieces rearrange themselves and slide into place.

"You killed Annabelle!" I manage to shout.

Then something explodes into my side and I'm knocked backward to the floor. I can't breathe. The pain is like an electric shock.

In the strange, silent numbness that follows, I'm vaguely aware of the door bursting open and a man appearing.

It's Senator Dawson. His dress shirt is unbuttoned at the top and his hair is rumpled.

"What happened?" he shouts at Honey.

"I did it for you!" she cries. She moves closer to me. I can see the gun rising in her hand again. I start to fumble in the bag still strapped across my body for my own weapon, but my fingers are slow and clumsy.

The senator comes up behind Honey, knocking her gun to the floor and wrapping her in a bear hug. She thrashes for a moment, then sags in his arms.

But this isn't like Annabelle's funeral, where he was comforting her. Even in my dazed state, my body suffused with agony, I see his arms tightening.

"You're hurting me!" she cries.

He looks at me. "Why did you say she killed Annabelle?"

The edges of my vision are receding. Every breath is agony. I'm about to pass out. But I have to tell him what I realized after Honey reacted to my comment about collecting the senator's DNA from Annabelle's room.

An investigation would also test samples of Annabelle's DNA to rule out her hair or body fluids in the room. And those two DNA tests, side by side, would turn up something incendiary.

The senator's rumpled appearance confirms my suspicion. He probably hurried downstairs straight from Honey's bed.

"Because she didn't want anyone to know you were Annabelle's father," I gasp.

My words find their mark, true as Honey's bullet.

The senator's face turns ashen.

"No, no, it wasn't like that! I did it for you!" Honey yells. "Annabelle began to suspect. She took one of your cigar butts and got your saliva tested. The company emailed her the results the night of her birthday. She wanted to confront us together, to tell Stephen. She said she was sick of this family's lies. Don't you see, darling? I only tried to keep her quiet so Stephen wouldn't know."

I start to swim in and out of consciousness, feeling my mind drift into a dreamlike state.

"I didn't mean it!" Honey is begging now. "It was a horrible accident. But I did it all for you!"

Love can look so many different ways, I think. It can be reflected in a man walking a baby through the darkness of night to provide comfort to the little being who doesn't even belong to him yet. It can mean a mother who looks up every time her daughter comes through the door with a smile so big it's like someone is delivering a gift.

It can also mean protecting a daughter, like the senator did to Annabelle.

His methods were harsh, but he didn't interrupt Colby's night with Annabelle because he wanted her for himself. He did it because he didn't want Annabelle to date her half-brother.

"You took away the only person I've ever loved!" the senator roars.

Honey's face collapses. His words seem to eviscerate her.

"You love *me*!" she cries. "We still have each other!"

His silence provides his answer.

Annabelle was the only person the senator loved, but it seems as if the senator was the only one Honey loved. She killed her own daughter in a fit of rage to preserve her affair and reputation.

The last thing I see is the senator violently shaking Honey, her head whipping back and forth, as he screams obscenities at her.

Then I slip out of consciousness.

CHAPTER SEVENTY-FIVE

GEORGIA

Patty lied about almost everything, but she told you the truth when she spoke of the joy in simple moments.

That first inhalation of fresh air, misty from a recent rain shower, when you step outside the hospital. The symphony of noises filling your ears—a car's radio playing reggae music, two women laughing together, a crow squawking up on a telephone line. The alternately distracted, happy, and worried expressions of passersby. Every moment is so beautifully rich and real. It conjures in you a sense of radiance.

You soak it all in and think about how often the tales we tell ourselves are fictions. We're both the unreliable narrator and the gullible listener in our own life stories.

Annabelle learned that lesson when you and she forged a new relationship before Honey killed her in a flash of rage and panic. But you were every bit as guilty of seeing things through a warped lens as Annabelle.

You now know the senator rushed to her side on the night of his wedding anniversary because she texted him, hysterical, in the back of a police car on the way to a holding cell. She'd been pulled over and gotten a DUI after making the bad decision to drink a third glass of rosé at happy hour. She knew Senator Dawson was the only one who could get her out of it. He met her at the police station and got the charges to disappear, then drove her home. Tony Wagner's men captured the video of him leaving her apartment after he'd gotten her settled.

You saw something different about that night because you expected to.

Senator Dawson told you the truth himself after he finished giving his statement to the police. He personally came to the locked ward to secure your immediate release.

At first you thought it was a publicity stunt: the senator heroically helping the wrongly accused woman. But no paparazzi were hovering around to document your release, which means he didn't tip them off. And when he apologized, it sounded sincere.

"I'm sorry you went through this. It couldn't have been easy."

"It still isn't," you reply as you inhale another breath of precious, free air. You haven't even begun to mourn Annabelle, or try to reassemble your life.

"Can I offer you a ride home?" he asks as you stand in front of the hospital together.

You shake your head. "No thanks."

The hollowness around his eyes ages him a decade since you last saw him. He'll be in mourning for the rest of his life.

But he won't mourn losing his relationship with Honey. He turned on her in an instant when he learned what she'd done.

It all makes sense now. The powerful love and longing on the senator's face when he watched Annabelle was that of a father for his only daughter, one he could never publicly acknowledge. The puppy he brought her, his murmured words of adoration that night in the antechamber, him checking out the men she dated—none of it was salacious. Had you peered into the antechamber for a few moments more on Christmas Eve, you would have seen him kiss her forehead or cheek, not her lips. And to her, he was like a much-beloved uncle.

He starts to walk away. Then he turns back. "I vowed to get justice for Annabelle. And I will."

His steely gaze tells you Honey has no chance.

"Good," you reply.

The media is feasting on the scandal again, but this time there's a new angle: Honey confessing to the murder of her beloved daughter. The details are so juicy they're bursting all over the internet: Annabelle was the result of a tryst between the senator and Honey. She was the secret that bound them together.

What surprised you was that the senator did the right thing by turning Honey in to the police and confessing to the affair. Whether the senator rises above this political and personal stain and claims the presidency has yet to be seen. But you wouldn't discount him. Now that Annabelle is gone, the only thing in life he adores is power.

Which means Patty, the senator's fixer, will be more dangerous than ever. But you decide not to think about that today. You've been suffused with terror about the future ever since Annabelle died. Right now, you want to live in the moment.

You stand on the curb by the hospital's main entrance, watching a minivan pull into the parking lot and a man run around to open the door for his very pregnant wife. They both pause halfway to the entrance, huffing out breaths together, the man encouraging her through the contraction. You look in the other direction and see a burly guy with tattoo sleeves walking a tiny, fluffy dog down the street. You feel laughter bubbling up inside of you for the first time in far too long.

You take another long look at the messy, beautiful life surging around you, drinking in every last drop. Then you turn and walk back *into* the hospital.

The first floor feels so different from the fifth, where the locked ward exists: The patients here are in light blue gowns, visitors and staff roam around freely, and you see only one security guard, a bored-looking woman.

You approach the desk and wait until the guard looks up.

You speak the words aloud for the first time: "I'm here to visit my sister Amanda Ravenel."

CHAPTER SEVENTY-SIX

MANDY

When I open my eyes, I see Georgia's face.

For a moment, I think I'm still asleep. She was just in my dream; we were floating together in the ocean, the baby waves lapping warm and soft against my skin. Georgia and I were holding hands; it was just the two of us in that endless swath of deep blue water.

I blink a few times and realize I'm lying in a hospital bed, an IV threaded into my forearm, my midsection swaddled in a white wrap. The room is dim, with only one soft light glowing. I try to move, then groan. Even breathing hurts.

"I have to admit, now that you're the patient, I like this role reversal better," Georgia says, smiling.

She's curled up in a chair pulled close to my bed, wearing the sweats I took out of her closet and brought her. I don't know how long she's been here. I don't even know how long *I've* been here.

"You slept for ten hours," she says, answering my unspoken question. "You've got a few broken ribs, but you're going to be fine."

"How long have you been here?" I ask my twin.

"A couple hours. Senator Dawson convinced the cops to release me after he gave his statement incriminating Honey and the charges against me were dropped. Luckily I didn't have far to travel to reach you, even though the elevators in this place are really slow."

A tiny laugh escapes me, and I wince.

"Sorry." She winces, too. "They said you could get pain meds when you woke up."

She reaches for the nurses' call button and pushes it.

"Want some water?" she offers, picking up the tumbler on my nightstand. I nod, and she adjusts the straw before putting it to my lips. I drink deeply. Swallowing hurts, too.

Georgia must intuit that from my expression. Or maybe she feels it. She puts down the tumbler and walks into the hallway. A moment later, she returns, bringing with her a nurse.

"How are we feeling?" the nurse asks brightly.

"Like I was run over by a bus," I tell her, far less brightly.

"Broken ribs are no fun," the nurse says.

Fuzzy recollections float back to me: The wail of sirens approaching the Cartwright estate. Paramedics rushing me into the ER on a stretcher, an oxygen mask strapped over my face. Someone cutting away my clothes, then looking up in bewilderment, saying, "There's no blood."

The nurse injects something into my IV, and I feel a warm rush sweep through my body. Suddenly I'm drowsy again.

I know I was shot. I felt the explosive punch of the bullet. It slammed into me, throwing me to the floor and breaking my ribs. I passed out from the pain.

How is it possible I didn't bleed?

"Go back to sleep," Georgia tells me. "Maybe I will, too. I was having the best dream right before you woke up. We were together, floating in the ocean."

I fight against the tide of medicine pulling me back beneath the surface of consciousness. I want to tell her I've read about this phenomenon, called shared dreaming. It came up during my research into twins. It can happen when two people are deeply linked. When they are haunting each other's subconscious.

I struggle against the undertow pulling at me, but I'm no match for it. My eyelids are so heavy. I'm already starting to drift, even though I have so many questions for Georgia.

Before I can voice a single one, I lose consciousness again.

★   ★   ★

The room is brighter when I awaken. I smell the rich, earthy scent of fresh coffee. Georgia is still sitting vigil next to me, staring down at something in her hands.

"Morning," I croak.

She reaches for the tumbler again and I shake my head. She gestures to the Styrofoam cup of coffee on the nightstand and I nod.

"I would give my firstborn for that," I manage to say.

"Speaking of, who do you think was born first?" she asks.

We answer in unison: "Me."

"To be continued," Georgia says. She sets down the item she was holding in her lap, then plucks the straw from the tumbler. She dunks it in the coffee and holds it to my lips. I take a sip, then grimace.

"What kind of sadist drinks it black?"

"Stop being so high-maintenance," she teases. "They didn't have almond milk."

"When am I getting out of here?"

"Today. But you're coming to stay at my place for a day or two. Just till you're back on your feet."

"I don't understand," I say. "Honey shot me. I felt the bullet hit me."

Georgia picks up the item she was holding earlier and passes it to me.

"This was in your bag. Senator Dawson arranged to borrow it so I could show you, but the police will need it back as evidence."

My hand closes around the familiar shape of the fierce archangel Michael. This is the metal figurine my parents gave to Georgia as a baby, the twin of the one I have.

All in a rush, I understand.

My ribs broke beneath the shot's impact, but the bullet Honey fired never pierced my skin. That's why there was no blood.

I made a last-minute decision to grab the little statue my parents gave Georgia out of her closet and tuck it into my cross-body bag before I went to the Cartwrights'. Maybe it was superstition. It could have been intuition. But I think something bigger was behind it, something I can't fully explain.

The bullet tunneled into the solid metal instead of me; I can see the tortured path it left.

I stare at it, a lump rising in my throat, thinking about all the questions I still want to ask my parents. I'll never be able to get a full explanation of their motivations or challenge their decision to keep me from knowing about my sister.

But of this I'm certain: They loved me deeply.

More than that, I still love them.

I think about the words on the statue's leather pouch: *Protect Me Always.*

I close my eyes, and with everything I have, I will a message to my mom and dad: *You did.*

CHAPTER SEVENTY-SEVEN

GEORGIA

In a little while, you need to pick up Mandy from the hospital and bring her to your apartment. But these moments, right now, are for your other sister.

You sit beside Annabelle's grave, staring at her headstone and aching for the woman you barely had the chance to know.

When she was killed by Honey, you and Annabelle were in that first, heady rush of discovering each other. The truth is, you probably would have had a complex relationship, like many sisters. Both of you could be hotheaded and defensive. And even though you said you didn't hold anything against her, you stored a bit of lingering resentment. She probably did, too. In the years ahead you would've fought and made up. Been each other's support system and driven each other crazy. Like sisters do.

There would have been so much history for you two to unpack. Honey prized Annabelle, but hadn't truly loved her, either. Annabelle was the thing that tied her to the senator, and Honey was willing to sacrifice her daughter in an instant to preserve her decades-long affair.

It explains why Honey was so determined to eliminate the young widow the senator was falling for. It wasn't to help Dee Dee. That bit of vindictive revenge was for Honey alone.

Now she has no one left. And in the sweetest of ironies, Honey is reportedly planning to launch a temporary-insanity plea. She may be the one to live out her years in a locked ward.

Maybe you should feel sorry for Honey, but you don't. Your heart sewed itself closed to her long ago.

You stand up and brush off your jeans, sliding the handles of your tote bag over your shoulder. You walk away in the dappled sunlight, beneath birch and hickory trees, knowing you'll be back before long.

Inside your bag is the formal letter you've written detailing Opal's treatment of you and your suspicion that she planted the piece of wire in your room to make you look dangerous. It should be enough to get her fired, and you're going to insist the letter be part of her permanent file. Many of the patients in the locked ward are truly sick. They need help, not the machinations of a deviant health aide.

At the entrance of the cemetery, you turn and look back at Annabelle's grave, remembering your final moments together. Just before she died, Annabelle opened the gift you gave her. Then she gave you one in return, with her whispered words in your ear.

"I think you should call Mandy," Annabelle had said.

"I'm going to," you promised.

"She's going to love you, Georgia. How could she not?"

Your family used to make you cry all the time as a little girl. You'd promised yourself they never would again. But that night, you couldn't hold back your tears. Could it be possible after so long without even one sister, you could have two?

You'd hurried to the bathroom, leaving Annabelle staring at her phone. You now know she'd just received an email from the DNA lab confirming the samples she'd sent in of the senator's cigar butt and her own cheek swab proved he was her biological father.

You didn't hear a thing from inside the bathroom, but when you stepped back out, the world had tilted on its axis.

★ ★ ★

As you walk down the path toward the parking lot, a man slowly approaches, his spine curved by grief. Then he lifts his head and you realize it's your father, Stephen. The surprise dawning on his face reveals he didn't expect to discover you here, either. You both stop short.

At the same moment, you resume walking, meeting in the middle.

"Georgia." His voice is hoarse, like he's ill. He appears fundamentally changed. It's as if all the emotions he repressed through the years are finally seeping out, dragging down the corners of his eyes and his mouth, staining his hair and eyebrows an ashen gray, and pulling weight off his frame.

"I called you," he begins. "And I stopped by your apartment yesterday, but they said you weren't home. I left a message with the doorman . . ."

His voice trails off. You received his messages, but you ignored them. Just as he ignored you when you needed him as a child.

Then, like a contagion, it spreads to you. *Your* suppressed emotions come pouring out: Anger at the father who should have protected you. Disgust at him for being too weak to defy Honey. And beneath is a bottomless crevasse of hurt.

"How nice you tried to visit," you say, your voice icy. "Where were you the rest of my life?"

He bows his head, and you struggle against the lump rising in your throat. He looks completely broken.

"I know I made mistakes," he says haltingly, as if openness is a foreign language to him. "I thought if I provided for my family, I was being a good husband and father. I was taught that's what a man did. But you deserved more."

You feel your anger pop like an overfilled balloon, allowing pain to rush in and fill the void.

"Honey made it seem like I was evil!" Your voice sounds childlike to your own ears. It's as if you're aging in reverse, while your father is speeding ahead. "You loved Annabelle best because you thought she was your real daughter!"

Stephen shakes his head. "No."

You don't want to admit it, but you hear the ring of truth in his simple, powerful denial.

"You are my daughter, too, Georgia. You have always been my daughter."

You close your eyes, and his words wash over you like a balm, soothing the ragged surface of your wound.

Then Stephen says the last thing you'd ever expect.

"I knew Annabelle wasn't my biological daughter, either. But I loved her just the same."

Your eyes fly open. "You *knew*?"

"From early on. I saw how Honey acted around Dawson, and I know the way he is with women . . . Plus, Annabelle looked a little bit like him as a baby. It's easy to test these things to prove them."

Worlds fail you as you stare at the father you never truly knew.

You finally find your voice. "But why didn't you divorce her? And why are you still friends with him?"

Stephen shrugs. "Because deep down, I didn't care. I never truly loved Honey. Our marriage has been over for a long, long time. I'm not sure we ever actually had one to begin with."

Your mind swims as you realize what this means. Honey killed Annabelle to stop her from telling Stephen. But Stephen knew all along. So Annabelle died for no reason.

A hoarse cry escapes your throat. You see an echo of your pain wash across Stephen's face. He takes a step closer to you.

You grow dizzy. This is all too much to take in. "I should go."

"Maybe we can talk more sometime?" Stephen asks. "Or I can give you space . . . But I'll be here for you from now on. I promise."

The two of you stand there, the only remaining shards left from a shattered family.

"We could have lunch sometime," you say haltingly. Then you remember Stephen doesn't eat lunch—he prides himself on working straight through.

"Any day you like," he replies.

When he dropped you at boarding school, you left him reaching his arms out into empty air. But now you step forward and lean into him while he wraps his arms around you. You hear him take in a deep, shuddering breath.

Then your father says, "I have loved you since the day you were born. I didn't know how to show it. But I promise I'll learn. And I'll never stop trying to make it up to you."

CHAPTER SEVENTY-EIGHT

MANDY

"Why did Annabelle begin to suspect the senator was her biological father after so long?" I ask.

I'm sitting in a straight-back chair—it's easier on my ribs than curling up on the couch—sipping the sweet hibiscus iced tea Georgia made for me.

"Maybe she subconsciously knew it for a while. Kids tend to pick things up. And when I told her about you, it might've made her wonder what other huge secrets Honey had," Georgia says. "I explained how a DNA test confirmed you were my sister, which must have given her the idea to send in her own samples. And I was remembering years ago, our families took a vacation and the lake was surrounded by patches of poison ivy. Everyone got it except Dawson and Annabelle and Colby. I was so jealous because I was itchy and miserable for the rest of the week. I looked it up today. Immunity to poison ivy is a dominant genetic trait. Maybe Annabelle remembered things like that, too."

I nod, then wince. I never realized how many muscles are attached to my torso. Even tiny movements hurt. "I can't believe he and Honey were together for so long."

"Gross, right? I don't think Dee Dee had any idea. But it makes sense he was at the house when you showed up. He could only truly mourn Annabelle in front of Honey. And creepy DuPont was there to make sure no one caught them."

I take another sip of tea. The retro turntable is spinning Keith Urban's greatest hits, and the wall composed of windows showcases the city lights around us. Georgia is on the couch, her long legs folded beneath her, finally looking peaceful.

"Did you suspect Honey because she was left-handed?" I ask Georgia.

She shrugs. "No, I figured whoever did it was setting me up with that detail. Besides, there had to be others at the party who were left-handed. Ten percent of us are. Can you name even five other people you know of?"

I think about it for a second, then shake my head. "I guess I never really notice things like that."

I'm trying to be present for our conversation, but a sense of lethargy is overtaking me. I gave a statement to the police today, which took a lot out of me. I answered all their questions truthfully, but I didn't volunteer any additional information.

They were focused on pinning the murder charge on Honey; they didn't react when I casually mentioned that Georgia and I were twins who'd been adopted into different families as infants and that's how I got pulled into everything. I detailed Honey's drinking, her rage, and how the senator had stopped her from shooting me again.

"How are your ribs feeling?" Georgia asks.

"Perfect, unless I breathe or move," I tell her. "I've only ever broken my nose, but this is worse."

"Ouch. How'd you do that?" she asks.

"A marital arts sparring match last year. It wasn't that bad, but I kept getting nosebleeds for a week."

"I've only ever had a few stitches—" Georgia cuts herself off. Her eyes widen as she stares at me. "When exactly did it happen?"

I try to remember. "Last March, I think."

She picks up her phone and taps on it. "Was it a Saturday afternoon? March 16? Around 3 P.M.?" Intensity fills her voice.

"All the matches were on Saturdays, so probably. That timing sounds right. Why?"

She puts down her phone. She's turned so pale I'm glad she's sitting down.

"I was meeting a client at the florist that afternoon and I got this nosebleed. It was awful; I had to run to the bathroom to clean myself up. Just out of the blue, and it *hurt*. Like someone punched me in the face. I've never had a nosebleed in my life before. But all that week, I kept getting them. I finally went to the doctor, and he couldn't find anything wrong."

I have no words. She doesn't seem to, either. We just stare at each other.

"I've read about stuff like this happening to twins," she says haltingly. "I just didn't realize it was happening to us."

Georgia and I were wrenched apart at birth, but we stayed invisibly linked all along. I'm surprised by how much comfort that gives me.

I think about how I always wanted one best friend, someone as close as a sister.

Maybe my subconscious was seeking Georgia.

We talk for a while longer, sharing more of ourselves. I'm wearing a pair of her soft pajamas, and I already feel closer to Georgia than I ever have to anyone other than my parents.

Close enough that when a silence falls between us, I immediately sense a shift in her energy. She no longer feels at peace.

"What are you thinking about?" I ask.

"Remember that woman who faked her way into being a patient with me? She works for the senator, but not officially. Her name is Patty, unless she came in under an alias."

"Right."

"I asked her for help. And she relished telling me I didn't have a chance. If Tony Wagner's death wasn't from natural causes, I know she's behind it."

I put down my tea. "You think she killed him?"

"She would've hired someone. It's easy enough to do."

Georgia is twisting her hands together. Maybe she's thinking that Tony would still be alive if she hadn't asked him to track the senator.

"He was a nice guy, Tony," she says. "He pretended to be a curmudgeon, but he wasn't. I don't think he had any family, but he found you for me. He told me he'd had a brother who'd died in his forties, so he recognized the importance of siblings."

I nod, remembering that he sounded like a good guy when I spoke to him, too. "And Patty may have decided to exterminate him like a bug because he tried to help you."

Georgia blinks. "Wow, you're really angry."

"I despise the Pattys of this world."

"I don't know if the coroner has released the cause of death. But it'll be easy enough to find out. Do you think there's anything we can do?" she asks.

Yes, I think. It's important to always fight back hard. I feel a hitch in my pulse.

But I'm circumspect with my words. "If she did it, she needs to pay. More than that, she knows a lot about both of us and I don't like that. I still don't know if she had someone break into my apartment or car to leave a listening device. I need to search."

"If Patty had someone do that, it's probably gone by now," Georgia tells me. "She seems to pride herself on not missing a single detail."

"Let's give it a little time so we can think clearly. It's never a good idea to plan revenge when you're upset," I say.

Georgia gives a little laugh. "Not like we have a lot of practice planning revenge, but okay."

I smile but remain silent. There are a few things about myself I will never share with Georgia or anyone else.

Georgia pulls herself off the couch. "You look wiped out. You need to go to bed."

I watch as she shakes a few Advil into her palm, noticing how quickly she has reverted back to herself. Her red-gold hair is smooth and shiny, and her shirt and skirt drape across her body as gracefully as if they're couture.

She hands me the Advil, and I wash it down with the last of my sweet tea.

"You take the bed. I'll sleep on the couch," I offer.

"Don't be a fool, we're sisters. We're both taking the bed. But if you snore, I'm going to suffocate you with a pillow."

I smile. "Ditto."

"Can I ask you to do one last thing? Delete that video and destroy the thumb drive Tony sent," Georgia says.

"I'll do it tomorrow," I promise.

I stand up, bracing myself against the arms of the chair and enduring the stab of pain in my midsection, then shuffle to the bedroom.

As I brush my teeth, I hear her moving around the apartment, clinking silverware as she fits it into the dishwasher and clicking off the lights.

When I turn off the sink water, I hear another sound: soft sobbing.

I walk back into the living room. She's on the couch, her head in her hands, crying like her heart is broken. I walk over and rest my hand on her shoulder.

"I had to hold everything in at the hospital." Georgia looks up, her cheeks damp and her eyes reddened. "I guess I need to finally let it out."

"I get it," I tell her. "Do you want to be alone?"

She shakes her head. "I'm glad you're here."

She wipes her eyes, then looks down at the broken nail on her left index finger. She has filed away the rough edges, but it's still much shorter than the others.

"Do you know how this happened?" she asks, tapping her finger.

I shake my head.

"I was fighting off Honey. She killed Annabelle, then attacked me and tried to pin it on me. What sort of mother could do that to her children?"

I was the lucky twin, I remind myself again. But all I say is, "Honey was never your mother. She doesn't deserve that title."

Georgia nods and wipes her eyes again as fresh tears stream out.

"I feel guilty I didn't protect Annabelle in the end," Georgia says haltingly. "That's what big sisters are supposed to do. If I'd come back a minute or two earlier from the bathroom, maybe I could've stopped Honey . . . When I was in the hospital, I kept thinking about that. I even prayed to Annabelle, telling her I was so sorry."

I sit down on the couch beside her, wincing as my ribs protest. I stay there with my sister, my hand on her back, as she cries for everything she lost.

EPILOGUE

MANDY

I slip out of bed early the next morning while Georgia is still sleeping. I gaze at her for a long moment before I leave, finding it hard to tear my eyes away from her face. She's utterly familiar and an enigma all at once. She's endured so much throughout her life, yet you'd never know it to look at her.

But our surfaces are mirages. They project lies. Everyone has hidden layers, including me.

Especially me.

A few paparazzi are clustered around the entrance of her building, but no one knows who I am. My identity has been kept out of the news so far. A guy with long dreadlocks yawns and stretches out his arms as I walk past him and his colleagues. They're waiting for Georgia, so they miss the bigger story as I move down the block and climb into the back of an Uber.

"You live in that building?" the driver asks me, indicating the paparazzi. He turns down the radio as I reply.

"No, just visiting a friend," I tell him.

In the rearview mirror, I see his eyes flick to me. "Not her, though? That woman who killed her sister?"

I frown. "She didn't do it, you know. Her mother did—Honey Cartwright."

The driver pulls away, heading in the direction of the strip mall parking lot where I left my car. I hope it hasn't been towed.

"Yeah, but I was just listening to the radio, and this guy says he thinks the mother sacrificed herself to save Georgia. That's why she confessed even though she didn't do anything," the driver tells me.

"That's quite a spin," I say.

"I mean, I could totally see that. A mother's love is fierce, right?"

"It should be." Then I hear the name Dawson on the radio, and the driver turns it up as we both fall silent.

"Thirty-two years ago, I committed an indiscretion." The senator's deep, warm voice is confiding. "My terrible moment of weakness resulted in something good and beautiful: Annabelle Cartwright."

The driver shakes his head. "Are any politicians faithful these days?"

"My beloved wife, Dee Dee, forgave me long ago, as did my dear friend Stephen Cartwright," the senator continues. I muffle a snort. "And now I ask for the public's forgiveness, too."

The senator talks for another minute or so, announcing a new tax cut he's pushing on Capitol Hill, clearly trying to give the press something else to write about now that he's delivered his mea culpa.

The driver pulls into the lot, and I see my Honda waiting for me. I exit the Uber and slide into my front seat. Before I drive off, I do the thing I've been dreading. I send Scott a text: Talk tonight?

I don't know what—if anything—might happen between us. I don't think I'm cut out for a serious relationship, let alone marriage and kids. The truth is, there's a hollowness inside me I've hidden from everyone I've ever known. I felt like it filled up with a missing piece when I met Georgia. But I think that was only part of the reason.

The other was because of the location. The secret part of me that has always felt wild and ferocious somehow *fit* in the locked ward.

I'm so lost in thought it doesn't seem to take long at all to drive to my bank. A teller gives me access to my safe-deposit box. As I open it, he steps away, allowing me privacy. I remove the silver thumb drive sent by Tony Wagner and tuck it in my purse. I'll destroy it with a hammer as soon as I get home, like I promised Georgia.

Then I reach for the second item in my hiding place: the envelope of Polaroid photos I took more than a decade ago at college. I took Polaroids that night so they couldn't be traced to me through my phone. It was one of many details I considered while I waited to execute revenge on Beth's attacker. Like I told Georgia, it's important for your mind to be clear, past the first red-hot flush of rage, to enact a solid plan.

I've already begun to consider one for Patty. She needs to be discredited in the mind of the senator. I can't have her working with him, not when she may decide at some point that Georgia and I are threats to her. Depending on the cause of Tony's death, Patty may require more punishment.

I look down at the first picture, staring into the intoxicated face of Bradley, the guy who raped Beth, shattering her life and leaving me bereft and alone. He had no idea what was coming when I put myself in his path at a campus bar one weekend night. Bradley was pretty clueless; he hadn't noticed me following him for days, seeking out for the right opportunity. I don't know if he knew I was friends with Beth, but if he did, he didn't care. Maybe he didn't believe he'd done anything wrong.

It was easy to lean forward and stare into his eyes, giggling at his dumb jokes. I ordered rounds of shots, making sure he drank many more of them than I did. When he went to the bathroom, I took the strong dose of sleeping pills I'd ground up and stirred it into his beer. I needed him compliant so I could strip off his clothes and make him pose in humiliating ways. I planned to photocopy the pictures and spread them all over campus.

I was burning up for the way he'd abused Beth when she was helpless. For the way he'd taken my friend away from me.

When he finished his beer, I suggested we take a dip in the big fountain on campus before going back to his room. It was a tradition for students to dunk themselves in the fountain, but I pretended I hadn't yet.

"You know you want to see me in a wet T-shirt," I giggled, lacing my arm through his as we left the bar. I was practically dragging him by the time we reached the fountain with its high spray of water providing both noise and a visual shield against anyone approaching. I propped him up against the base while I wrestled him out of his clothes.

I made him pose several different ways, positioning his limp limbs to reveal everything, and documenting it all with my camera.

When I was done with him, I heaved him up over the side of the fountain. I figured the shock of water would wake him up and I'd get one last picture of him naked and vulnerable and afraid. Just the way he'd left Beth when he was done abusing her.

But he didn't wake up.

A feeling of deep peace swept over me as I watched him float face down. I thought about turning him over, but I didn't. I just watched the man who'd raped my roommate die.

No one ever discovered what I did to him.

Now I stare at the photos, including the last one I took of his lifeless body in the water, then tuck them back into the envelope and lock them up.

"Got everything you needed?" the bank employee asks as I walk through the main lobby.

I smile at him. "I sure did."

I pass a round table and chairs in the waiting area by the front door and notice a copy of today's paper on the table.

The headline is about the Cartwright murder. Pictures of Honey, Annabelle, and Georgia are splashed above the fold—including one of Honey with both girls when they were babies, looking sweet and loving. The picture of Georgia is far less flattering; she's caught off guard, frowning. It seems like the paper is deliberately stoking speculation about who was Annabelle's real killer.

Some people will always believe Honey sacrificed herself to save

Georgia in a heroic act of maternal devotion. They'll look at Georgia and think, *She's a killer.*

One of us got away with murder, but it isn't Georgia.

They have the right idea, but the wrong twin.

Sisters share so many things in common. But deep down, in a hidden place no one can ever see, they're often exact opposites.

ACKNOWLEDGMENTS

This book wouldn't exist without the extraordinary help of a nurse and book blogger, Dr. Michelle Jocson, RN, DNP (aka Nurse Bookie). Michelle has in-depth field knowledge of locked wards for individuals accused of violent crimes, and she has my deep appreciation—as does her colleague Professor Edgar Barawid, RN, BSN, for answering my countless questions. My thanks also to Dr. Philip Candilis of Saint Elizabeth's hospital in Washington, DC, for his valuable insight and generous time.

I'm the luckiest author around to get to work with Jennifer Enderlin, my brilliant and beloved editor, and the rest of the St. Martin's Press dream team, including publicist Katie Bassel, marketing gurus Erica Martirano and Brent Janeway, Robert Allen, Alexis Neuville, Steven Seighman, Jeff Dodes, Marta Fleming, Olga Grlic, Tracey Guest, Sara La Cotti, Christina Lopez, Kim Ludlam, Kerry Nordling, Erik Platt, Gisela Ramos, Sally Richardson, Lisa Senz, Michael Storrings, Tom Thompson, and Dori Weintraub. And on the audio side, huge thanks to Guy Oldfield, Mary Beth Roche, Emily Dyer, and Drew Kilman.

My fantastic team at William Morris Endeavor includes my literary agent, Margaret Riley King; my film agents, Hilary Zaitz Michael and Sylvie Rabineau; foreign rights director Tracy Fisher; and Celia Rogers. Thanks also to my manager, Robin Budd of Viewfinder, who has taught me so much about the world of TV and film. My gratitude to entertainment lawyer Darren Trattner.

Laurie Prinz is my first reader and all-around sounding board, and her generous help improved this novel. My gratitude also to my beta reading team: Jamie des Jardins, Suzy Wagner, and Napheesa Collier (who happens to be a brilliant reader along with being the four-time All-Star of the WNBA). And to the friends and family who buoyed me while I wrote, especially Rachel Baker, Laura Hillenbrand, Amy and Chris Smith, Lucinda Eagle, and Anthony B.

Cathy and Sydney Hines—thank you for making sure my Charlotte references rang true! A heart tap to Suzy Wagner and Karlee Rockstroh for helping me up my social media game, and to my good pal Alex Finlay for the Paris Writing Retreat, where I wrote several of these chapters.

To the folks who keep me physically and mentally supported, including the team at International Thriller Writers, Germaine Williams, Pam Rudat, and Club Pilates Bethesda. And to the staff at Planta Bethesda, who are accustomed to seeing me tapping away on my laptop while I eavesdrop on everyone around me.

This will be the first book I've written that my mother, Lynn Pekkanen, won't be able to read. Mom, thank you for everything. You are missed every single day.

To my sons, Jackson, Will, and Dylan, as always. There aren't enough loving words to describe you three.

And to my family at RRSA India, especially Dr. Bhavesh and Anjali, who inspire me every day with their heroic commitment to saving the millions of street dogs in India.

And finally, to all the Bookstagrammers, social media friends, librarians, booksellers, and readers—a high point of my day is chatting with you on Instagram and Facebook. I can't wait to hear what you think about *The Locked Ward*. Please tag me so we can connect!

ABOUT THE AUTHOR

Bill Miles

Sarah Pekkanen is the number one *New York Times* bestselling author of fifteen solo and coauthored novels. Her books are sold in thirty-six countries, with several optioned for TV and film. Sarah also cowrote the screenplay for *The Wife Between Us* for Amblin Entertainment. She serves on the board of directors of International Thriller Writers and is the founder of the nonprofit India Street Paws, which rescues injured and abused street dogs in India. She lives just outside of Washington, DC.